Leave of My Duty

Leave of My Duty

Piper Falls: Station 28

Nikki A Lamers

Copyright

This is a work of fiction. Any names, characters, events, incidents, businesses, places are either the product of the author's imagination or used in a fictitious manner. Any resemblance to actual events, locales, or persons, living or dead is purely coincidental.

Text Copyright © 2024 Nikki A Lamers, Nicole Mullaney
All Rights Reserved

No part of this book may be reproduced or transmitted in any form or by any means, electronic or mechanical, including photocopying, recording, or by any information and retrieval systems, without the written permission of the publisher, except where permitted by law.

Cover Photo by Creative Instincts
Cover Model Vinny Varden
Cover Design by Carter Cover Designs

Frey Dreams an Imprint of Nikki A Lamers
ISBN: 978-1-951185-26-8

Dedication

To the men and women in blue.

Prologue

♡ Noah ♡

Striding into the bullpen, I go straight for one of my best friend's desks. He looks up from the files he's studying as I approach, his blue-eyed gaze meeting mine. "Hey, Matt. Interesting case?"

He arches his eyebrow in question, knowing something is coming his way. "What's up Noah?"

I laugh. "So, it's my anniversary this weekend and I wanted to surprise Mallory and bring her up to Aurora Heights for dinner. I thought she'd appreciate returning to where we got engaged for a nice romantic night out away from the kids."

"You're just trying to get laid."

"Mal and I are good in that department." I smirk.

"What do you want from me?"

"My sister has to work, so I was wondering if there was any chance one of Amber's sisters would be around this weekend?"

"You want me to ask Amber if her sisters can babysit?"

"Yeah. Do you think Olivia or Parker would want to?"

"Maybe. I guess they're old enough now, right?" he asks, shaking his head in disbelief. "But Parker definitely won't be around. And Amber and Olivia are both staying in Georgia this weekend. I don't think they'll be out this way until Katie is on break. I was planning to head that way on my days off this week to see my daughter."

"I knew it was a long shot." I heave a sigh, shaking my head. "Thanks anyway. How is Katie doing?"

A smile tugs at his lips. It's obvious how much he adores his daughter. "She's good. She looks more like her mom every day."

"I believe it."

"Why don't you ask your parents?"

"Yeah, I guess I'll have to. The three of them can be a lot on my parents with all their energy, so I try to exhaust everything else first. Short spurts works best for them."

He laughs. "That I can believe."

"Thanks anyway. I have to get back out on patrol and let Jake or Brian grab lunch. Don't want Caden on my ass." We both laugh, but not 'cause he wouldn't get on us for it, but because it was an adjustment for all of us when he became my lieutenant. There's six of us who went to high school together and came back after college to attend the academy together. Five out of the six of us are here at Station 28 in Piper Falls, Texas. "I'll catch you later."

"Later." He waves as I spin towards the front door. The same station I now work at as a patrol sergeant with people I consider family; a couple of the guys have been there for me my entire life.

My phone beeps with a text message. I look down at the screen, an image of my wife and kids lighting it up and bringing a smile to my face. I'm a lucky bastard. Mallory is beautiful, her long brown hair falling over her shoulders in waves, her caramel eyes sparkling with her bright smile. She's about half a foot shorter than my six feet, fitting perfectly underneath my arm. Her breasts and ass have a little more than a handful which she hates, but I love.

Our youngest daughter, Mia looks just like her, but she's going to be more of a handful, like I had been as a kid. I can already see the signs at only three years old. Ollie also has my energy at five, but he looks exactly like me with his strawberry blonde hair and green eyes, but Mal's smile. Our oldest Tiegan is already nine and has my strawberry blonde hair, my mom's blue eyes, yet she seems to be looking more like Mallory in other ways as she gets older and I love every second of it. I'm looking forward to seeing what they're like as they grow up.

We may have been through a lot having our kids so young, but I wouldn't trade it for anything and I know Mal feels the same, despite the turmoil we went through. Tiegan definitely came as a surprise. We found out she was pregnant at the end of our sophomore year of college. After that, she decided she would keep going to school for teaching but decrease her workload so she could be there for our kids.

I worked my ass off to finish and get in the academy so we could start our life together here in Piper Falls. With me working at the local police station, she was able to pick up more classes and finish school before she took over as one of the new Kindergarten teachers. It's a perfect fit for us.

My family gave us a hard time when they found out, but they remained supportive. Mallory's family wanted nothing to do with her or me. They didn't even come to our fucking wedding. It broke her more for our kids and I hate that for her.

Every day, I look at my wife, awed by everything she has done without the support of her family and I fall in love with her all over again. She's the most amazing woman I know.

"What's got you smiling?" Reid Flanagan, another one of my best friends asks as he strides towards the station.

I hold up my phone and shrug. "Mal."

"Ah, tell her I'll be stopping by for some cookies."

I laugh. "Eat too many and you'll never find a woman like her."

"She's got me covered."

"Like hell she does." He laughs and I flip him off, grinning wide. "See y'all later."

I slip in behind the wheel and finish my squad safety check before calling into dispatch. "Squad twenty to Dispatch."

"Squad twenty, go ahead."

"Squad twenty is ten-eight."

"Squad twenty is ten-eight at thirteen-hundred-hours."

Taking a deep breath, I pull out of the parking lot, my mind on Mallory and our anniversary this weekend. I can't wait to get some time alone with her. We need it.

Driving down Main Street toward the edge of town, I expect the day to be uneventful, but sometimes I'm surprised. As I loop around, passing through one of the residential neighborhoods, a white van flies by me heading towards the warehouses. "What the hell?" I mumble under my breath.

Making a U-turn, I hit my lights and siren as I follow him. Just after we pass an abandoned warehouse he pulls over and I pull in right behind him, silencing the siren and reaching for my laptop as I call dispatch. "Squad twenty to dispatch."

"Squad twenty, go ahead."

"Traffic Stop at Carey Street and Tarif Avenue. White Ford Transit with Texas plates. Number is Delta, Gamma, Alpha, 4, 3, 2, 1." I type in the information as I speak, running the plates.

"10-4. Traffic Stop at Carey Street and Tarif Avenue. White Ford Transit. Texas. Delta, Gamma, Alpha, 4, 3, 2, 1 at thirteen twenty-seven hours."

"Huh, Tombstone Pass. Wonder what he's doing in Piper Falls." Finding nothing unusual, I step out of the car, only seeing the silhouette of one person in the driver's seat, appearing to be a male, barely moving.

Slowly, I approach, making my way over to the passenger side of the van. The moment the man starts to come into my view, he moves. The black steel is the only thing I see as he pulls the trigger. A loud noise pierces the air. Gasping, I reach for my gun and lurch back, but it's too late.

My upper right chest is hit, my arm suddenly moving like sludge. I'm hit again before I'm able to react, pain slicing through me. My eyes widen and my knees give out. Desperately, I gasp for breath as I hit the ground. Gravel hits me as the van speeds away. I begin to shiver, my breath slowing. Mallory and our kids slam into my thoughts, the only things on my mind.

I'm sorry. I'm so fucking sorry Mal…

I love you all so much. The guys will take care of all of you. I know they will.

Please, let them be okay. I love you. I'll always love you.

Mallory and our kids remain my last thought as my body becomes numb and my world goes black.

Chapter One

♡ Griffin ♡

(Two years and two months later)

"I'm so glad y'all are here," my mom whispers, as my two sisters hug her from each side. She looks around the room, glancing at me, my three brothers, and sister-in-law. We quickly fill this sterile, white room, but we all wanted to be here. We all needed to be here.

"Of course, we are, Ma. we wouldn't be anywhere else," Colton, my oldest brother declares, pulling his wife, Robin tightly to his side. These are the times I'm grateful we have a big family, a family that would do anything for each other, that you know you can depend on to the end, and even then, we would keep fighting.

There's no denying any of us are related. We all have varying shades of brown hair, mine so dark, it's nearly black like my dad's but I have my mom's blue eyes, like my sister Harper, and everyone except Sage has brown like our dad, while her green eyes shine like our grandmother.

"Where are the twins?" Ma asks, glancing at Colton and his wife.

"Asher and Mason are at my sister's," Robin answers.

"You should go get them and bring them home so they can sleep in their own beds tonight," mom insists.

"Mom's right, it would be good for the boys," Colton advises, pulling Robin closer like he doesn't want to let her go. I don't blame him.

"And for you Colton," mom interrupts. "Go home with your family. Dad will be okay." She looks pointedly at each of us, knowing none of us will leave without encouragement. "I'm sending all of you home."

Colton nods obediently and walks over, giving my mom and sisters a squeeze, kissing them each on the top of the head. He squeezes my shoulder and gives my brothers, Wyatt and Beau a firm pat on the back, needing to do something for each of us to show his support. Soon, my other siblings follow and I'm the last one remaining. Stepping into my arms, my mom rests her head in the middle of my chest. "That means you too, Griffin. Go home and rest. I'm going to do the same, only I'll be here."

"I can stay tonight, Ma."

"No, I sleep better when I hear your dad snoring." I chuckle softly as she steps out of my arms, looking up at me. "With everything going on, I didn't even ask you, what about the station?"

"I took an emergency leave of duty."

She shakes her head. "You didn't have to do that."

"Yes, I did. I wouldn't be able to focus on work and besides, they'll survive without me." I pause, taking in my mom. She's still beautiful but her body sags as if willing the floor to consume her. The dark circles under her eyes show how tired she is and the number of wrinkles and worry lines has increased significantly since the last time I came home making my stomach turn. Instantly, I make a decision. "I'm putting in for a transfer."

She straightens, looking me in the eyes. "What?"

"I'm requesting a transfer home to Piper Falls." A gasp escapes her lips as I watch her fighting back the hope in her eyes, only solidifying my decision. "I've mentioned it to the chief already and I just have to sign the paperwork." Or submit the damn paperwork, but she doesn't need to know that. At least I'm not lying about talking to the chief about it. "Apparently one of the lieutenants is retiring soon at Station 28." Hopefully, soon, will be in the next couple months.

"Really? Who? I didn't think any of those boys were old enough to retire."

My lips twitch in amusement and I shrug my shoulders. "I don't know, Ma. You would probably know better than me who's ready for retirement. I can tell you it's none of my friends. I'm not that old. Besides, Chief will put in a good word for me and a lot of them know me. So, unless someone comes in and bumps me, the job should be mine."

"You are really coming home Griff?" A tear escapes out of the corner of her eye, but she ignores it, likely willing me not to notice, squeezing my heart.

"Yeah, Mom. I'm coming home. And I think I'll try to extend my leave until the transfer goes through. You need me here."

Her hand falls to my forearm. "Griffin…" she attempts to interrupt.

"Drop it, Ma. It's done. You need me, whether you want to need me or not. Let me be here for my family. Colton has his own family stuff to worry about with Robin and the boys. Harper and Beau are still finishing their degrees, Sage will lose her job if she takes more than one week off."

"Wyatt can help."

I nod. Wyatt and I already talked about it. He's only two years younger than me and has always wanted to come back and work on the family farm, his head full of ideas. "He can, but he needs to go back for a little while to tie up some loose ends and we have no idea how long that will take." Her eyes widen in panic. "No one is leaving yet, Ma, don't worry."

She sighs in defeat. "I know. I'm just glad you're all here now. So is dad." Her voice cracks as she looks towards him lying in the hospital bed, connected to various tubes and beeping machines.

Looking completely vulnerable, he appears to be the opposite of the man we usually see. He would hate it. I hate it, but only because I'm not ready to lose him. "And you know this is exactly where I want to be." It's where I need to be.

A sad smile crosses her face as she nods her head in acknowledgement. "I know Griff. I know."

The door swings open and a young male nurse walks in, "Excuse me. I'm sorry to interrupt, Ma'am, but I'm here to check Mr. Erickson's vitals."

"Hi, Eddie. Thank you." My mom smiles, sad, but appreciative. "Did you meet my son, Griffin?"

"We met earlier, Ma. Are you sure I can't stay here?"

She shakes her head. "Go home and get some sleep."

I hesitate, but know this isn't an argument I would win, or one I want to have after such a long day. At least I think it's only been a day. "I love you, Ma. We'll take care of everything at home, just please let us know how things are and we'll all be back. Let us know what we can bring up for you tomorrow."

"Just as long as I see all of you sometime tomorrow, it will be okay. You're all I need when you have time."

"Ma…"

"I just mean, the farm doesn't wait for emergencies, Griffin. You can't all come back and stay here by my side all day. We haven't scheduled any extra help."

Nodding, I emphasize, "You don't need it. That's what all of us are for." She gives me a look I know too well, my lips twitching at the familiarity, without turning into the normal smile. I just can't. Leaning down, I give my mom a kiss on the cheek. "We can get the help set up for when anyone needs to go back. I love you."

"Thank you." She tries to smile, but it looks more like a grimace, squeezing my already battered heart. "I love you too. We're so glad you're home, Griff." Reaching up, she pats my cheek, giving me an adoring smile and some comfort even when I can see she's practically shoving me out the door so she can take a moment of her own, praying for the man who has been her rock, just as she will do everything to be his, now and forever. We hope his forever remains with us for much longer before the next step.

Gulping down the lump in my throat, I trudge out of the hospital towards my pickup. Every step I take feels heavier than the last, the weight of everything that happened in the past twenty-four hours holding me down. By the time I climb into my truck, my body is dragging.

As I pull out of the lot and turn towards home, my mind drifts, barely able to focus on the road. In the blink of an eye, I'm making my way down the long dirt road towards the back of the large white farmhouse, instantly flooded with memories. Shaking it off, I quietly make my way inside, but my efforts are unsurprisingly fruitless. Wyatt, Sage, Harper, and Beau sit at the long wooden kitchen table with bowls and toppings in front of them, watching as Wyatt flips a perfect scoop of homemade vanilla ice cream into a bowl, his eyes raising to meet mine.

"What are y'all doin'?" I ask accusingly.

Wyatt's eyes narrow. "Making ice cream sundaes. You joining us or not?"

I toss my keys and wallet onto the counter and flop into the chair across from Wyatt. "Well, are you going to give me a bowl or are you planning on eating it all?"

His lips barely twitch as he slides a bowl across the table before filling another for himself as the rest of us add our favorite toppings. Slowly I pour the hot fudge over the top, watching it thicken instantly with the shock of the cold.

"What about Colton?" Harper asks, always wanting all of us together.

"He needs time to help Robin put the boys down," I advise. She nods, her movement bringing my attention to Beau and his bowl overflowing with toppings, his ice cream looking more like something from Elf than something edible. "Don't you think you have enough, Beau?" He lifts his gaze and I nod towards his bowl.

Without answering he heaves a sigh and lifts a spoonful holding it towards the middle of the table and waiting for the rest of us as we mirror his actions. Clearing his throat, he forces the first words out. "To Dad."

"To get better soon," Harper squeaks.

"For a quick recovery," Wyatt adds.

"To smile and laugh again," Sage whimpers.

"For him to come home soon," I finish, all of us raw with emotion. We clink our spoons, as per our usual, all taking a bite.

"Ewe, I got some of Beau's stuck to mine," Harper complains.

"More for me if you don't want it," he claims, grinning, attempting to lighten the mood.

Sitting back, I poke at the ice cream, listening to my siblings banter. The mood, quickly returning to somber. "What are we going to do?" Sage asks the question all of us are thinking.

"We come up with a plan. It will be fine," Wyatt chimes in.

"He will be fine," I emphasize. Sighing, I add, "And Wyatt's right."

His bowl clatters to the table. "Did you hear that? Even Griff says I'm right, so it must be true."

"Shut the fuck up, asshole," I retort. He smirks, shrugging.

"I guess I'll be the grownup," Sage interrupts, rolling her eyes. Whipping out her phone, she begins tapping. "I'll write a list of everything we need to do and who's responsible and share it with everyone."

In no time, we have the chores we don't have regular staff for broken down, a list of plans for when everyone has to go back to their daily lives, and a list for checking on mom, making sure she takes care of herself, and of course visiting dad.

With a satisfied smile, Sage taps send and announces, "Done."

Our phones beep with her message followed by a response from our brother.

Colton: You better not have made homemade ice cream sundaes without me.

We all laugh, easing some of the tension. Beau sends a picture of his bowl in the group. Colton replies instantly.

Colton: WTF is that?

Wyatt: Beau's concoction.

Colton: 'Nuff said. I'm fine without that. But don't let it happen again.

We know he's joking, but I'm having trouble finding anything funny tonight. The sequence of events is on repeat in my head. I'm grateful the call came in when it did so I was able to get back to Piper Falls so quickly, but even then, it wasn't fast enough. What if the worst had happened? I wouldn't have made it in time and I would never be able to forgive myself.

Moving back here is the right move. Nothing is more important than family. I need to make it happen.

There's no other option.

Chapter Two

♡ *Mallory* ♡

"Ollie, where are your pants? It's almost time to go."

"I don't know, Mommy," my seven-year-old son answers, as he kicks his soccer ball around his bedroom.

"Don't play ball in the house."

"I'm not."

"Ollie," I warn, arching my eyebrows as I reach into his dresser and pull out a pair of the tan cargo pants he loves.

Heaving a sigh, he stops and picks the ball up, setting it on his bed adorned with a soccer ball quilt. As he turns back to me, his strawberry blonde hair flops over his forehead and he looks up at me, his green eyes shining innocently like his dad's used to do when he was trying to win me over or get away with something. The simple gesture squeezes my heart. I gulp down the sudden lump in my throat and spin towards the door. "Get dressed and grab your things."

My eyes close momentarily as I pull the door closed and take a deep, calming breath. "He looks more like you every day, Noah," I mumble under my breath.

"Mom?" my oldest asks as she steps into the hallway.

Pushing away from Ollie's door, I quickly shake off my thoughts. "Ready for school, Tiegan?" She nods, her strawberry-blonde ponytail bouncing. Her hazel eyes, more of a mix of the two of us, look up at me imploring. She sees more than I'd like her to at only nine-years-old. Being the oldest, she's been through more than any child her age should have to endure.

"Are you okay?" she asks so soft I almost don't hear it.

Guilt crashes into me, making it difficult to breathe. Forcing a smile, I insist, "I'm just tired this morning. I'm glad it's Friday."

Her shoulders visibly relax and she smiles. "Me too. We have a sleepover at Aunt Carla's on Saturday."

My eyes widen. "Oh, I forgot about that."

She rolls her eyes at me. "I'm hungry." Without another word she bypasses me, making her way to the kitchen.

"There's a bowl of berries on the counter and the pancakes are covered to keep them warm."

"Pancakes!" Mia, my five-year-old mini me pops out of her room wearing a frilly pink princess dress and a tiara on her head. Charging towards the kitchen, she holds her wand out like it's a sword and she's ready to fight for breakfast.

A burst of laughter echoes down the hallway as Ollie's door swings open and he runs past me. "Save some for me!"

As I step into the kitchen, Tiegan points a fork at her sister, frowning. "Mom, she can't wear that to school. It's embarrassing."

"She's not embarrassing. She's five."

"Mom…"

"I'm sorry, Mia, but you can't wear this to school."

Mia whines, "But Mommy…"

I step towards her, my hand falling to the back of her head. "Sweetie, you won't be allowed to wear that at school today."

"It's not a costume. I'm a real princess."

An adoring smile lights up my face. "I know honey, but you can wear it after pre-K. You only have a couple weeks left of school before summer starts. Besides, what if something happened to your dress or the crown?"

She frowns, an exaggerated pout on her perfect little face. "Okay."

Reaching for a handful of blueberries, I pop them in my mouth and make my way around the counter to grab my coffee. As I take a sip, I glance at the time, my eyes widening in surprise. "Finish eating and I'll get you something to wear," I add, nodding at Mia.

I return with another pink dress in hand and take her crown off followed by her dress and slip the other on in seconds. "Come on, y'all, we have to go."

We rush to the garage, the kids quickly piling into my white minivan. I glance at Ollie as he climbs in with only a lunch box and a soccer ball. Fighting my smile, I ask, "Ollie, where's your backpack?"

He turns in a circle as if willing it to appear before answering. "It's still inside."

"I'll go get it."

"Thanks, Mom."

A few minutes later we're making the short drive to school, the sun barely over the horizon. "I don't want to be the first one there today," Tiegan complains.

"What's so different about today?" I ask, glancing at her in the rearview mirror before focusing back on the road.

She shrugs, staring out the window. "Aaron went home sick yesterday, so he won't be there."

Ah. Her best friend. She tends to play with the boys whenever Aaron is around but when he's not, the boys don't always include her and she plays with the girls. "I'm sorry he's not feeling well, but you know I have to get to school before the other kids get there."

Heaving a sigh, her body sags, melting into the leather seats. "Yeah, I know."

"Besides, summer vacation starts in a few weeks." She nods, still frowning. "And you have a lot to look forward to this weekend." A smile tugs at her lips.

"Hey! Ollie!" Mia screeches, making me jump.

I glance back, finding Mia's arms swinging towards her brother with tears already streaming down her cheeks while Ollie laughs, holding something away from her, taunting her. "Mom, Mia brought her crown."

"Give it back!"

"Mom, Mia hit me."

"Mommy!"

Turning towards my kids, I reach my hand back, attempting to separate them as I pull off to the side of the road. "Both of you stop!"

"Mom!" Tiegan yells, eyes wide.

I spin back towards the road and slam on my brakes as two large hands come down hard on the hood of the car, the booming echo of a man's fists hitting metal startling me. My heart hammers against my ribcage as my eyes drift up the corded muscles and colorful ink covering his right arm, and flowing onto his broad chest and shoulder, slick with sweat. I lick my lips watching the shadowed scruff on his face move as he clenches his jaw. My wide brown eyes lift, finally meeting his shocking bright blue ones, staring at me, and making my mouth water like I've been starving for years.

Another piercing scream echoes in the confines of the car, jarring me out of my stupor. "Are you guys okay?"

"Mom, you almost hit him. Are the police coming? Will we get to see Uncle Matt?"

A gasp escapes my lips as my son's words slam into me, as if dousing me with cold water. "I need to see if he's okay." As I reach for the seatbelt, the corner of his lip tugs upwards and he winks before spinning around and taking off in a run. "Wait!" I call, but it's already too late. Slightly stunned, I sit behind the wheel, my eyes glued to his firm backside as he disappears around the corner. Who the hell was that?

Turning in my seat, I shake my head and give each of my kids a pointed stare. "No fighting or yelling in the car. Ever! Do you understand?"

"Ollie started it," Mia whines.

"I didn't do anything!" Tiegan argues, while Oliver remains unusually silent.

"Do you understand?" I repeat, ignoring their outbursts.

The defeated sound of all three of them responding almost in unison echoes in the car, "Yes, Mom."

"Good." I nod, turning back towards the road.

As I pull away from the curb, my thoughts drift to the muscles and piercing blue eyes that moments ago stood before me giving me chills. Who was he? I've never seen him before and Piper Falls is a small town. Maybe he's here visiting family or a friend or something. I feel terrible I didn't even get the chance to apologize.

My stomach flips, letting me know that's not the only thing I feel bad about. A wave of guilt washes over me as I force Noah to the forefront of my mind. He would want me to date again. He would want me to find someone, so why does my heart feel like dead weight because I find a stranger so attractive? Okay, let's be real, he was panty melting hot. And

Noah is gone. My stomach twists with both shame and the excitement of possibilities. The hard part is figuring out which one should win. I'm pretty sure I might already know what one will.

Exhaling slowly, I shake my head and park next to Tanner's car, not only the assistant principal, but a close friend I grew up with a few towns north of here. With all the vandalism going on recently, he's here like clockwork every day waiting for me and the kids when we arrive. He's always watching out for us, just like Matt, and the other guys at the station. Reid is always there too, but I think Tiegan still blames him some for not saving her dad since he's the one who found Noah. It doesn't seem to matter how many times we've said there was nothing he could've done. I'm honestly incredibly grateful for all of them. I don't know if I would've survived without them.

I wave before I grab my things and climb out of the car, Tiegan, and Ollie already out of their car seats while Mia kicks her legs in anticipation as she waits for me. "Hi, Mr. Pratt." Tiegan grins as Ollie gives him a high five in greeting.

"Good morning! How are y'all doing today?"

"Mommy hit someone with her car!" Mia announces, handing him her bag without asking.

"What?" His eyes widen, his eyebrows nearly hitting his dark hairline. "Is everyone okay?"

Heaving a sigh, I grab my tote filled with a few things I brought home last night to work on and my purse. "We're fine. He's fine. I didn't actually hit him, but it was close. The kids were fighting and his hands came down on the hood."

"Who was it? Do you think he'll sue?"

I shake my head. "I have no idea who it was. He ran off, so I guess he's fine."

His eyebrows draw down in confusion. "You don't know who it was?"

Reaching for Mia's hand, I instruct, "Hold hands." Tiegan instantly follows directions.

"But my soccer ball," Ollie complains.

"You don't need that right now."

"But I want it for before and after school."

Tanner lifts his hand and offers me a comforting smile. "It's okay, I got him." His hand falls to his shoulder protectively, bringing a smile to my face as we all walk side by side to the front door of the school.

When we reach the gym, Mr. Sylvin stands in front of the door, unlocking the gym. "Good morning, y'all," he greets us.

"Good morning," we all reply with a smile.

I glance at Tanner, grateful for his help. He's always been there for me for as long as I can remember, but after Noah died, he really stepped up, helping out whenever we needed anything. I can't imagine how different things would have been without him here in Piper Falls. "Thank you."

His lips tug up at the corners. "My pleasure, Ms. Bailey."

Mia laughs. "That's not her name, silly. Our last name is Dolan. Why does everyone at school call you that?"

They all set their things down against the wall as Tiegan rolls her eyes, answering before I have a chance. "Bailey was mom's last name before she married dad. That's what they call her at school."

"Oh. I thought that was just what her class called her this year," Mia claims, scrunching her face up, clearly puzzled.

My chest tightens. I don't want to confuse my kids, but I needed to find some of myself after struggling so much the first year and taking my name back at school is one thing that seemed to work for me. It feels like I'm me again, not Noah's widow. How do I explain that to a five-year-old?

"I love you," I say and hold my arms out wide. All three of my kids rush into my arms and I hold them tight, not caring that I can't breathe. I kiss the tops of their heads, all of them coming closer to my chin at my five-five height every day. It won't be long before they're all taller than me at this rate. For a moment, I relax, relishing their love and sharing mine. This is by far one of the best parts of my day, every single time.

A mumbled chorus of, "I love you," follows, bringing a broader smile to my face.

My kids break free. Ollie spins, running for his soccer ball, and kicking it across the gym, while Tiegan walks to the table for the drawing paper and Mia finds a princess coloring book and jumps up and down in excitement, holding it up like a trophy.

Turning towards Mr. Sylvin, I sign my kids in and smile. "Thank you."

"Have a good day."

With one last glance at my world, I exit, Tanner following right behind as I head to my Kindergarten classroom. "Now that the kids aren't around, I have to ask, are you okay?"

My eyebrows draw down in confusion when suddenly the memory of chiseled arms with firm muscles adorned with colorful ink slams down on me, startling me. "Oh, yeah, um, the guy. Yeah, the kids were fighting and I was pulling over to deal with them, but I didn't see him. His hands hit the hood, but he just looked at me and then went back to his run." I shake my head remembering his wink making my breath catch. Who even does that?

"You sure that's it? Mal?"

"Um, yeah, yeah, that's it." I shrug. "I have no idea who he was, but…"

"But?" He arches his eyebrows.

"Nothing." My teeth dig into my lower lip as I shake my head. I don't want to talk about him.

"I know that look." He narrows his eyes at me. "I admit, I haven't seen it in a while, but I know it well." Glancing at him out of the corner of my eye, I purse my lips, not sure what he's insinuating. "You might be interested in this guy you've never spoken to. So that's what it takes to get you interested? Let you hit them with your car?"

My head falls back in laughter as I playfully shove him towards the exit. "Just go."

He chuckles, moving towards the door. "I think that could be a good thing for you, Mal."

I blush, ignoring him and begin setting up my classroom centers for the morning. I want to have it ready before my teaching assistant, Ms. Garcia gets here, so we can work on the Kindergarten graduation celebration with any free time.

Chapter Three

♡ Griffin ♡

Wyatt sets the last box next to one of the tables and stands next to me as we look around the park. Saturday mornings have always been an array of activity with the Farmer's Market in addition to our everyday farm duties. There appears to be a little bit of everything today like, fruits, vegetables, jam, honey, beer, wine, bread, pies, and other pastries, as well as baskets, quilts, and woodwork.

Sage steps between us, flicking us both on the ear.

"Squirt," I warn as we spin towards her, Wyatt sweeping her off the ground.

"Put me down! Y'all need to stop reminiscing and help me get this stuff set up before the crowd barrels down on us."

Laughing, he sets her on her feet. "This ain't no rodeo, Sis. Pretty sure the only barrels will be from a local vineyard."

Narrowing her eyes, she argues, "You'd be surprised how busy this gets now. The restaurants and stores love it and not just people from town show up. Everyone wants fresh food. Plus, the Bluebonnet Bakery has a tent sometimes and those desserts are out of this world."

"Piper Falls Farmers' Market. Who'd a thought?" I quirk a brow.

"You'd know if you came home more often," she claims, glancing between the two of us.

"I'm working my ass off so I can move back and expand the Vodka company," Wyatt proclaims, shrugging. "Well, more like start the Vodka company, it's not much of one yet."

Sage turns her glare on me. "And what's your excuse?"

I hold my hands up in surrender. "Look, I know I haven't been around as much as I should, but work is busy. We've been short-staffed, so I've been picking up some patrol shifts to help out."

"And it has nothing to do with…" she trails off as I cross my arms over my chest, narrowing my eyes in warning. "You can't ignore it or this town forever Griff." My gaze doesn't waver. I relax the moment I see her relenting. "Fine." Heaving a sigh, she redirects, "I don't understand why you don't apply at the station here."

"Actually, I told Ma I'm moving home."

Both my siblings drop what they're doing and spin on their heels, staring at me wide-eyed. "What?" Sage questions.

"You said you were taking a leave of duty, you never said you were moving home," Wyatt states, needing clarification.

Huffing, I reach into a box and begin sorting the vegetables onto one of the tables Sage already covered with a red tablecloth. I need to do something while I talk. "It's too much. I was covering someone's shift and out on patrol when I got the call and couldn't answer right away. Then, by the time I got back to the station and called… the traffic…" My voice cracks with emotion and I pause, clearing my throat. Recalling the helpless and guilty sensations consuming me, I shake my head, glancing at them with the desperation I feel in the moment. "What if something happened and I didn't get here in time? It's happened before, but with them… I'd never forgive myself."

Sage flicks away a tear and wraps her arms around my waist as Wyatt looks away, gulping down his own emotions. "Are you leaving the force?" she asks.

"No, just taking a break. Wyatt and I talked about it some."

Sage's head snaps towards Wyatt, her eyes narrowed. "You knew?"

"No!"

"We only talked about me taking a leave of duty and helping out on the farm while dad recovers and mom is busy with dad."

"He's going to hate that," Wyatt mumbles under his breath.

"Understatement." I huff a humorless laugh.

Wyatt adds, "I just can't come home yet, but I will be back soon to stay and dive further into Vodka."

"Don't you drink enough already?" Sage snarks.

"Smartass." Wyatt smirks. "I want it to be more than something we bring as a gift to the Walker estate for dinner or the town fair. I've been working on a business plan for a long time and I'm almost ready. I'm going to give my job notice, but it will take a couple months because we're in the middle of a project. It's time for me to leave, anyway. I just can't leave them hanging when they've been so good to me."

"Ma would be proud," I tease, although it's true.

Ignoring me, he adds, "Besides, I can still make it home on the weekends if I'm needed. If not, I'll work my ass off to get back faster. With me home, Griff will be able to go back to work."

"Yeah, go back to work, but I need to stay here. There's not really anything in Waco for me anyway besides the station."

"Or anyone." Sage arches her eyebrows in challenge.

"Or maybe it's too many someones." Wyatt laughs.

"Well, no one I want to stay there for. It's an easy call. I already mentioned it to my chief and since I'm on leave, it seems like the perfect time to set everything in motion. Besides, I heard Bill Camden is retiring this summer."

"Really?" Wyatt questions.

I nod. "Matt mentioned something."

"He's been trying to get your ass back here to work with him since you left."

The corners of my lips tug upwards. I was so determined to get away from Piper Falls and do my own thing after everything, but the thought of coming home, being close to my family and working with a few of my friends is exactly what I need right now. Hopefully, the position will be mine.

"Well, the job's not mine yet, but it would be ideal."

It's not long before the three of us get the farm stand set up with early summer fruits and vegetables, along with some herbs, all neatly placed and exhibited in wooden display crates. Dusting off my hands, I take another look around the park lined with small tents and tables at the edge of the grass, people milling about. "This is definitely a lot bigger than I remember."

"And we're about to get slammed," Sage announces, pointing towards the parking lot, quickly filling up.

"You got the register, sis?" Wyatt questions as our first customers approach.

We attempt to get lost in the work, but nearly every customer asks, "How's your dad?" followed by, "It's good to see you boys home."

"I'm going to take the pickup back to the farm. Beau texted something about a broken fence," Wyatt informs us, leaving the keys for the farm truck.

"Griffin Erickson, I heard you were back."

I spin towards the feminine voice, grinning down at Tara Maxwell. "Hey, Tara. How are you? How's Leo?"

"I'm good," Leo comments as he steps next to his wife. "How have you been, man? It's good to see you." Grinning, he steps towards me, slapping me on the back with a one-armed hug, I return.

"You, too."

"Matt told us about your dad. How's he doing?"

I fight my flinch. "He's doing okay. We're hoping he'll be able to come home soon."

"That's good news."

Forcing a smile, I nod in response. "What's new with the guys?"

"Not much. Everyone is good. Tonight a few of us off shift are going out for a beer. You should come."

"Maybe."

"It'd be good for you to get out if you can."

I pinch my lips tightly together knowing he's right. I wonder if Matt or Reid are planning on stopping by.

"Tag, you're it!" A little girl with long brown hair wearing a fluffy pink dress bumps into my legs as she runs by giggling.

A boy, taller than her by a couple inches with wavy strawberry blonde hair halts, pouting. "I'm not playing, Mia." He spins around, bumping into a crate full of potatoes. I reach out and grab it before any fall to the ground. His eyes go wide as he stares up at me. "Sorry."

"It's okay, cowboy."

He turns and runs out of the tent as if he's in trouble. My siblings and I used to do the same thing here when we were kids. Leo waves, bringing my attention back to him. "I'll text you."

I nod in acknowledgement as Sage calls, "Griff, can you help with these crates?"

"Coming."

A few minutes later, I'm carrying some empty boxes back to the truck, when a soft whimper catches my attention. Following the sound to the other side of the truck, I find a ball of pink sitting beside the wheel. Crouching down, I keep my voice gentle, not wanting to scare her. "Hey, princess."

With a gasp, her head snaps up as she stares at me with wide eyes and tear-stained cheeks, squeezing my heart.

"Are you okay?"

She nods, more tears spilling down her cheeks. "Ollie was s'posed to find me."

"Maybe you're too good at hiding, but I can help you find him."

Tilting her head to the side, she purses her lips in thought. "Okay, but you have to pass my test first."

My lips twitch. "Okay, little darlin'. I can do that. What's the test?"

"Are you a knight or a prince? If you are one of them, you can help me."

A low chuckle escapes. "Well, then I guess I'm the right man for the job. I'm a knight and a prince."

Wiping her tears, she rolls her eyes dramatically and pushes herself off the ground. "You can't be both."

"I can't?" I quirk a brow.

"No." She shakes her head. "I know how to tell. Put your arms in the air." Indulging her, I do as she says. "Stand on one foot and jump up and down." She watches me as I listen to her orders. "Good job. Now spin around." I put my foot down, and she laughs.

"What?"

"You put your foot down, so you can't be a knight. You must be a prince." She puts her tiny hand in mine, trusting me.

"You must be right." She beams with pride. Now maybe we can find her parents. "Well, I saw your brother, but what does your mom or dad look like? They might be a little taller and easier to find."

"My daddy is an angel and my mommy looks like one," she answers without pause, making my own eyes widen and my heart break.

I open my mouth to ask for further explanation when I notice a beautiful woman with her long, brown hair flying as she looks around frantically, grasping the hand of the same boy as before. "Is that your Mommy?"

She shrieks in happiness, smiling brightly. "Mommy!" Gripping my hand tighter, the little girl tugs and I willingly follow.

The woman's gaze finds her daughter as we step in front of the tents prompting her to exhale in relief. "Mia!" She drops to her knees in front of the little girl, hugging her tightly, still refusing to release her son's hand. "You can't run away like that. You scared me half to death."

"Ollie and I were playing hide and seek."

"No, we weren't," the boy retorts, narrowing his eyes at his little sister.

"I don't care what y'all were doing, you do not run away from me."

"But Mommy, Prince Charming found me," the little girl announces, looking up at me with pride, bringing a small smile to my face.

The woman's gaze finally lifts to mine and the same caramel eyes as this morning look back at me in stunned recognition. She stands slowly, her short brown cowboy boots and jean shorts, bringing my attention to her legs. My eyes drift up, traveling every luscious curve of her body. Damn. Pausing on her full lips, I lick my own, and I swear I hear her breath hitch making my cock twitch.

"This place isn't that big Mia." A girl about nine or ten with the same strawberry blonde hair as her brother claims, rolling her eyes, and grabbing our attention.

"Tiegan," her mom warns, taking a deep breath. She opens her eyes and stares into mine. "Thank you, Mr...."

"Erickson," I supply, her eyes widening, obviously familiar with the family name. "Griffin Erickson, Ma'am."

My lips curve up in a slow, easy smile as I reach to shake her hand. She releases her son's hand, meeting me halfway, heat shooting up my arm at her gentle touch. "Mr. Erickson..."

"Griffin," I repeat, wanting to hear my name on her lips.

Her cheeks turn pink. "Griffin," she corrects. "I'm sorry about this morning."

"So, you do remember me?" My grin grows.

Her face turns a deeper shade of red as she attempts to ignore my comment. "And thank you for finding my daughter." Her voice cracks and before I get a chance to say more, she yanks her hand free of mine and crouches, returning her attention to her daughter. "And Mia, you can't run away even if y'all are playing."

"But Mommy…"

"No buts. And if you get lost again, ask a police officer if you can or a teacher or at least someone you know. You know almost everyone at these tents, sweetheart."

"He works here Mama and now we know him too."

Her mom sighs warily as she stands. "We'll finish this at home." She raises her gaze, her eyes no longer playful. "Thank you again, Mr.–I mean Griffin."

"No problem, Ma'am."

My eyes remain glued to her as she turns around with her three kids connected through a chain of hands as they walk away. Too busy taking her in until she's gone, my brain takes a moment to register she never told me her name, but this town is small, I have no doubt I'll soon find out.

Chapter Four

♡ *Mallory* ♡

My kids drop their bags and charge for the kitchen. "Slow down!" I warn, knowing they won't until the food sits in front of them. A soft moan leaves my lips as I inhale the scent of pepperoni pizza. "Smells good, Carla."

"The kids' favorite aunt is really good at ordering." She grins, shaking her phone in front of me.

"Are you sure you want all three of them for the night? Can I help you with anything before I go?"

She laughs, shaking her head. "No. The kids are staying with me so you can take some time for yourself for once. Why don't you go out and have a good time instead of cleaning the house or running errands."

I frown at her accurate assumption. It's rare I do something that's truly for me anymore. "That's not what I do," I argue in spite of myself, my face heating.

She arches her eyebrows in challenge. "Oh, really? Have anything fun planned for tonight?"

I glance at the woman who used to be my sister-in-law, and still treats me like I'm family. I don't want to disappoint her. She's a couple of inches taller than me with long, auburn curls, the same green eyes as Noah and curves garnering constant attention she wished she didn't receive. "Actually, a friend from work asked if I wanted to join her and her friend for drinks," I declare, my defiance obvious.

Her eyes widen in surprise before narrowing on me. "Where? What time? Are you going?"

"You know me well."

"You're going and I will be asking you for a report." I roll my eyes and she steps closer. "I'm serious Mal. Noah wouldn't want you to stop being you."

I flinch and look away, my heart squeezing. She's right, I know she is. Taking a deep breath, I exhale slowly. My lips breathe my response before I even realize what I'm agreeing to, "I'll go." I feel her triumphant grin before I even look at her. "They're meeting at Papi's Lock 'n' Stock," I say like it's no big deal.

But we both know it's a big deal. Besides making treats for the guys at the station, or hanging out with her, Matt, or Tanner, everything I do is focused on work or our kids. If I'm busy, I don't have to think about it too much. It never really leaves my mind entirely.

Her smile widens as she steps closer, putting her arm around me and guiding me to the door. "You better go then, girl. Your mom is leaving," she calls towards the kitchen.

A chorus of mumbled responses ensue. "Bye, Ma. Love you."

I laugh. "I love you. Be good for Aunt Carla!" More incoherent sounds follow, making me chuckle. "Mia has been hiding lately. If you need…"

"Bye, Mallory." She waves as I take another step back and carefully closes the door in my face.

"Love you, too, Carla."

Her laughter travels through the closed door. A smile tugs at my lips as I turn, walking down the block to our house to keep my promise. I think.

Three hours later, dressed in white shorts, a pale pink tank top with a slightly ruffled V-neck collar and my tan cowboy boots adorned with pink stitching, I approach Papi's, glancing at the police station across the street. I should bring brownies in for the guys, but my chest tightens at the thought of walking through the doors.

Maybe I can ask Matt to come by and bring them for me. I'm not ready to go inside knowing he never will again. Sending treats to everyone once in a while is my way to let them know how much I appreciate every single one of them, hoping one day I don't need a delivery boy.

They became my second family because that's who they were to Noah. When we lost Noah, they were all there for me and the kids. That time went by in a blur, but I still know they were there and I will never forget it.

Momentarily, my eyes flutter closed as I spin around and take a deep breath, refocusing my thoughts before opening them and forcing my feet to move, walking towards the bar.

A cacophony of music, laughter, voices, clinking of silverware and ringing of glasses as they meet in a toast, echoes in my ears as I search the sea of faces, most of them familiar, but not who I'm looking for until my eyes fall on her golden hair. Breathing a sigh of relief, I weave my way through the crowded bar, a mix of cologne, sweat and beer attacking my senses.

"Hi," I greet Jen and her friend as I squeeze in next to them.

"You made it!" I smile in response.

"Mal, this is my girlfriend, Dani."

"Oh, girlfriend?"

She shrugs, giving me a shy smile. "It's new."

"I'm so happy for you guys. Jen is amazing."

"I think so." Dani grins. "It's so great finally meeting you."

"You, too. My kids keep me busy."

"Oh, I'm sorry about your husband." She grimaces, obviously uncomfortable, but no one ever is.

Forcing a smile, I attempt to put her at ease. "It's okay. He's been gone almost two years," I say knowing it helps others feel better, although it does nothing but turn my stomach. Then again, the last time I came out for a drink here, I was with Noah. "It's busy."

"It's Saturday and karaoke is about to start."

My eyes widen. I'd forgotten about that. "Oh, yeah."

"Are you going to sing? You probably want a drink before that starts."

Nodding, I mumble, "No, yeah, or I'll go grab a drink and then I'd love to hear how you two met."

I turn and walk away, not waiting for a response. Finding an empty spot at the bar, I wave to the bartender, TT, short for Tobi Tyler as he approaches. He towers over me at six-foot three with fair skin, brown hair, and brown eyes. Between him and the owner, Jason, a lot of women come in here just for the view.

While the other bartender, Ruby, reminds me more of what my mom might look like now if she were still alive, sharing advice my mom may have given. I see her more than anyone when I pick up food for me and the kids. TT's lips curve up in a smile as he leans towards me. "Hey, darlin'. It's good to see you."

"Hi, TT."

His eyebrows draw down in confusion. "Are ya' here to pick up food?"

I blush, shaking my head and force a smile. "No, I came to meet friends." I point towards the girls. "Jen and I work together."

His grin grows. "Glad to hear it. What can I get ya'?"

"How about a Margarita on the rocks?"

"Absolutely." He nods, turning to make my drink.

I fall back on my heels, taking it all in, and feeling completely out of my element. My breath hitches as my eyes land on the same blue eyes from the farmers' market this morning, staring straight at me. Frozen, I stare back, my heart pounding. The corner of his lips tug up in a crooked smile, his gaze feeling like a caress, giving me chills.

TT sets my drink in front of me, breaking Griffin's hold. "Thank you," I mumble, reaching for my purse.

"This one is on me." I shake my head, opening my mouth to argue. "It's good to see you out."

My cheeks heat and I drop my purse to my side, wondering when everyone will stop feeling sorry for me. "Thanks."

"Maybe it will encourage you to come out more often."

He turns, going back to work, the blue eyes returning to my line of sight only a foot in front of me as he leans against the bar, a cocky grin lighting up his face. "Well, now this is becoming a habit, or maybe third time's a charm?"

A snort escapes, my hand flying to my mouth in horror as his lips twitch in amusement. Quickly brushing it off, I drop my hand to the bar, and shrug. "It's just a small town, Mr. Erickson."

"It's Griffin," he reiterates.

"Right. Griffin."

"I missed your name the last few times we met."

"Oh, I'm sorry. I'm Mallory Bailey."

"Well, Mallory, how about I take you out?"

"We are out."

He chuckles, the low sound vibrating through me. "On a date with me."

My eyes widen in surprise. "You're asking me out?"

He grins, tilting his head to the side. "Why not?"

"After I almost hit you with my car?"

He chuckles softly. "True. You do owe me for hitting me with a minivan…"

"Almost hit you, not the same thing."

"Okay, almost, but add being your daughter's knight in shining armor…"

"Knight? She said you were her prince charming." My lips twitch.

He runs his hand along the scruff of his jaw and I bite my bottom lip, holding back a groan as I watch the simple movement, my mouth watering. "I'll take prince charming. That and a near death experience." I huff a laugh eliciting his sexy grin. "After all that, I think I deserve a date at the very least."

Without a word, I take a sip of my margarita, needing a moment to think of a subject change. "Thank you for finding Mia. That girl is going to be the death of me."

"I hope not."

Ignoring him, I continue, "She's just not afraid to try anything, or talk to anyone and she has a very creative imagination which can get her into trouble. When I saw her holding your hand…" I gulp down the lump in my throat, not able to finish my sentence as a mix of relief and fear wash over me at the memory.

He tilts his head to the side and quirks his brow, assessing me. My face heats and I look away, finishing my drink, in hopes it will cool me off. But the moment my gaze veers back to him, my body ignites all over again as my eyes roam the colorful ink etched into the hard muscles of his arms drawing my attention. I wouldn't mind seeing the rest of that ink up close and tracing the lines with my tongue.

Swiftly shaking the heated thought out of my head, I shove up my walls and blurt out, "You meet a woman who has her three kids with her and you ask her out? Aren't you curious about my husband, or are you just a player who doesn't care?"

My face turns beet red, but I hold my breath, needing his explanation, the realization further scrambling my brain.

Arching his eyebrows, he questions, "Excuse me?"

"You see me with my kids and you think it's okay to flirt and ask me out?"

He nods slowly as understanding and a spark of something else flashes in his eyes. "When we were looking for you, your daughter told me her daddy was with the angels and her mommy looked like one."

"What?" I gasp, my mouth hanging slightly open.

"I'm sorry for your loss, but I'm not about to ask for details because that's none of my business unless you wanted to share, so yeah, I think your daughter's right about you and it's okay to flirt with and ask out a beautiful, single woman." I don't miss the fact he didn't answer my question about being a player. "Am I wrong?"

My body burns being so close to this man, Noah flashing through my mind again. I shake it away, desperate to escape the past, if only for a moment. Straightening my shoulders, I answer with a confidence I don't yet feel, "No."

"So, about that date…" His lips twitch as his eyes sparkle with mischief. This man could be trouble for me.

"I don't owe you anything."

He leans closer, his lips hovering over my ear and his heated breath on my cheek. "You're right. You don't owe me a damn thing. So, how about you go out with me because you want to," he rasps, giving me goosebumps.

I open my mouth to respond when Jen and Dani step up to us, hand in hand. "Are you okay, Mal?" Jen asks, glancing towards Griffin. "Hey, aren't you Sage's brother?"

He chuckles, nodding. "One of 'em."

"How's your dad doing?"

His smile falters. "Getting better."

The karaoke starts up, drowning out their voices. I glance at my friends, grateful for the reprieve, attempting to calm my racing thoughts and cool the flames Griffin ignited. I have no clue what to do.

Chapter Five

♡ Mallory ♡

"Y'all were fantastic!" I grin, praising Jen and Dani as they walk back towards me in a midst of cheers after singing *Creepin' In*.

"Thank you." Dani blushes, her eyes focused on Jen.

"That was fun," Jen declares.

"I think I'm going to head home. I have to be up to pick up the kids in the morning."

"I'll take you," Griffin offers, stepping up behind me.

My head snaps up, eyes wide. "Oh, hi."

"I'll be right back and we can head out."

I bite the inside of my cheek, slightly stunned. There's something about him that makes my stomach twist the moment I know he's nearby. Am I ready to contemplate something new? Then again, I have no idea what his intentions might be. My eyes remain on him as he walks away. "What the hell just happened?"

"You know you can trust him; you can bet the farm on it." Jen claims, interrupting my thoughts. I turn to her, standing with her arms crossed over her chest, arching her eyebrows in challenge. She obviously noticed my hesitancy, but trust has nothing to do with my indecision. Or maybe it does; trusting myself to be ready to move on. Laughing, she urges, "Nothing will happen that you don't want, but if you're not comfortable, we'll walk you home."

I shake my head. I'm not about to interrupt their night. "No, stay. You two don't get to see each other that often. I'll be fine."

"I'm sure you will." She smirks.

Ignoring her comment, I wave and spin on my heel. "Y'all have fun."

The moment I step outside, I feel him before I see him out of the corner of my eye. "Trying to leave without me?"

"No."

"You shouldn't walk home alone at night."

"I'm fine. It's a small town and I'm not far."

"Doesn't matter."

"Are you lecturing me, Mr. Erickson?"

Stuffing his hands in his jeans pockets, he shrugs, his muscles rippling with the movement. "It's true."

A shiver runs down my spine and I tear my gaze away, looking straight ahead.

"Are you cold?" he asks, stepping closer.

My body heats, my heart pounds, and my stomach churns. "I'm good." I squeak, picking up my pace.

His low chuckle rumbles over my skin as if it were his tongue. Ugh, his velvety tongue on my lips, my neck, my chest…I can't breathe.

"You sure you're okay, darlin'?"

"Yup," I proclaim, popping the p. Desperate to redirect my dangerous thoughts, I blurt out questions, not giving him a chance to respond. "So, do you like working on your family farm? How many siblings do you have? I heard you have a big family, but I only know Sage and Colton and of course, Robin and the boys. Well, I've seen your parents too, but I don't know them well. You just moved back from Waco? What did you do there?"

His fingertips land on my chin making me gasp and halting my footsteps as he tips my head up to meet his gaze. "Slow down, Mal. This isn't a race." His eyes sparkle with mischief as his lips twitch in amusement. "Besides, I have much better ideas for your mouth."

"What?" I gasp, my body igniting in response.

"When I take you out on our date, we could eat lunch, dinner, both; your choice. Why? What were you thinking?" He gives me a crooked grin making me blush from my head to my toes.

He's messing with me. "You're trouble Mr. Erickson." I take a deep breath, walking the rest of the way to my pale, yellow ranch.

"Griffin."

"Oh, I know."

He chuckles softly and finally answers some of my questions. "I've always enjoyed working on the family farm. I have two sisters and three brothers; there's six of us and Colton is the only one married with kids."

"Oh, wow. That is a big family."

"How do you know Sage and Colton?"

"I met Sage through my sister-in-law and Colton and Robin because I had Asher in my class last year."

"Oh, you're a teacher?"

I nod. "Kindergarten."

"Never thought I'd be jealous of my nephew."

Giggling, I unlock my front door and spin, leaning against it as I look up at him, arching my eyebrow in challenge. Big mistake. I suck in a sharp breath, his eyes piercing me as he steps closer. I should've said goodbye. "Jealous?"

Nodding, he affirms, "As hell." He licks his lips, my eyes tracking the movement.

As he moves further into my space, a soft whimper escapes. He leans towards me and I panic, turning my head. What the hell am I doing? I'm not ready for this; whatever this is. My body on the other hand isn't listening, curving towards him, vibrating with heat and anticipation from his close proximity. My breathing picks up its pace and I'm no longer able to focus on anything but him.

His lips brush my ear, causing goosebumps to erupt across my skin. "I know you feel this between us," he whispers, his voice a low rumble. My answering nod is nearly imperceptible. "Fuck, that's good. But I'm not going to push you. I'll respect your wishes and back away. But first, tell me why you don't want me to kiss you, Mal."

I suck my lower lip into my mouth, releasing it slowly between my teeth and relishing his low groan as he watches me through hooded eyes. Taking a deep breath, I confess before I have a chance to think about the consequences. "Griffin, I can't. Because if I start, I don't think I'll ever want to stop."

His blue eyes ignite, indecision passing over his handsome features as he wars with himself.

My body burns, preparing to combust and I'm no longer able to hold back. I don't want to. "Screw it." I push up on my tiptoes and at the same time, reach up, tugging his head down. His lips crash into mine as my body sags into his in relief.

His hard body pushes me into the door. My lips part and our tongues collide, licking, tasting, and diving in deep. Our lips move together in a frenzy, wanting, needing, bruising as we begin exploring, trying to claim each other through our kiss.

I lift my leg, curling it around him and bringing him closer, making him moan. He kisses me harder and I push back, my body alive. "Griff," I whimper, gasping for breath, my lips going right back to his like a magnet.

He groans, his hands falling to my hips as he pushes my body barely away from him, creating space and causing my foot to fall. He pulls back further, breaking our kiss as he mumbles over my lips, "Fuck, Mal. What are you doing to me?"

As he kisses me again, he slows the pace, his head falling to my forehead as we both catch our breath. "I'm not taking advantage of you."

"I'm pretty sure I'm a willing participant."

His face scrunches up, his doubt obvious. "But the drinks we had tonight and your earlier hesitation tell me we need to wait before I come inside and…"

"Griff…" I whimper, hating how desperate I sound.

"We have all the time in the world for me to be able to take my sweet time with you. I'm sure as hell going to wait until that time to make sure you want this as much as I do."

My stomach drops, his rejection bringing me back to reality. My hand falls to his chest, my fingers twitching over his hard muscles. Gently, I nudge him back, not looking up. "I should go inside. Thank you for walking me home."

His fingers run along my jawline, stopping on my chin, and tipping my head up until I meet his gaze. "No, Mal. That's not happening. I want you. Damn, I want you. But I'm taking you on a proper date and both of us will have our heads on straight when this goes further and it will if you want me half as much as I want you. You hear me, darlin'?"

I nod, pursing my lips. His head tips down and he presses his lips to mine, kissing me soft, and slow until my body feels like jelly. He breaks the kiss, and rumbles over my lips, "You hear me?"

"Yeah," I concede breathily.

"So, about that date…"

"We'll see. I have to figure out my kids before I agree to anything."

Thankfully, he nods in acceptance. His lips brush mine once more, but I quickly push him away. "My neighbors…"

He smirks. "I guess we gave them enough of a show for tonight."

My face heats instantly. "Goodbye, Mr. Erickson."

He chuckles, stepping back into my space. "First, let me see your phone."

I pull it out of my purse and hand it to him without question. He arches his eyebrows. "No security?"

"I want my kids to be able to call for help if they ever need it."

"That's what the emergency call button is for on the lock screen."

"It's fine."

"Add the security."

I watch as he enters a number and presses call, his phone immediately ringing. He ends the call and hands my phone back, giving me a sexy smirk. My stomach twists but I ignore it. "Let me know. I'll be looking forward to it."

"Okay."

"Goodnight, Mallory."

"Goodnight, Griffin." Reaching back, I push the door behind me open and step inside, needing space.

He chuckles, his blue eyes sparkling with amusement. Our eyes remain glued to the other as he stuffs his hands in his jeans pockets, stepping back, waiting until I close the door.

Heaving a sigh, I close my eyes and lean against the door. I'm in so much trouble. That kiss, those lips, that body. "Mm…" I moan.

Why do I keep running into that sexy as sin man?

Chapter Six

♡ Griffin ♡

Sage sits down at the kitchen table between me and Beau and across from Wyatt. "We just need Colton," Harper comments, the door swinging open on cue, revealing our brother.

"Good morning." He grins, overly cheerful for what we've been going through the last few days. "Dad's coming home from the hospital today."

A collective sigh of relief fills the room, the stress beginning to melt away. "Thank fuck," Beau mumbles.

Reaching over, I flick him in the back of the head at the same time I'm almost positive Wyatt kicks him under the table and Colton warns, "Watch your mouth."

"Hey!" he grunts at all three of us, but we ignore him.

"We have a list of things to do to help get ready," Colton adds. He begins divvying up the tasks as he grabs a plate and piles it with food, sitting down next to Sage.

I'm ready to throw myself into some hard work. Charlie and Jimmy, our long-time farmhands, help out with the animals and crops on opposite days, with additional help when the crops come in. I remember when we used to all help growing up, but we've all been so busy figuring our shit out, or avoiding everything around here like me, that they had to get extra help. The thought only makes me feel like an asshole. I shouldn't have let anything or anyone impact how often I came home.

"I'll take Colton with me out to the fields so we can bring in some things for the next few days. We don't have much left after the farmer's market and you guys have eaten everything we had in the kitchen," Sage comments.

"I'm a growing boy," Colton snarks, patting his stomach.

I eye him, pausing at his flat stomach, and insinuate it's anything but. "You sure are. Is Robin feeding you too much?"

He smirks. "I could never have too much of her."

The table erupts, Harper the only one clearly disgusted by his comment. "Ew." She grimaces. "I think I'm going to throw up."

"I stopped in at Papi's last night with a couple friends," Beau comments, glancing at me out of the corner of his eye with a shit-eating grin on his face.

"I heard you were old enough now to walk through the door. Congratulations," I grumble.

"TT mentioned I just missed you."

"What's your point?"

"I heard you left with some hot chick."

My eyes narrow. "Watch yourself."

"You just got home, and you're already getting into trouble Griff?" Wyatt taunts. He shakes his head as if disappointed at the same time his lips twitch in amusement.

"Who were you hangin' out with?" Sage asks, arching her eyebrows.

I wave my hand, attempting to brush it off. All my siblings stare at me as I shovel another bite of food into my mouth.

"I'm pretty sure we can ask around and we'll know in a few minutes. So, you're better off just telling us. Who was it?" Sage pushes.

"Let me take her out first, then y'all can be assholes… to me anyway."

Chuckles sound around me.

Ignoring them, I finish my breakfast and stand, bringing my dishes to the sink. "Beau, you've got kitchen duty."

"No, it's your turn."

I turn, narrowing my eyes. "Nope. After starting that, it's yours. I'm going to start moving some furniture."

"Griffin, can't you take a joke?" he calls after me, but I keep walking, his groan in frustration soon following.

It doesn't take us long to get the empty first floor bedroom set up to accommodate dad while he heals. "Knowing dad, he'll be sneaking up to his bedroom by day three, but then he'll have to deal with Ma," Harper comments, making me chuckle.

"Or we'll find him in the barn. Y'all know he can't sit still," I add.

"Speaking of the barn, we should head out and muck the stalls," Wyatt reminds us.

"But you're so good at that shit." I smirk.

"I'm not tackling that alone."

My phone pings with a text and I pull it out of my back pocket, a smile curving my lips at the site of Mallory's name. "Yeah, fine, no problem, but I've got to take care of something first," I tell him, without bothering to look in his direction.

Wyatt swings his arm around Harper as they walk out of the room with me trudging behind. "Let's go, bean."

"Ugh, don't call me that."

"Would you rather Harp?"

I tune out my brother's lingering laughter and read.

Mallory: Thank you so much for the flowers.

Stopping, I sit down on the couch, typing out a message for the woman controlling my thoughts without strings.

Me: You're welcome darlin'.

Mallory: I usually buy flowers at the farmers' market on Saturdays but my kids had me leaving forgetting everything but them.

Me. I'm glad I could do that for you.

Maybe I should put together some more things that I think she might need or want for the week. She did say she forgot everything but her kids and I'm sure she went there to buy something. I quickly send another text.

Me: Mal?

Mallory: Mr. Erickson?

I chuckle softly, knowing she's already fucking with me and loving every second of our easy banter.

Me: Griffin.

Mallory: Oh, right. Griffin. Kids are home and we're trying to decide what to do for dinner.

Me: Speaking of dinner, what about our date? When are you free?

Mallory: Impatient, Mr. Erickson?

Me: You like testing me sweetheart?

Mallory: Maybe.

My head falls back in laughter.

"Are you sexting her now?" Beau teases as he walks into the room. I flip him off and keep my focus on my phone.

Me: So, when are you free to go out with me?

I watch as the three little dots dance on my screen, disappear and dance again before a message finally pops up.

Mallory: I'm not sure.

The corners of my lips curve up in a smile.

Me: Is that a yes?

Mallory: Maybe.

Me: I'll take it.

Mallory: I didn't say okay.

Me: Sounded like a yes to me. We can pick a day later.

Mallory: You're unbelievable, Mr. Erickson.

Me: Griffin.

A towel smacks me in the back of the head. Swiftly, I reach up, grabbing it before it hits me again and yank, Beau tumbling over the back of the couch. "Hey!"

I laugh. "You started it."

Standing, I slip my phone back in my pocket, wiping off my grin as I head out to the barn. Don't need to give my siblings any more ammunition.

Chapter Seven

♡ Mallory ♡

"Only a couple more weeks," I mumble the words that have become my mantra the last month. The bell rings, vibrating through me causing my body to sag in relief at the same time I paste a smile on my face. It's not the kids fault I've had a rough day.

I love teaching Kindergarten but I can't help it, I can't get Noah out of my head. Well, Noah and Griffin, which is the problem. Griffin Erickson is consuming my thoughts. My lips tingle, remembering his heated kiss. The way he made me feel is just lust, right? It's the thought of a sexy man wanting me again, kissing me, touching me, making me primed and ready to combust. Or me feeling like a born-again virgin?

What I'm struggling with is it wasn't just any man that did this to me, it was him. It feels like Griffin came from out of nowhere. For the first time in years, a man other than Noah takes root in my dreams and I wake up hot, bothered, and unsettled and I have no idea how to handle it. I've never felt more like an inexperienced teenager than I did standing in front of him on wobbly legs, breathing heavily.

Taking a deep breath, I attempt to push both men out of my mind and focus on my class. "Okay, everyone, it's time to clean up the center you're working at."

Grumbling and cheering of little voices ensue as my classroom of twenty-one five and six-year-old kindergarteners begin picking up and getting ready to go home. "Ms. Bailey, Connor took my crayon," a sweet soft voice complains.

"I was cleaning up like Ms. Bailey told us to," he argues, scowling at her.

"But I wanted to put the pink one away."

Focusing on the two of them, I smile and advise, "Lily, Connor was just trying to help and Connor, you know Lily's favorite is the pink crayon. I appreciate your help, but maybe next time you could ask her if she wanted to put the pink one away?"

Both frown but nod in agreement. "Thank you. Now grab your things and then sit down quietly at your table so we can line up to go home."

They do as I say as Tanner sticks his head in the classroom. "Good afternoon, everyone."

"Hi, Mr. Pratt," a few kids respond.

"Ms. Bailey, could Ms. Garcia take over dismissal for a couple minutes?"

My eyes widen and my heart drops into my feet, already knowing I'm reading too much into the request. Everything is fine. "Of course, Mr. Pratt."

I glance at Izzy who smiles and nods in agreement, already taking over.

My knees wobble as I step into the hallway. "Tanner?" I question, my voice cracking.

He glances at me, his eyes instantly softening as he places a comforting hand on my arm. "Everything is okay, Mal. Your kids are fine."

I breathe a sigh of relief knowing I can get through everything else. "I love that you know me so well that you tell me that first. Thank you. Unfortunately, I know the but is coming. What's going on?"

He grimaces, exhaling harshly. "Yeah, sorry, but Mia poured a jar of glitter glue on Topher's head."

A groan escapes my lips and I push my long brown hair behind my ear as if seeing him better will change what happened. "She did what?"

His hand drops to his side as he gives me an apologetic smile. "Would you come down to the office? Miss Falk brought her and Topher down from class, but Topher is in with the nurse getting cleaned up."

My heart sinks. "Yeah, okay. Thanks Tanner."

"I'm sorry to have to deliver the bad news, but I'd rather it be me to soften the blow."

I frown. "It helps that I don't feel like I'm being judged or in trouble because it's you, but Mia is going to keep me on my toes."

"No surprise there." I give him a look out of the corner of my eye, making him chuckle. "Do you have a busy week? I know you've been working on kindergarten graduation. Like I've told you before, I'd be glad to help out with anything you need."

"Thanks. Yeah, I'm sure I'll be working on it most evenings if you're around." I give him a small smile, grateful for his offer.

"Of course, I could bring dinner for you and the kids one night if you'd like?" he arches his eyebrows in question.

Pausing, I grab his hand and look him in the eyes making sure he knows how much I appreciate him. "You know you don't have to do that."

His cheeks tinge red as he holds my gaze. "Of course, but you know I like to help you out. You work so hard, Mal." He shrugs, smirking. "Besides, my parents would likely find a way to have my hide for dinner if I didn't watch out for you."

We laugh, momentarily lightening the mood and continue walking. "True. Your parents are so sweet. I still think they love me more than you. I am the one who brought your mom flowers and you and your dad supper when your mom had pneumonia when we were in high school."

"I can't argue with you there and I wouldn't really blame them." He smirks and my cheeks heat. "I was thinking we could take the kids to the sports center this weekend so Ollie can kick his soccer ball around."

"Oh, that sounds great, but I um, I might have a...a date this weekend." I scrunch my nose up, anxious about what he might say.

His footsteps falter and his eyes go wide. "A date? Mallory, that's great. This is your first one, since..."

"I know. I think it's time."

He reaches for my hand, giving it a squeeze as he gives me a comforting smile. "I'm proud of you. A first date can't be easy."

My cheeks heat as I offer him a shy smile. "Thank you."

"Anyone I know?" He quirks a brow, curious.

"Umm... I don't think so."

"Is he from Piper Falls?"

"Yeah, but he just moved back. Griffin Erickson," I blurt out while I have the guts to say his name out loud.

"One of the Erickson's." He nods thoughtfully. "I'm happy for you Mal. I hope you have fun and let me know if you need anything."

Nodding, I agree, "I will. Thank you."

He smiles, pushing the door to the office open. I catch a glimpse of Topher out of the corner of my eye, his blonde locks covered in pink and purple glitter and the nurse applying coconut oil. "Oh, Mia," I mumble under my breath with a heavy sigh.

"Good luck," Tanner advises, his lips twitching as he opens the second door to the principal's office.

Mia sits next to her teacher assistant, Miss Falk and across from the principal, Christina Cabarillo, with her head down and her legs swinging.

"Mama," Mia whimpers, as she lifts her tearful gaze meeting mine. I crouch down next to her, wiping away her tears. "I just wanted to make his hair pretty."

I bite the inside of my cheek to stop myself from laughing. She can get into a lot of trouble for such a little ball of pink sunshine. She must get that from Noah.

A few minutes later, I'm walking out of the office tightly grasping Mia's hand. "I'm sorry, Mama."

"You need to apologize to Topher. You can't do things like that, Mia."

"I'm sorry, Mama," she cries, eliciting a heavy sigh from my lips. There's no point trying to talk to her until she's calmed down if I want her to hear me.

"Everything okay?" Tanner asks, peeking out of his office.

I smile, giving my head a slight shake. "It will be."

"Mia can stay with me in my office while you finish up with your class, and I'll meet you at the gym for aftercare."

"Are you sure?" Admittedly, sometimes I feel like I'm taking advantage of his friendship without meaning to. He offers, but I know it's a lot.

He nods and walks over, crouching down in front of Mia. "I refilled my treasure chest this morning."

She smiles, bouncing on her toes. "Yay!"

"But," I interrupt her excitement, giving them both a pointed look, "maybe she could stick to one of the old books or coloring books today since she already had her fun trying to give Topher a glitter makeover."

"Oh, of course, I'm sorry, I know better than that." He nods, frowning at Mia as her face falls. "But you could always look through and put a few things to the side to save for when you're not in trouble."

She brightens again. "Okay."

Sighing, I give in. "You will apologize to Topher when he comes out too." She nods in agreement. Grabbing Tanner's hand, she waves as I repeat, "Thank you, Mr. Pratt." He smiles and I watch as they disappear inside his office.

I step outside the office and right into a man a few inches taller than me with dark blonde hair and brown eyes dressed in blue jeans, brown cowboy boots and a plain, wrinkled, black t-shirt. He grabs my arms with his rough hands and steadies me. "Whoa, there, darlin'. Whatcha' running from?"

Gasping, I step back, eyes wide in apology. "Oh, I'm so sorry about that. I was just going back to class."

He gives me a crooked grin, his eyes sweeping over my body, his hold barely loosening. "Oh, so you're a teacher here?"

"Yes, I'm Ms. Bailey." Uncomfortable, I jerk back, his hands finally falling to his sides. I step away, attempting to hide my relief. "I'm one of the Kindergarten teachers. Do you need help with something?"

"I'm here to pick up my son from the nurse's office. He's not sick or nothin', but he got into some trouble with a girl he likes and my ex-wife couldn't be bothered to pick him up, so here I am," he announces as if he's a hero.

My heart drops into the pit of my stomach as realization hits like a punch in the gut. The similar features of the boy without the bright glitter glue poured over him blaring like a neon sign. "You're Topher's dad?"

His lips curve up before dropping almost instantly. "Yeah, I am. Frank Borato."

"I'm Mia's mom." His eyebrows arch in question. "Mia Dolan and yes, my daughter was the one who poured glitter glue on Topher. I'm so sorry."

His eyes light up with understanding as he nods his head slowly, processing the information. "I didn't realize it was that Mia."

"That Mia?" My eyebrows draw down in confusion.

Nodding, he clarifies. "I'm sorry about your husband."

I pinch my lips tightly together and give him a firm nod in acknowledgement. "I have to get back to my class for dismissal, Mr. Borato. I'm really sorry about Topher and my daughter will be apologizing."

"Well maybe you can help make it up to us?"

Shaking my head, I blurt out, "I'm sorry but I don't date students' parents."

He chuckles, making my stomach twist and not the way it does when I see Griffin. "It's good you're not my son's teacher then." I shake my head and open my mouth to argue again when he interrupts, "I'm teasing, but there's nothing wrong with a playdate for the kids."

He's right, except for the fact that he makes me uncomfortable as hell. "Well, Mia is grounded."

Grinning, he leans towards me as if about to tell me a secret. "She'll have to be free sooner or later." He leans back and winks. I bite the inside of my cheek so hard the coppery taste of blood hits my tongue. "Have a good day." He slips past me into the office, and the tension finally leaves my body.

Of course, she had to pick the one boy who has a dad that makes me squeamish and torture him. "Oh, Mia," I sigh as the bell rings and I rush down the hall towards my class, already filing quietly down the hallway towards me.

Chapter Eight

♡ Griffin ♡

Driving back towards the farm after leaving a couple bags of fresh fruits, vegetables, and herbs on Mallory's doorstep, my mind drifts to the spitfire. She has a way of keeping me on my toes. I wonder what her story is. I'm sure I can find out in a heartbeat, but hearing about anything secondhand is not the right move. The words should come from her. Mallory telling me her story would let me know she's comfortable with me. That's what I want.

A grin tugs at my lips knowing I definitely kept her relaxed the other night pressed up against her front door. Damn, I need more of that, more of her lips, her tongue, her taste, her everything. Licking my lips, I groan at the thought as I turn down our dirt driveway to the main house.

My phone rings just as I park the truck. Glancing at my phone, Mallory's name flashes across the screen making my heart speed up. "That was fast," I mumble under my breath. Turning off my truck, I answer. "Well, hello, darlin'."

"Griffin," she breathes my name, the sound going straight to my dick and making me readjust.

"I see you got my name right this time."

She huffs a laugh. "You didn't have to bring us all this food. That was so sweet."

"You mentioned you were too upset about your daughter the other day to grab what you wanted at the Farmers' Market. I'm sorry I wasn't able to drop this off to you sooner, but I sure hope you like everything."

"That's true, but it's only a few more days before it's Saturday and there's another Farmers' Market."

"What you're trying to say, sweetheart, is thank you."

She laughs, the light, airy sound dancing over my skin. "Thank you, Griffin."

"You're welcome."

A tiny voice sounds in the background, "Mommy, I'm hungry."

"Me too. Can I have this?"

"You're always hungry, Ollie."

A small smile tugs at my lips, enjoying the kids banter in the background.

"I'm sorry, but I have to get dinner going."

"Before you go, I'm asking again, go out with me."

Giggling, she accuses, "That doesn't sound like a question Mr. Erickson."

"We're back to Mr. Erickson, huh? Okay, Mallory, will you please go out with me, darlin'? Let me take you to dinner this weekend. Friday, Saturday, or even Sunday."

I hold my breath, waiting for her response, exhaling as I hear the words I've been waiting for. "Okay, Griffin. I'll go out with you."

"Yes, you're stuck with me now."

"Let me see if I can get a babysitter."

"If you need a sitter, I know several people I can call for help."

The grin in her voice is apparent as she responds. "It's okay, I have some friends I can call. I've got it."

"All right. I'm here if you need me. Let me know when you find a babysitter for the kids. I promise I'll take good care of you."

She clears her throat before responding. "I'll text you. I promise."

"I'm holding you to it. Goodbye, Mal."

"Bye, Griff."

I disconnect the call, not able to wipe the smile off my face as I finally step out of the truck. Thankfully she said yes before all my siblings went back to their lives. I need to take advantage of the time I have while they're still here.

Just as I open the back door to the house, my phone pings with a text.

Mallory: I have a babysitter for Friday night at 6pm.
Me: I'll be there to pick you up at 6:01.
Mallory: How about I meet you wherever you want to go?
Me: I'd rather pick you up, Mal.
Mallory: Okay… How about you text me when you get here? I don't think it's a good idea for you to meet my kids yet.

Should I remind her I already met her kids? This would be under much different circumstances, and she did say, "yet". Does that mean she's already thinking about it? With a shake of my head, I willingly concede.

Me: I can do that.
Mallory: Thank you. I'll see you then.
Me: You can count on it.

"What's got that smile glued to your face?" Wyatt asks, arching his eyebrows as he helps Sage set the table for dinner.

"I'm pretty sure I know what or I mean who gave you that look."

My steps falter as I pocket my phone, my eyes narrowing on my sister. "What do you mean, Sage? What do you know?"

She rolls her eyes dramatically. "Oh, come on, Griff! We knew who she was the moment you talked to her at Papi's last weekend."

I huff in disbelief, crossing my arms over my chest. "Really? Why didn't you say anything before then? Or are you trying to get me to tell you who she is?"

"Seriously, Griff? We live in Piper Falls. Small town, USA. You know the moment you came back into town, everyone knew your business and if they didn't, they did everything they could to find out. Hell, some of them worked to find out what you were doing when you weren't here. We just know better than to push you, but it's just us."

I groan, running my hand along my jaw in thought. "Well, shit. Everyone knows?" She nods and I heave a sigh.

"Listen, you really seem to like her, but…" she trails off, hesitating.
"But what?"

"She's not someone you can just hook up with, Griff," Sage warns, unapologetic.

"Hookup? What? Me?" I question, feigning innocence. She rolls her eyes, making me chuckle. "I'm very aware, Sage. There's a lot more to think about when it comes to her, but I'm not holding back. I can't. Besides, I wouldn't cross that line with any woman who has kids if I didn't see her as more."

Wyatt laughs, shaking his head in amusement. Taking a deep breath, he tilts his head to the side, assessing me. "Huh. You really do like her, don't you? It's not just because you're watching out for Noah's family?"

My hand falls to my chest as it squeezes, making it difficult to breathe. I look at my brother, eyes wide, hoping what he's insinuating is anything but true. "What the fuck did you just say?"

Both of them gasp, dropping what they're doing to give me their full attention. "You didn't know?" Sage asks.

"Didn't know what?" I push, needing to hear it.

"Mallory is Noah's widow."

"Fuck! I should've known." I begin pacing next to the counter. "Maybe if I would've come back for the wedding or met his family when I came home, or even given her my fucking condolences at the funeral, but I was too focused on my own grief, blaming myself for not being here for him."

"It wasn't your fault," Wyatt interrupts.

I shake my head, blurting furiously, "I know that, but that doesn't take away the guilt. When I got the call from Matt, it was already too late. If they wouldn't have caught the fucker so fast, I would've been hunting him down myself."

"Well, I for one am glad you weren't chasing down a murderer," Sage mutters. I give her a look and she shakes her head in denial. "The less I know, the better, Griff. The asshole murdered his girlfriend and was trying to flee before they found her body. After killing Noah, he mugged and killed a fourth-grade teacher. I refuse to think of you going after someone like that." She shivers, quickly shaking it off.

My stomach turns, almost wishing it were me instead of Caden that arrested him that night several hours after the BOLO, or Be On The Lookout was issued. Although, the asshole didn't go down easy. "It fucking kills me that I couldn't get over my own bullshit when I should've been here."

"Does it matter, Griff?" Sage asks.

"Of course, it matters."

She takes a step closer, her voice softening, "No, does it really matter? You know Noah. He wouldn't want his wife or his family to be alone. What better person to watch out for them than one of his best friends?"

"Matt, Reid, and everyone else at the station has always watched out for her and the kids. They're doing well," Wyatt adds.

"What does that even mean?"

"It means from what I heard about the two of you the other night, she's ready to move on and apparently she wants to move on with you," he grumbles, his sarcasm thick on his tongue.

With a heavy sigh, my hand returns to my chin, running along my jawline in thought. "Does she, though? You think she'll date another cop after everything that happened?"

"Fuck if I know." Wyatt laughs. "But we're not the ones you should be asking."

Can I even go there? Mallory runs through my mind, her bright eyes, her full lips, and her sassy smirk every time she calls me Mr. Erickson. I clench my jaw, stifling my groan.

"You have to think about the kids too," Sage comments.

I glare at my sister. "You know me, Sage. I've already been thinking what it would be like to date a woman with three young kids. They were at the Farmers' Market on Saturday. Her youngest seems to do her own thing. She tries to lead, but her brother is not having it. I can already see her mind creating an entire world of new things and she already trusts me."

"Damn, just talking about them your face went from a scowl to a grin and you've barely spent five minutes with them." Sage laughs.

"I don't know much about the oldest, except she looks exactly like Noah. How the fuck did I not see it? His son too, except he has her eyes." I shake my head. "What the fuck is wrong with me? How did I not know?"

"How could you? It seems obvious now, but I never realized…" Wyatt shakes his head, his voice trailing off.

"I'm an asshole." I huff a humorless laugh. "Honestly, I don't know much about any of them, but fuck I want to know more. I want to know everything."

"It sounds to me like you've already made your decision." Sage comments, fighting her smile.

"Now you just have to let Mallory make hers." Wyatt states, arching his eyebrow in challenge.

"It's not betraying him? She's Noah's…"

"She hasn't been Noah's for over two years. She's his widow and the mother of his children. He's not their future. She needs to move on for her and her kids. It's good for all of them. Noah included," Sage proclaims causing my heart to squeeze for more reasons than I'm able to register.

"Besides, she likely will be someone's again. She's gorgeous, smart, works hard, a great mom…"

"All that and so damn much more," I interrupt my brother.

He smirks. "And after the assholes in town saw you hitting on her and leaving with her, they all figured that meant she's now fair game. At least that's what I heard." He shrugs like it's no big deal. "I'd act fast." Wyatt laughs as my body tenses.

"Fuck," I mumble under my breath just as Beau and Harper walk in from outside. There's no way in hell I'm letting that happen, at least not if I can help it.

"I'll get mom and dad," Beau offers, striding right through the kitchen. "Dad said he was eating at the table tonight."

"Hey, guys," Harper says as she makes her way to the oven to pull out the roast. "I was talking to mom earlier and before everyone leaves on Sunday, we're doing a family breakfast. Colton said Robin and the boys will be able to come with him then too, so it's perfect."

"What if I have plans?" Wyatt taunts.

"Change them," she demands, planting her hand on her hip, leveling him with her glare.

Is this what it's like for dinner at Mallory's house? The banter, the friendship, the chaos, the love. Everyone coming together to help. I wonder if she has her family close by. Is she close with Noah's family? Carla? My stomach twists. Damn, I wanna' know.

She should have family to depend on, but does she?

Chapter Nine

♡ Mallory ♡

By the time Thursday comes around, it feels like the week has lasted the entire month of May. "Shouldn't school be over already?" I question, feeling more like one of my students than their teacher.

Ms. Garcia laughs as we wave and smile watching Connor walk away, his hand in his mom's. "It has been a long week. I think the kids are ready for summer."

We turn to walk back towards school when a booming voice calls out, "Ms. Bailey, could I talk to you for a moment?"

Spinning around, I smile at Lily Salvatore's dad, Ms. Garcia stepping back, but waiting. With all the vandalism that's been going on in town lately, I appreciate it. "How can I help you Mr. Salvatore?"

He grins, glancing nervously in Ms. Garcia's direction before focusing back on me. "Rich, please." I nod in acknowledgement, knowing I would never call him by his first name while his daughter is in my class. I don't care that there's only a couple weeks left. "I just wanted to say thank you. You've been a wonderful teacher for Lily."

"Of course, she's been a joy to have in class. She's a smart girl."

"She is." He nods, shifting on his feet. "She definitely keeps me on my toes. She's had a rough year with her mom gone, you know." He glances at me, practically begging for me to relate to him.

My eyes soften. "I do understand. My kids have all had their ups and downs the last two years. If you and Lily ever need anything, please let me know."

His eyes brighten, returning to mine. "Well, actually, I was thinking maybe you'd like to go out for dinner or something sometime? With me," he adds on quickly as an afterthought.

My heart squeezes for him. He's clearly stepping out of his comfort zone. "I'm really sorry, but I don't date my students' parents."

"Well, the year is almost over." His lips twitch in amusement, watching my reaction, hopeful.

Without thought, I shake my head, already knowing my reason why. He's not Griffin. He's the only man I seem ready to step out of my comfort zone with. "I'm sorry, but I don't think that's a good idea."

His face falls, but I stand my ground. I'm not about to go on a date with someone because I feel bad for them. I wouldn't want anyone doing that to me. I know exactly what that pity feels like. "Thank you for being so honest. I appreciate it."

Forcing a smile, I nod. "Have a good night."

He walks away and I turn towards Ms. Garcia, finding her covering her mouth with her hand, obviously holding back her laughter. "Did he just ask you out?"

I shrug, and she laughs, no longer able to hold back. "Why is that funny?"

"You're exhausted and want nothing to do with it, but I'm pretty sure that's the third, no fourth man who asked you out this week."

"What do you mean four?"

"That's what's holding you up? Four is Mr. Pratt. I know you don't count him."

"That's because he doesn't count. I've known him my whole life. He's like my brother."

"Sure," she laughs. "It's like there's something in the water this week. Hey, all eligible bachelors, Mallory is starting to date again. Act now before you lose your chance. Or maybe they just all heard you were out with that sexy hunk of a man last weekend."

I roll my eyes dramatically like Tiegan would. "Funny."

"If you're not going out with him, I sure as hell will."

"Stop."

"Does that mean you're going out with him?"

"You know, I can finish up here. Tanner will wait for me."

"Smooth subject change," she taunts. "Okay, I can take a hint, but you have to let me know when you finally say yes to a date with that man so I can live vicariously through you. My dating life is nonexistent."

"Not because it has to be." I wave her away laughing. "Get out of here."

As I finish cleaning up my classroom for the day, I stop at the office first to get everything from my mailbox. Tanner waves as I walk in. I reach for my mail and lean against the wall, sifting through. A small, plain white envelope grabs my attention, my first name in black block lettering. Slipping my finger underneath the flap, I tug, ripping it open and flinching as the paper slices my finger. "Ouch," I mumble, instinctively putting my finger to my lips.

"Paper cut?" Tanner asks, locking his office and moving towards me.

"Yeah, I'm fine," I grumble, unfolding the paper, trying not to get any blood on it.

He gives me a cheeky grin and reaches under the secretary's desk, pulling out the first aid kit. My focus returns to the letter as he grabs my hand, gently attending to my small cut.

My eyebrows draw down at first glance, the short letter written in the same black block lettering.

Darlin' Mallory,

It's been a long time since I've been this excited about summer break, but this year, I'm ready to shoot out the lights with you. I've been watching you strut around this school all year, sweetheart but our wait is over. We're finally free to be together. No more husband, no more school, no more barriers. It's no longer forbidden for us to date, to kiss, to fuck. Get ready, gorgeous, because the moment I lay my hands on you will be sweeter than stolen honey.

My heartbeat pounds out of my chest, my breathing picking up its pace. What the hell is this? Tanner finishes the task at hand, wrapping a sparkly silver Band-Aid around my pointer finger and kisses the tip. "Better?"

"Thanks," I mumble, my eyes focused on the letter in front of me before shifting, uneasily taking in everything around me, but it's just me and Tanner.

"What's wrong?"

Gulping down the lump in my throat, I shake my head, not able to form the words. My eyes widen as he looks at me, my fear reflected in his eyes. He rips the paper out of my trembling hand, his eyes widening as he reads. "What the fuck? Where did this come from?"

"I…I don't know," I stammer, pointing towards my mailbox.

He reaches for me, pulling me into his arms and holding me tight. "We need to call the police."

"No!" I argue, planting my hands on his chest and pushing him away. The thought of going to the police tamps down my fear. "We can't."

"We can. You need to report this, Mal. This," he holds up the letter, "isn't something to mess around with."

"I don't want to worry any of the guys. You know how protective they would be over something like this, especially with me and the kids."

He huffs a humorless laugh. "Yeah, as they should be."

"The guy is probably harmless; a jerk, but harmless. Worst case scenario, he'll ask me out and I'll say no. End of story." His eyes narrow on me. "If anything else happens, I'll report it, just please don't make me say anything to anyone at the station yet. They'll likely put someone on me twenty-four, seven. Hell, Matt would probably move in and that wouldn't be good for me or the kids. They would be terrified. What would I even tell them?" I see the hesitation on his face and close the distance between us once again, grabbing his hand and squeezing. "Please, Tanner?"

His hold tightens on my hand, searching my eyes. A heavy sigh escapes, his entire body sagging in defeat. "Fine but call me at any time of the day or night if you need anything and don't you dare even think about hiding something from me."

"Of course," I concede knowing he would want me to do all of that anyway. "You already promised you're coming over tonight anyway to help me with kindergarten graduation plans," I remind him, attempting to lighten the mood.

"Fine. Why don't we order pizza? I'll stop home and change before I come over."

"The kids will love that."

After a few hours, the pizza had been devoured and the kids were dressed in their pj's ready to watch the new animated movie that released last week. I press play and give Tiegan the remote. "Pause if anyone needs to use the bathroom. I don't need y'all fighting tonight."

"Okay," she huffs, rolling her eyes.

I make my way back to the table, Tanner looking over my folder with the schedule and assignments for each of the students. "Looks like you've already done all the hard parts."

"Yeah, but I was hoping you could help me with the programs. You know I'm not the best with those."

"Of course, I'll just need a copy of this schedule." He pulls his laptop out of his bag and turns it on. "Is this on your computer so I can transfer it easily or should I type it in?"

"Well…" I begin, scrunching up my nose.

He laughs. "No worries."

"Thank you, Tanner."

"No problem."

My phone pings with a text and I reach for it, my lips tugging upwards at the sight of Griffin's name.

Griffin: I can't wait to see you Friday.

Me: So, I shouldn't cancel?

Griffin: You won't.

Me: And why is that?

Griffin: Because you don't want me coming over to your house yet with your kids.

Me: You wouldn't.

Griffin: Try me.

Who's that?" Tanner asks, arching his eyebrows.

"What?"

Tanner steps closer, "Who are you talking to? Whoever it is got you smiling."

My cheeks heat. "Um, Griffin Erickson."

He smirks. "Does that mean you've agreed to go on a date with the poor bastard?"

"Yeah, this weekend."

"Want me to watch the kids for you? I'd love to spend some time with them."

I shake my head. "No, Olivia Connery is going to watch them."

"Amber's sister?"

"Yeah, Matt said she's looking forward to it. Besides, I shouldn't have to depend on you for that stuff."

"You know I don't mind, Mal. I love those kids."

"I know and I appreciate it, Tanner."

Chapter Ten

♡ Griffin ♡

I pull up in front of her house, staying back from the front windows. I don't care if anyone sees me, but I want to be respectful of Mallory and her kids. They are what's important. Well, them and Noah. Fuck. Will he always be at the back of my mind? I sure as hell hope not, I already have no idea what I'm supposed to do about it. So, for now, I'll force him out and send a text to Mallory because I know I can't let this thing with her go. I'm pulled to chase her like thunder chases lightning in the middle of a thunderstorm. It will happen no matter how far away the possibility seems.

Me: I'm here and parked out front. It goes against everything I believe in to keep my ass in this truck and not come to your door to pick you up properly. I promise, I will make it up to you.

Mallory: Thank you. I'll be right out.

I grab the flowers and step out of the car walking around and leaning against the passenger side door, waiting. It's the least I can do. As the door swings open, I push off my truck and Mallory steps outside wearing a white sundress with eyelet daisies along the edges and scattered around the material, the length making her legs look a mile long. Her feet are adorned with the same tan cowboy boots she was wearing the other night. My eyes drift up her body, the dress showing off her curves, and exquisite chest. Fuck, I'm in so much trouble.

"Hi!" She grins.

I lick my lips and take a deep breath, whistling on my exhale. "Damn, you look gorgeous, Mal."

She blushes, the color making my dick twitch. "Thank you. You clean up nice yourself, handsome."

I glance down at my dark blue jeans, cowboy boots and navy-blue button down, with the sleeves rolled up to my elbows and smirk. I'm glad she thinks so. Dressing up is not my thing. "These are for you," I tell her, holding out the flowers.

"Thank you. I should go put them in some water."

"No. I'm not letting you out of my sight for the rest of the night."

She giggles and I emphasize. "I'm not kidding, darling. There's more where those came from. Let's go."

"Okay." She nods and moves towards my truck.

I reach my arm around her and tug the door open, my other hand falling to the small of her back making my fingers tingle. She climbs in and I shut the door behind her. I jog around the front, slipping in behind the wheel and looking over at her once again.

"Where are we going?"

"Just give me a minute to appreciate the beauty in my truck."

Her head falls back in laughter sending chills down my spine. The sound, the movement, the warmth in her eyes, everything about her is the most beautiful thing I've ever seen. I'm so fucked with this woman.

"That sounds like a line Mr. Erickson."

"With anyone else it would've been, but I promise it's not with you."

Her lips part, a soft gasp escaping drawing me in. "Another line," she whispers.

A smile tugs at my lips as I lean towards her, my hand reaching up and cupping her face in my hand. My thumb runs over her lips before I replace it with my mouth. Soft and slow I move my mouth over hers, breathing her in, tasting her on her vanilla lip gloss. Keeping our kiss simple is one of the hardest things I have to do, but I'm determined to do right by her and force myself to pull back. "Damn. I've wanted to do that again since the last time."

"That was nothing like last time, but still so good," she admits, bringing a smile to my face.

"I'll take it." I give her another chaste kiss and move away with a heavy sigh. "Okay, dinner. I'm taking you to dinner."

She giggles. "Are you telling me or reminding yourself, Mr. Erickson?"

Chuckling, I start the truck and slowly pull away from the curb. "I thought we could go to Aurora Heights for dinner. Great food, incredible view of the falls and perfect company. Is that okay with you?"

Her smile falters and her face pales. "Umm…"

"If you don't want to go there, we can go somewhere else," I offer, as my heart plummets into my gut, already feeling like I'm losing her.

She shakes her head, "It's not that I don't like it there. It's beautiful and the food is amazing, but…" she pauses, gulping down the lump in her throat. "I just haven't been there since my husband, and he proposed to me there."

"Ah." I nod, hating myself for the jealousy slamming into me. I'd give anything to have him back and I can guaran-fucking-tee she would say the same. Get over yourself asshole. "It doesn't sound like it's a good first date for us."

"Maybe some other time."

"Sounds like you're already scrounging for another date," I tease, attempting to lighten the suddenly tense mood.

She gives me what I'm looking for, laughing softly as her petite body slowly eases, melting back into the seat. "Yup, you got me, Mr. Erickson."

Damn, I'm starting to like hearing her call me that; at least the way she says it. Her voice sounds like liquid heat. Quickly, I shove the thought out of my head and focus on where I'm driving. "What about Abuela's Outpost? I know it's more casual, but it is my speed."

I watch her out of the corner of my eye as she exhales slowly, the color finally returning to her cheeks. "Dinner at Abuela's without kids sounds perfect."

"You got it." My body relaxes and I make a U-turn, driving towards Abuela's. "So, tell me more about your kids." Not only do I want to know more, but it's the perfect topic to get us back on track and keep my head out of the gutter.

A soft smile lights up her face at the mention of her kids. "Tiegan is my oldest, she's smart and she's such a good big sister. She's protective, more wary than the other two."

"Doesn't trust easily?"

"Definitely not." She laughs as if just remembering something, the sound hitting me square in the chest. "Ya' sure about this? I could talk forever about my kids."

"I'm positive." I nod, smiling. Reaching over the console, I give her hand a gentle squeeze. I could listen to her talk all day, but the way it brightens everything around her is something I could bask in for the rest of my life.

"Tiegan has gotten quieter since her father passed. I guess being the oldest, she remembers more. She looks just like him." Pausing, she gulps down the lump in her throat, while I do the same. "Anyway, she's always been a big reader, but she takes her time wading into anything now, unless her brother and sister are involved."

"My son Oliver, we call him Ollie. He reminds me so much of his dad with his looks and what he likes to do. Everything except his eyes are my husband. He's smart too and loves sports. Right now, he's really into soccer, but he'll play anything and loves getting dirty. He gives his sisters a hard time, but you know he'd do anything for them, even at just seven-years-old."

"Mia, my youngest, she's the one that is going to give me gray hair." She laughs.

"Why is that? She was sweet."

"Yeah, but she does her own thing, just like she did when she ran off that day. She gets so focused on what she wants to do, that she doesn't listen to anyone else. Plus, she seems to have no fear and loves to explore or run off. The pink dress she was wearing when you saw her is her favorite. Dressing up like a princess, and then rolling down a hill are normal with her. Honestly, she'll start kindergarten in the fall and I think it will be good for her."

I park my truck next to Abuela's, turning to look at her. "They sound like incredible kids."

"They are." She smiles back at me, my heart lurching in response.

Taking a deep breath, I let go of her hand and instruct, "Wait here." I jog around to the other side and open the door, holding out my hand. As she slips her hand in mine, and steps out, my body warms. It feels like this is where she was meant to be, but how can that be when she used to be married to one of my best friends? I pull the front door of Abuela's open and shake the thought out of my head. "After you."

"Thank you."

We step onto the polished concrete floors and walk towards the back near the wooden bar taking up most of the wall. Mallory waves to Eduardo, wiping down the bar. He grins, both of us exchanging a head nod. She slips into a high-back booth and I regretfully release her hand as I slide in across from her, the worn vinyl seat squeaking under my weight. The familiar stucco walls painted blue and yellow add to the homey atmosphere.

"I haven't been here in a while. I'm suddenly craving a steak burrito."

"Their chicken tacos are my favorite," she comments.

"Do you like guac or queso?"

"Mm, yes to both."

"So, I guess we don't need a menu."

A young waitress steps up to the table, her black hair pulled up into a high ponytail. "Hi, y'all, I'm Rose. Welcome to Abuela's Outpost. Would you like anything to drink, while you look over the menu?"

"Hi, Rose. I think we're ready to order," I tell her, nodding towards Mallory.

We both order and wait for the waitress to walk away before continuing. Mallory leans on her elbows, angling towards me, the movement pushing up her chest and drawing my attention to her already ample cleavage. My body heats and I readjust, clearing my throat and focusing on her caramel eyes. "Do you come here a lot?"

She shakes her head. "No, but my kids do love tacos. We used to order from here a lot, and we do come sometimes."

"So, you spend all day with kids and all night with kids. What do you like to do when you're doing something just for you?"

She bites her lower lip making me clench my jaw before I lean over and suck it out from between her teeth. Slowly, she releases it and I practically breathe a sigh of relief. "Um, honestly I love music you can feel, movies that make you laugh and some that make you cry, relishing in the outdoors, going to the fair, good food and animals, but family is the most important thing in the world to me. Nothing else really matters."

Her statement squeezes my heart. Hurting for her loss and feeling how much she loves her kids. "You're right. The little things make the time with family more fun, but family is the most important thing to me too."

"Good." She smiles, thoughtful. "For so long, I've been good with things being about my kids. I need to make sure they're okay. Ya' know? They've been through so much."

"Kids are resilient and it's obvious you're a great mom."

Her cheeks turn a beautiful shade of pink as she sits a little taller, her pride evident. "Thanks. I'm lucky I have a lot of support though. My sister-in-law likes to take them sometimes and tonight Olivia is babysitting."

"Olivia?" I ask, arching my eyebrow. I know that name.

"Yeah, my friend Matt, his… well he connected me with Amber's sister, Olivia. She's babysitting. Matt has helped out a lot. He's really good to me and the kids."

"Is that right?" I ask, another wave of jealousy washing over me for another one of my best friends. Matt has called to check on my dad, but I haven't seen him since I've been home, and it makes me feel like an asshole.

I haven't really had any time with all my spare time spent helping my family. That might be only a partial truth, but Mallory is the one consuming the rest of my thoughts. If I'd already talked to Matt, I would know how close they are, and not have to decipher whatever he is to her.

"Yeah, Ollie adores him. He comes over all the time and helps me out with the kids and stuff. They love hanging out with Uncle Matt. He's not their real uncle or anything, but he is like family to us."

"Hmm… That's great. I'm glad you have that." I am happy she has that, but I need to talk to Matt before I get in too deep. She smiles brightly, the sight hitting me in the chest. I think it's already too late.

"Me too."

Chapter Eleven

♡ Mallory ♡

"Mm," I mumble, licking my lips as we finish eating. "That was delicious."

"Are you testing me, Mal?"

My eyebrows draw down in confusion. "What?" He stares at me, his body taut as he takes a deep breath, clenching and unclenching his fist. "Are you alright?"

He chuckles softly, the deep sound vibrating over my skin, eliciting a soft sigh from my lips. He shakes his head as I take another sip of water, trying to cool my thoughts, but having Griffin's eyes on me does the opposite. My body burns like it's coming alive for the first time all over again. Looking across the table at him has me losing my train of thought and my heart racing out of control. I almost forgot what it was like to have this feeling; the butterflies, the anticipation, the excitement, and the intense attraction. The two of us have an undeniable chemistry. I like feeling like this again; I like it a lot, but I'm also terrified.

Am I ready for something like this?

Maybe I should know what this is between us before I decide. I know better than to make assumptions. I've got to know more about this man.

"So, Griffin, I feel like tonight has been all about me. I'd love to get to know more about you. You grew up here?"

"I did." He nods, wiping his mouth and setting his napkin on the table.

He must've known Noah, but I've never met him before. I don't remember seeing him at our wedding and it felt like the whole town was invited. He's not someone I would forget, even on my wedding day. Maybe they weren't close. I pinch my lips tightly together in thought. I'll never know if I don't ask. "Did you…"

"Dance with me," he interrupts. Standing, he holds his hand out to me and patiently waits, his sexy crooked smile curving his lips, making me lick my own in anticipation. But of what, I'm not exactly sure. Yes, it's been a helluva' long time, but I can't exactly jump him in the middle of Abuela's. This town talks enough without my help.

I put my hand in his, tingles shooting up my arm. "Lead the way, Mr. Erickson." I don't know why I started calling him that, but now I can't stop. Teasing him has become my new favorite hobby. I enjoy the spark and heat it ignites in his eyes. Knowing it's me who put that look there, just urges me on. I've always been told not to play with fire, but when it comes to him, that's like telling a fish to stay out of the water. It seems to be impossible.

He spins me around and pulls me close in one swift move, pulling a laugh out of me. "Smooth Mr. Erickson. Real smooth."

As I tip my head back to look up at him, he leans down, our lips only a millimeter apart. My breath hitches, the room suddenly feeling like a furnace. "This was a bad idea," he murmurs, his deep voice barely audible.

My eyes widen and I flinch. Steeling myself, I plant my hands on his hard chest, and shove, attempting to push him back, but he holds me close, unmoving. "What?" I squeak, barely heard over the music.

Tipping his head closer to me, he whispers in my ear, his heated breath eliciting goosebumps across my skin. "Not what you're thinkin'. Having you this close makes me want to do things to you I'm not about to do in a public place, let alone things I don't think you're quite ready for."

My heart jumps up to my throat. With his words, his voice, his touch, and his hard body pressed up against mine, I'm struggling for air, my body comes alive with awareness and my panties are suddenly soaked. This man takes me from zero to sixty in two seconds flat. I can just imagine what it would be like to be with him and damn do I want it. I want to know what it's like to be touched by a man again.

A soft sigh escapes as I boldly ask, "What kind of things?"

A slow easy grin lights up his face. Reaching up, he runs his thumb along my lower lip and my tongue flicks out. Heaving a sigh, he chuckles humorlessly. "You're going to be the death of me, darlin'."

I laugh. "That doesn't answer my question."

He shakes his head, clearly amused, but I don't find it funny. My entire body is on alert, all too aware of how long it has been since I've been with anyone. My heart squeezes momentarily and I exhale slowly, letting it go. My body seems to already know the time is coming. It's so close, it's within reach. I don't want to wait anymore.

"Next time I need to bring you somewhere I can at least kiss the hell out of you without half the town watching."

I arch my eyebrow in challenge, my lips twitching in amusement. "Who said there's going to be a next time?"

He smirks. "I did. You haven't figured out that I don't give up easily?"

"It's not like I gave ya' a hard time."

"Eh." He shrugs, making me laugh.

"What? Not as easy as you're used to?" I taunt, arching my eyebrows, my voice thick with sarcasm.

The music picks up and I give his chest another nudge, but this time he reluctantly loosens his hold and instantly, I feel the loss. The simple emotion suddenly feels like too much. "Everything okay?"

"It's just fine, Mr. Erickson, but it's starting to get crowded in here. Plus, I have to get up for my kids early in the morning."

His hand slides to the small of my back as he guides me back to our table, his gaze shifting around the room before landing back on me. "Looks like it. Let me pay and we'll go before it gets too busy."

I nod in agreement. "Okay." He lays money on the table, his hand returning to my back as he follows me outside. "Thank you," I repeat the moment we're sitting in his truck. "That was a lot of fun."

His lips twitch, his cocky grin slipping through. "You're right about that, but tonight went way too fast, Mal. I'm not ready for it to end."

My cheeks heat and my heart skips a beat. "I like hanging out with you too."

He chuckles softly. "I'm taking a beautiful woman out to dinner. Call it what it is, Mallory, a date."

I nod, repeating it in my head before saying them aloud. "I had a lot of fun on our date." My nerves return the moment the words leave my lips.

"Let me take you out again."

"Don't you think we should finish this date first?"

He shakes his head. "Doesn't matter. Go out with me again."

Laughter erupts from my chest and I shake my head in amusement. "Persistence is definitely not your weakness."

"I know what I want."

"Lust will do that to ya'," I blurt out before I think better of it. My body floods with heat, embarrassed. I shake my head, willing the past ten seconds to be erased from existence.

He huffs a laugh as he pulls up near my house and parks the truck. "Yeah, I'm not the only one feeling that." He looks over at me, his gaze heated.

"No, but I have my kids to think about."

"You think they're not on my mind?" He arches his eyebrows in challenge. "I thought about them the moment you hit me with your car."

"I didn't hit you."

His lips twitch and he continues. "My point is, I knew you were a mom right from the start. And thanks to your daughter, I knew you were a single mom." I gulp, breaking our gaze. "I'll be blunt, Mallory, so you know where I'm at. I'm not the kind of asshole who screws over a single mom for a fuck." I flinch and his voice softens. "Yeah, there's no denying how much I want you, but I want to get to know you. I want you to say yes to another date with me."

Lifting my head, I meet his gaze, his sincerity overwhelming, squeezing my chest. He leans closer, his hand slipping into my hair as he cradles my face, my body leaning into his touch without my consent. I'm so confused. I want this, but even though I know it's not, it feels like a betrayal. With the way my body is reacting to him when we haven't done anything but kiss, how can it not? But damn, I wanna kiss him again.

"You brighten the room with one of your smiles. When you laugh, everyone who can hear you looks to see what's so funny. The moment you open your mouth, there's a crowd pushing in to listen whether you see it or not. It's blatantly obvious I'm not the only man interested from the few times I've been around you. And there's no way in hell I want to take a step back and let my chance slip through my fingers. I want to know everything about you. I'm shootin' my shot, Mal, and I'm not going to stop showing up for you, unless you tell me you're not interested. Then again, even then, I'll be there in a heartbeat if you need me or just want me to be because you've already pulled me in."

This man. By the time he's finished talking, I don't hear anything except the flow of blood in my veins and the pounding of my heart. I close the distance between us, pressing my lips to his as a soft moan escapes between us. Our mouths move together in a slow, sensual kiss, further igniting me. His tongue slips into my mouth colliding with mine, licking, tasting, and exploring.

"Griffin," I whimper as I pull back, gasping for breath.

His forehead falls to mine, my face still cupped in his hands. "Let me walk you to your door."

"I'm sorry, but not tonight. Not yet."

"Then, go out with me again tomorrow." He lifts his head, looking into my eyes, his sexy grin in place.

My stomach twists as I reply. "Okay, if you can do dinner again."

"Dinner is perfect. I have the farmer's market in the morning and I'll get everything else done before that. What about your kids?"

My chest tightens, loving that he really does think of them. "The kids are going to dinner with their grandparents. They're picking them up at four and they'll probably be gone until about seven."

"Good, I'll pick you up at four-fifteen."

"For dinner?" I question, wide-eyed. "I understand all of them going that early, but why would we?"

"Because I want all the time with you I can get, darlin'. I'll come up with something else for us to do before we eat." He winks, making me blush.

I nod, my response barely a squeak. "Okay." I move to get out of the truck and his hand falls to my thigh, squeezing, and halting me.

"Wait," he rasps.

I do as he says, my body taut, my nipples standing at attention and my panties desperately needing to be changed. His hand falls away and he clears his throat, jumping out of the truck. Moments later, he yanks the door open and helps me down, my body vibrating from his touch. "Thank you, Griffin."

His eyes flash as his hands weave into my hair, tilting my head back. He leans down pressing his lips to mine, kissing me soft and slow. A soft whimper escapes as he lifts his head, ending it all too soon. "I'll see you tomorrow."

"Bye." My hand shakes as I wave awkwardly. Spinning on my heel, I stride towards the house, his eyes burning into me with every step. I unlock my door and slip inside, wondering if I'll make it another day before I wrap my legs around that sexy man.

Chapter Twelve

♡ Griffin ♡

As I get ready to leave for town to pick up Mallory, Noah consumes my thoughts. The guilt of not being there for him because of my own fucking ego hits me hard. Why couldn't I get over myself? We were just kids. I should've dealt with it, with her, years ago, then I would've been here for you. Maybe if I was here that day I… I huff a humorless laugh. You what asshole? There's nothing I could've done, it was what any one of us would assume was a common traffic stop. Doesn't make me feel any less guilty.

I'm the asshole who didn't show up for the funeral. Well, technically I did, but I couldn't even tell my best friends I was there, hiding in the back and running out before it ended. I texted Matt and lied to him like a fucking coward. All because of her. She stopped me from being there for him while he was still alive and then again when we were all grieving, just trying to get through and understand your useless fucking death. Why did I let her? And why the hell did it have to be you?

"It was never supposed to be you Noah!" I grit through my teeth, slamming my hands against the wall next to the bathroom mirror in frustration. Closing my eyes, I take a few deep breaths, attempting to get my heartrate under control.

Then again, if it wasn't you, I wouldn't be taking your wife on a date and that thought is fucked up on so many levels. I open my eyes, glaring at my reflection. "Your *wife*, Noah. What the fuck am I supposed to do with that?"

I feel guilty as hell for wanting her, but that sure as fuck doesn't make me want her any less. The things I imagine doing to her. I'm hard just thinking about it. I run my hand through my hair in frustration. "Shit, Noah, I'm sorry, but I can't stop myself from going to her." I promise it isn't just about sex. You know I wouldn't go there if that were true. I want to be there for her, and protect her, if she lets me. And I know you wouldn't want her to be alone.

You always talked about her like she was your world and I see it. I stare into the mirror as if staring into the eyes of my best friend, desperate for him to see my intentions. Struggling for breath, I mutter, "I could fucking love her, Noah – her and your kids." Might be crazy, but I know it more than I know I'll take my next breath. The thought slams into me and my head drops as I grip the sides of the sink for support.

Am I good enough? Am I the man you would want to be here for your family since you can't be? Or maybe that man is Matt. Fuck.

I heave a sigh and stride back to my room. Grabbing my phone, I sit on the edge of my bed.

She may not even want to give me that chance. My hand hovers over her name, wondering if I should make up an excuse for tonight and figure my shit out. The thought makes my stomach turn. I'm not canceling, but I do need to talk to Matt. My fingers move before my brain registers my actions, deciding for me.

Me: You got a few?

Matt: Your dad okay?

Me: He's getting better. Hope he'll be home soon.

Matt: Good. Yeah, I've got time. I'm at my dad's. Luke and Aly are here too.

Me: On my way.

I slip my phone in my pocket, and grab my wallet, heading for the back door. I swipe my keys off the hooks in the kitchen and step outside, right into Sage. "Another date?"

"I'm going to see Matt."

"Really? You're not dressed up for Mallory?"

"Maybe. I'm picking her up later."

She grins. "Now that makes sense."

Heaving a sigh, I step past her and wave.

A few minutes later, I'm pulling into the driveway at the Bradley Farm. The familiar large white farmhouse looms in front of me with the same tire swing hanging from the oak tree appearing much larger than it had been the last time I was here. I spent many days and nights here over the years, just as Matt did at my house. More than anything, I love the simplicity here. Their list of chores was much smaller with the farm being more of a hobby for his dad. His dad treated the cows in the barn out back like they were family pets. A smile tugs at my lips, remembering each of them named after one of the Beatles.

As I step out of the truck, the front door swings open and Matt walks out with a wide grin on his face, his dimples showing. He's a few inches taller than me with a similar build, broad shoulders, and a narrow waist. He sets two bottles down on the wicker coffee table as I step up onto the front porch and turns to me. "It's good to see you man," he proclaims, meeting me with a one-armed hug and a firm pat on the back I return.

"Good to see you too, Matt."

His smile falters. "I'm just sorry it's under these circumstances."

"Yeah, me too, but my dad is doing better."

"Good. You wanna' sit out here?" He points to the worn wicker furniture that used to be white, the paint chipping, my eyes landing on the porch swing at the end.

"Sure, but I don't have much time."

He glances at me as if noticing for the first time that I'm dressed up and frowns making my stomach roil. Fuck, does he already know? It's likely. "Got a date?"

"Yup."

"Huh." He grinds his jaw and turns, dropping onto the nearest chair. I sit down next to him as he reaches for the beers he set down before, handing one to me. "Thought this might be the kind of conversation we'd need a drink."

Fuck he knows. I glance down at the label of the local beer, a pale ale I haven't tried and take a sip. Not quite ready to talk, I blurt out, "I can't believe your little brother is getting married."

"Yeah, Aly's good for him."

His hazel eyes bore into the side of my head, and I finally turn, meeting his gaze head on. "Go ahead, Matt, ask me."

"So, it's true?"

There's no point in denying it. "Yeah, I have a date with Mallory."

He exhales slowly, controlling his breath. I watch as he sets his beer down and turns, his accusing gaze meeting mine. "What the fuck ya' doin' Griff?"

I flinch, his accusation hitting its mark. "I didn't know." He huffs a humorless laugh. "I swear I didn't know Matt, not until yesterday."

"But didn't you go out with her last night? I heard you two went to Abuela's for dinner."

"Yeah…"

"She's not someone you fuck around with. You may be one of my best friends, Griff, but I'll lay you out in a heartbeat if I know you're fucking with her."

"Good." I retort, staring back. His eyes narrow and I quickly begin explaining, needing him to understand. "I knew almost immediately she was a single mom. You know me. I don't step in water over my head."

"So, what the fuck is this? You haven't been serious about a woman since high school."

I flinch, but he's right. "Why can't I be now?" He arches his eyebrows in challenge, his disbelief clear making me shake my own head in frustration. "I hear your name a hell of a lot when it comes to her. Is there something going on with you two? Is that what this is?"

His head falls back as laughter erupts. "I love that woman and those kids more than my own life and I would do absolutely anything for them, but Mallory is like my sister. We've always been close, but after Noah, we became family."

I breathe a sigh of relief knowing that's one less thing to worry about. "Thank God. I'm having a hard enough time knowing she was Noah's. I don't know what I'd do if I knew you two had something going on."

"I'm not the issue here. You are, Griff. I haven't seen you go out with a woman for more than five minutes in years. How do I know this is different."

"You don't," I concede, shrugging. "But I can tell you my attention is solely on her."

"What good does that do? You know that doesn't mean shit."

"What else am I supposed to say?"

"Do I really need to tell you?" With a heavy sigh, he runs his hand through his short brown hair, dropping it into his lap. "For starters, have you talked to Carla yet?"

I wince. "Not yet."

He shakes his head in disappointment. "I'd advise you to do that sooner than later. You will see her."

"Yeah, I know I gotta' settle things with her."

"Don't you think it's time? Damn, Griff. You've missed too much shit because of her. I'm still struggling getting over being pissed at you for missing the funeral. Seriously, how the fuck could you do that? The wedding, that was bad enough, but Noah's funeral?" he questions, his voice incredulous.

My chest squeezes, making it difficult to breathe. Shaking my head, I mumble, "I didn't miss the funeral."

His eyes widen. "What?"

"I snuck in the back of the church and left just before the end. At the cemetery, I stayed back, but I was there. You, Amber, Reid were with all of them. What was I supposed to do?"

"Griff–"

"I watched you with Mal, and I guess it was Tiegan hugging you. They were okay. You were protecting them like they were your own family. But I couldn't tell you, or anyone else. It damn near killed me, but Noah's funeral was not the day to start a war with his sister. That was her family, not mine." It doesn't matter how much it felt like that's what I'd lost.

He shakes his head. "Of all the bullshit things to do. I spent the last two years trying to figure out how the hell I was going to forgive you for that. I just knew Noah wouldn't want us to fight about it."

"You're right about that."

"I usually am."

"But seriously, asshole, don't lie to me about something this important again. You'll want to talk to Reid, he was pissed too."

"Yeah, I will. I haven't seen him around yet."

"That's easy to solve, text him. Man, I thought you were a cop." His lips twitch.

"I am."

"Not a good one apparently."

We both laugh, lightening the mood. "I'll text him, but that's not a conversation I'll have over text."

"Hell no. While you're at it, you should also deal with the one you've been putting off for the past–what–thirteen years?"

I huff a laugh and shake my head. "Yeah, you're right. I'll reach out to Carla soon. Just let me get my dad home and get through the rest of the weekend. Everyone is leaving tomorrow, then I'll get in touch with her."

"You better. Say hi to your family."

"I will."

"Now about Mal..."

Swiftly, I interrupt. "I like her, Matt. I really fucking like her. Honestly, it's already a bit surreal feeling and acting on anything is throwing me off, but to know she was Noah's wife." I wince, rubbing the center of my chest.

"Does that even matter? Aren't you leaving soon to go back to work too?"

I shake my head. "Nah, I'm done. I can't do this anymore. What if I didn't make it back?" His eyes widen and I hold his gaze, my own eyes watery, bleeding with emotion.

"You leaving the force?"

"I don't want to. You said Bill Camden is retiring…"

"Yeah," he mumbles, dragging out the word, urging me to give him more.

"I'm hoping I can lock in that position."

He grins. "It's about damn time! I'll be putting in a good word for you. Let's get the ball rolling."

"Do you think if we can work through everything with Noah that she would date another cop?"

Matt fists his hand and cracks his knuckles, repeating the process on the other side. "I don't know, Griff. I honestly don't know."

My stomach turns, but I appreciate his honesty. "Do you think Noah would be okay with it? Knowing I want to do right by her? It's like I just can't stay away from her."

"Well, if the feeling is mutual, I know Noah would just want her to be happy; her and his kids."

"I don't know man, I've only been out with her a couple times and I feel like an imposter with some of the looks I'm getting. How can I do that to him? It's like I'm betraying him just by being near her."

"If he had to choose the man to take his place with his family, we all know he'd pick me–"

My lips tug upwards. "Fuck you."

His lips twitch in amusement as he continues, "but that's not an option, so he'd likely settle for you."

"Thanks."

He chuckles, clearly amused. Taking a deep breath, he exhales, holding my gaze. "Griff, Noah wouldn't want it to be anyone else. What better man to be with his family, watch over them, love them, protect them, than one of his best friends, someone he loves and trusts with their lives."

Like he trusted us? Yet, here I am going after his wife. Would he really be okay with this now that he's gone? "Maybe…"

"What does Mallory say about it?"

I clench my jaw, attempting to hide my wince. "She doesn't know yet, but I'll tell her tonight."

He shakes his head. "You sure as hell better, Griff or I will."

Chapter Thirteen

♡ Griffin ♡

I pull up near Mallory's house, just out of sight, trying to be cautious. As I turn off my truck, I reach for my phone and pull up her name, refusing to let myself fall back down the rabbit hole. Tonight, I'll tell her about Noah and see how she takes it. Hopefully, that doesn't impact whatever is happening between us, but the sooner I tell her the better. I tap out a text and hit send.

Me: Are your kids gone?

Mallory: Yes. They just left.

Without another word, I jump out of the truck and stride towards her front door before I change my mind. I notice a small brown package on her front stoop and pick it up, finding nothing but her name on the top in black block lettering. "Hm…"

The door swings open before I have the chance to knock. My gaze swings to the gorgeous woman in the doorway, slowly traveling up her body starting at her now familiar tan cowboy boots. Holding back a groan, I bite the inside of my cheek as my eyes hit her bare legs until they reach her pale green sundress scattered with white daisies and barely covering her ass. It curves in at her hips, her full chest on display with the scoop neck and one-inch straps over her shoulders, drawing my eyes to her neck and a spot behind her ear I want to sink my teeth into. Her long brown hair falls loose around her shoulders, curling a little at the ends. Pink tinges her skin as I finally meet her golden gaze, any earlier trepidation instantly wiped away.

"Hi." She smiles sheepishly.

A wide grin covers my face. "Mal. You look absolutely beautiful."

Her cheeks turn a darker shade of red making me chuckle. "Thank you. You don't look so bad yourself."

I glance down at my chocolate brown boots, dark blue jeans, and pale blue, short-sleeved button down, shrugging like it's no big deal as I take a step closer to her, invading her space. "Thanks," I murmur. Reaching up with my free hand, I cradle her face in my hand as I tip her head back to meet my gaze. "I'm going to kiss you," I tell her, and wait, giving her a chance to say no. The instant her body curves towards me, I lick my lips and cover her mouth with mine, kissing her soft and slow, savoring her taste, the soft touch of her lips and the burning feeling it ignites inside me. With a satisfied hum, I pull back, an easy grin on my lips. "That's the way we should start every date."

She giggles, averting her gaze. "Sounds like you have a lot of plans, Mr. Erickson. Should we go?"

Suddenly remembering the package in my hand, I hold it up between us. "I found this on your front porch. Were you expecting something?"

Her eyebrows draw down in confusion as she looks at the package in my hands. "Um, I don't think so. Unless Tanner left me something for the graduation he was helping me plan. I can open it later." She steps inside and sets it down on a wooden bench just inside her house.

I don't want to worry her, but the nondescript label alone makes me wary. "Why don't you open it now and check, so you don't have to think about it," I urge, taking a step inside. Holding my hands up, I add, "Unless you don't want to open it in front of me. No pressure."

She shakes her head and sets her purse down on the bench, picking up the package. "Oh, I don't care about that and I guess we have time. I asked Katie to babysit. Matt will bring her over when Noah's parents bring them home from dinner so that gives us a little more time than the couple hours they'll likely be gone."

A smile tugs at my lips as I watch her opening the package. "So, you're telling me I have more time with you than I thought."

She blushes, nodding as she sets the ripped paper on the bench and opens a small white box, revealing a jagged, shiny, pink stone, shaped like a heart and the size of a softball. Her face falls, my heart dropping into the pit of my stomach right along with it. "Huh," she mumbles, sounding confused.

"What is it?" Hopefully she'll tell me what she's thinking. I don't like the sound of her puzzlement.

"It's a rose quartz crystal. It's known to open the heart, but I don't know why anyone would give this to me or where it came from."

"You don't see a note?"

She shakes her head and sets the box down. "Unless my sister-in-law came by and left it or Tanner."

"Tanner? You mentioned him before."

"He's a good friend of mine. We actually grew up together and now we work together at school."

"Why don't you text both of them and ask." I know I'm pushing, but I can't help it. It's in my nature with my line of work. Besides the fact that I'm naturally protective of everyone I care about.

She nods, reaching for her phone. I keep my eyes focused on her as she types a quick text and presses send before repeating the process. Her phone beeps with a text before she sends the second message. "Tanner hasn't been here and didn't send me anything." She frowns, another text coming through, followed by another. She shakes her head. "Carla didn't send it either."

Internally, I flinch, holding back any outward reaction. "There's no one else that could've brought it over?"

"There is, but nothing I can think of that makes sense." With a heavy sigh, she shakes her head as if trying to shake it off, but I'm not buying it. I don't want her to know it's bothering me too; at least not yet. But everything about it leaves me on edge. "I'm sure I'll figure it out. It's nothing to worry about."

Her words don't leave me uneasy, but her eyes do, betraying the appearance she wants to portray. Being married to a cop has obviously taught her to be cautious; careful. No matter how hard she's trying to hide it from me, I can see how nervous it makes her.

"Let's go," she urges, her hand falling to my bicep and shooting tingles throughout my body like an unrelenting current.

With a nod, I give her the reprieve she apparently needs as my mind begins to race. We climb into the truck and I turn towards home, reminding myself I need to focus on the here and now. I can worry about the strange gift she received a little later.

"Where are we going?"

I glance at her out of the corner of my eye, hoping to catch her reaction. "I thought we could have dinner at my family farm." Her eyes widen, possibly picturing my large family. "Don't worry, you don't have to endure dinner with anyone in my family, except me. I've got a private place for us to have dinner, just the two of us."

She relaxes into her seat, a sweet smile curling her lips. "Oh. That actually sounds perfect."

Chuckling, I arch my eyebrows in question. "You sound surprised."

She blushes a deep shade of red, the innocent look on her face going straight to my dick. "Um, not surprised, just impressed. It's not like there's a lot of places to go in Piper Falls that there won't be someone in town invading your space, pushing to know your business. I guess it's just a little strange."

As I pull into the long drive at the farm, I laugh. Veering right, I head towards the stables instead of left towards the main house. "True, especially if you're not used to it."

"Noah and I met in college, and moved here together, so it's definitely new to me," she comments as she looks out the window.

I park the truck near the barn and we climb out. Reaching for her, I wrap my arm around her waist and pull her close, kissing her on the top of the head before releasing her and grabbing her hand. I open my mouth to tell her about Noah, but the words don't come. "We're nothing like the corporate farms around here or ranches like Walker Estate, but we do have a few horses and the property is beautiful this time of year."

"I can see that, at least from everything I've seen, it already is, Griff."

My footsteps falter hearing my nickname on her lips in this setting; it sounds natural, right. I clear my throat, continuing towards the stables. "You've barely gotten a glimpse. Wait 'til you see more. I was thinking about riding, but I think we'll save that for another day."

"Why? I like riding horses. I dare you to find a girl from Texas who doesn't."

I chuckle, her enthusiasm catching. "Good, and believe it or not those women do exist, but I don't feel right taking you ridin' when you're wearin' that sweet dress." My eyes drift down her body to her bare legs. "Mm." I lick my lips and lift my gaze to meet hers. "I'd be a gentleman, but I don't control the elements."

Pink floods her cheeks, her eyes sparking with heat. "Oh."

"Damn. I can't even kiss you right now because someone will likely be here soon to feed the horses and with the way you're lookin' at me, I won't give a damn who walks in."

Her skin deepens to a darker shade of red as a soft gasp escapes her lips. "Don't make promises you can't keep, Griffin." My eyes widen and my mouth falls open. Did she just say that? "I may seem innocent, but I have three kids and it's been two years since I've even been kissed. My body doesn't want to wait anymore and honestly, neither do I."

After that confession, I couldn't stop myself if I tried. I need to kiss her. With a quick tug of her hand, she falls, crashing into my chest as my mouth covers hers. I kiss her hard, teeth clashing, lips bruising and tongues colliding, tasting, needing, desperate, but I don't let it last. I can't...yet. Pulling back, I look down at her as we both catch our breath, my heart bouncing around my ribcage like a basketball. "We need to get out of here," I rasp, my voice a low growl.

She nods, swaying on her feet. "Okay."

"Let me grab what I left in the office and we'll go." Taking a step away from her, I spin around and jog towards the office. I pull everything out of the refrigerator and set it in a crate we use for the farmers' market, quickly making my way back out to Mallory.

"Come on, we'll take the Gator."

"Gator?"

"Like an ATV, but more space."

Chapter Fourteen

♡ Mallory ♡

In a few minutes we pull up to an open area with a few scattered trees, and a pond, right next to a colorful garden full of flowers in various stages of growth. "Oh, wow, this is so beautiful."

"I thought you might want to pick your own flowers today."

"Really?"

He chuckles. "Of course. I didn't bring you any because I thought you'd enjoy doing it this way. Am I wrong?"

I shake my head, "No."

A smile curves his lips. "The shears are in the glove compartment and after, we can eat what's in the box."

"Thank you, Griffin. I love this."

"Good." We get out of the Gator and he grabs a large red and black checkered blanket I didn't see sitting in the back. Walking towards the water, he shakes out the blanket and spreads it out on the ground before coming back for the box and setting it down on the corner of the blanket.

I step up next to him and spin around slowly, taking in the beauty of our surroundings. "Wow. My kids would be in heaven here between the animals, the flowers, the pond and all this open space. They would love this."

"We'll bring them next time."

His casual remark leaves me off-balance. Am I ready to introduce him to my kids? My heart squeezes in anticipation, as if the moment is inevitable. But this is all so new to me, I don't know. Technically, I realize he already met them, but that was under very different circumstances. Wanting a subject change, I smirk, poking him in his hard abs. "You must've brought all the girls here when you were growing up."

He laughs, the sound making my stomach twist and goosebumps to spread over my skin. "Not if you were smart."

My eyebrows draw down in confusion and he shrugs, unapologetic. "The two places besides the house you never take a date is the stables and out here. I have five siblings and all of them know every piece of this property like they created it with their own hands. We used to mess with each other all the time." He shrugs and admits, "Still do."

"But I'm here, so what does that mean?"

He shakes his head. "You have nothing to worry about."

My stomach roils and my face drops. "Why? Because of Noah?" I challenge defiantly. He visibly flinches. "I hate when people walk on eggshells around me, Griffin. I thought you were different."

"No," he rasps and clears his throat, "not because of Noah. We just called a truce for things like this after Wyatt and I walked up on Colton and Robin. That scene is burned into my retinas and I wish I could erase it from my memory."

I blush, looking away, hating that I jumped to conclusions. "I'm sorry, I…"

"Don't apologize. Please." His voice cracks.

A shiver runs down my spine, the sound of his voice leaving me on edge. "Griffin?" I know something is coming, but I don't have any idea what.

He sighs heavily and runs a hand through his hair. "I have to tell you something, Mal and I need to tell you now before this goes any further."

"Okay," I mumble, dragging out the word, my trepidation making me queasy.

"It's something I found out the other day, something I should've realized, but I didn't until someone said something…"

"Who said what? I'm so confused, Griffin. I need you to spell it out for me. What are you talking about?"

As his hands drop to his sides, he exhales harshly. He meets my gaze as words I don't expect spew from his mouth. "Noah was one of my best friends."

I gasp. My mouth drops open and my eyes widen as I stare at the man in front of me. "What?" I shake my head. "That's impossible, I know

Noah's closest friends. In fact, Matt was the best man in our wedding and Reid was a groomsman."

"Yeah, they're also my good friends. We all grew up together."

"Then why have I never met you before?"

He shrugs. "The guys would come down to Waco to see me or when I'd come home, we would go out, just the guys."

"You were the friend from Waco?" He nods, pinching his lips tightly together. "Then why weren't you there? At our wedding? Or when our kids were born? His funeral?" I demand, confusion and betrayal washing over me, but is that even fair? He wasn't mine then. He's not mine now.

"There was no way I was going to miss Noah's funeral. I was there, but I stayed back." My eyes widen in surprise, but he stares out at the pond, lost in his own thoughts. "But the other things…missing the rest, every single missed moment involving him is one of my biggest regrets. I'd give anything to go back, but..." His voice cracks and he pauses, clearing his throat. "I should've been here. I should've been here for every damn memory."

"So why weren't you?"

He runs his hand through his hair again, looking lost. "I could say work, and that may be partially true, but I could've gotten out of it. In reality it's mostly because of my ex."

My heart drops into my stomach like a lead balloon. "What?"

Heaving a sigh, he closes his eyes, slowly opening them and holding my gaze. "This is not going like I want it to, Mallory. I'm not sure what I expected, maybe it's just the circumstances, but my ex is the last thing I want to talk about. I'm not hiding anything and I will talk when you want me to, but you could say we have a bad history and Noah always said he understood."

My lips press tightly together as I attempt to process his confession. What's a bad history? Bad enough that he wasn't here for someone he claims was one of his best friends? I don't understand. My stomach churns, my curiosity running on overdrive, wanting to know more about his ex, but I need to process what he said about Noah first.

"Ask me what you want to ask, Mal."

"How do I know you'll tell me the truth?"

He huffs a humorless laugh, looking more hurt than anything. "You may not know me that well yet, but I will tell you the truth. I'm not one to lie."

"You just delay telling the truth when it suits you?"

His lips twitch, his flinch almost unnoticeable, but it's there. He nods in acceptance, the movement subtle. "I deserve that."

I heave a sigh, coming to my own conclusion. "Look, Griffin, this is just a lot to take in, but in all honesty, I get why you didn't tell me right away when you found out…when did you find out?"

"Sage and Wyatt said something yesterday."

"You knew on our date?"

He nods. "I think I was a little in shock, although it seemed obvious the moment they told me."

"Because I'm a widow?"

"Maybe that's part of it, but more because of your kids. Your son looks just like him, your oldest daughter too."

A smile tugs at my lips, thinking of my kids. "They do."

"I don't know how I didn't notice."

"It's only easy because you know the truth. Everything comes easily in retrospect."

"If I only…"

"Don't," I interrupt. "I don't want to know what you're about to say. There's nothing good that can come from a sentence that starts like that when it comes to Noah. What happened to him was a terrible tragedy that I've endured and not only survived, but I believe I'm stronger. We've all prevailed in our own way." He cringes as if my words are an accusation, but they're the furthest thing from it.

"Ya' know, I think I like that you were close to Noah." He arches his eyebrow in question, searching my eyes for the truth. "And Griff? I don't think I would be here with you right now if I'd met you back then, even if it was just at the wedding or the funeral. The look everyone gave me no matter what they thought of me was almost always the same. They either felt sorry for me, or they felt the pain as deep as me and they are the ones that became my family."

"Like Matt and Reid."

"Especially them, Matt more than anyone. They helped us heal. Tiegan has trouble trusting, but she trusts Matt. He's been here consistently for us. Reid too, but she still gives him a hard time for not saving her dad. She knows it's not his fault, that he was already gone when he found him, but she needs someone to blame. I think…" I trail off, turning away as I'm suddenly overwhelmed with emotion and everything I'm feeling lodges itself in my throat like a tiny porcupine.

In seconds, I'm wrapped in strong arms and tucked perfectly underneath his chin as Griffin pulls me into his chest. "I'm still sorry I wasn't here like I should've been; for him, for you and the kids. I could've…"

"Please?" I whimper and he goes silent, pulling me closer.

His lips brush the top of my head, the simple gesture giving me hope for a future. It doesn't feel like something that someone would do if he just wanted to sleep with me. Then again, neither does this conversation. "I'm glad you're here now, Griffin." My hands inch around his waist and I hold on tight, relishing in the warmth and comfort of his embrace. His pounding heart beats against my cheek, the rhythmic sound calming me. My own heart matches his beat as I relax further into him, a soft, content sigh escaping through my lips.

"I'm glad I'm here now too."

"New rule. For the rest of the night, we focus just on us. No more talk of Noah or exes, or even my kids."

"I can get on board with that plan." He tilts his head down and nips at my ear, making me giggle.

"Griff."

His fingers trail down my arm, his hand clasping with mine. He kisses my neck again and then pushes away. "Let's go pick you some flowers."

Taking a deep breath, I exhale slowly and smile. "Whatever you say, Mr. Erickson."

"Whatever I say?" he challenges, quirking his brow and making me laugh.

"You're pushing it," I tease, squeezing his hand as we weave through the colorful array of flowers.

"Do you have a favorite flower?"

I shrug. "Not really. For my garden I usually plant zinnia and salvia, but I love sunflowers, daisies, the one flower that reminds me of a rose but it's not. It's a pale pink flower with lots of layers."

"Ranunculus?"

"What?"

He tugs, leading me. "Over here. These?" He points to the flower I just described.

I grin. "Yes, those. I love those."

"Better than roses?"

"Always better than roses."

Chapter Fifteen

♡ Griffin ♡

Mallory slips her hand into mine as we walk side by side to her front door. "Thank you for letting me walk you. I understand your reasons, but we were raised to pick a woman up at her door and drop her off the same way at the end of the night."

"I find that hard to believe you stuck to those rules."

My head falls back in laughter. "Those rules in particular or any rules?"

"You? All rules, but with the way you kiss, there's no way your dates looked the same at the end of the night as when you picked them up."

I smirk. "Wanna' test that theory?"

She laughs and instantly covers her mouth, her eyes going wide as we step onto the porch. "Shh!" she whispers, still giggling. "I can't shush you and keep a straight face. You're too big for that."

My lips curve up and I wiggle my eyebrows. "Thanks for noticing. I didn't even see you lookin'."

Her face flushes instantly. She sucks her bottom lip between her teeth, slowly releasing it, giving me my intended reaction. I step into her space and she backs up, right into her house. "Griff." Her breathing picks up as she tilts her head up looking at me. "I had a lot of fun with you tonight, even the tough stuff was good."

"Yeah?"

She nods. "Yeah. I'm glad you told me about Noah and I do think it's a good thing."

"Good, cause, I needed you to know the truth. And you should know I'm enjoyin' every minute I spend with you, even when we're trudging through the muddy waters. You sure tonight has to end?"

"Yeah…kids…" She exhales, her heated breath dances over my lips, the sweet taste of her earlier glass of wine a whisper on my tongue.

"I'm gonna' kiss you, Mal." I reach up with my free hand, my thumb grazing her full lips as I pin her hand I'm still holding above her head. Her breathing picks up its pace, as my fingers weave into her hair. Holding her stare, I lower my head. My tongue slips out, and I lick her lips, begging for entrance. I groan as her lips part and she allows me inside, my tongue diving right in to tangle with hers, licking, tasting, exploring.

The moment I release her hand, both her hands fall to my chest and begin to roam, working their way down to my abs, and around to my back, holding me close like I may slip away, but I'm not going anywhere. Her delicate but firm touch, igniting me and leaving a trail of goosebumps in its wake.

A soft whimper escapes her lips, the sound, the vibration mixes with the kiss, causing me to lose my sense, forgetting where we are as I push my body into hers. With a tilt of my head, I kiss her deeper, my hand sliding down, skimming over the top of her breast, down her side and anchoring it on her hip. Her soft moans urge me on as I mold her ass cheek in my other hand. My cock is ready for me to pick her up and fuck her against the wall.

That reality slams into me, reminding me where we are. She deserves better than this. I tighten my hold on her hips and force myself to slow our kiss.

"Griff," she whimpers, tugging my mouth back to hers and I'm done for, instantly lost in the feel of her velvety lips, the sweet taste of her kiss and the soft sounds she's making with each pass of my tongue.

The front door suddenly swings open, startling us and causing our lips to break apart, but I take my time releasing her and stepping back, trying to catch my breath, and hoping to give Mallory the same time to pull herself together. Clearing my throat, I turn towards the front door and find Amber's sister standing in the doorway with Mia peeking curiously around her legs. "You're back." Olivia breathes a sigh of relief.

Mia sees her mom first and smiles before looking up at me. She gasps, her eyes going wide. "It's prince charming! You came to see us."

I chuckle, enamored with her excitement. "Howdy."

"Come inside, please." She reaches for me and pulls, and I willingly follow.

"It's pretty late, Mia. What are you even doing up?"

"Mommy, I couldn't sleep."

"Okay, but you have to get back in bed."

"No!" she whines, hugging my legs, causing my heart to squeeze and Mallory to heave a sigh in defeat.

"Um, I'm sorry, but it's my fault she's up. I'm so glad you're home," Olivia interrupts, glancing between us.

"Everything okay?"

"Actually, I was just about to call Matt or the police or something. There was some guy lurking around outside and I screamed. After I saw the headlights from your truck, it looked like he ran off in the other direction. Then I went to check on the kids."

"I'm glad you didn't call the police. It's probably nothing to worry about," Mallory claims.

She turns away, avoiding eye contact with me as I quirk my brow in question. Why the hell wouldn't you want to call the police? But I don't ask aloud with Mia still in the room. Instead, I focus on Olivia. "Where did you see him?" I question, taking inventory of the doors and windows from where I stand as well as the point of view.

"Out the kitchen window facing the driveway."

I nod and look at Mallory. "Stay here and lock the doors."

"Where are you going?"

"Just outside to look around. No big deal. I'll be right back."

"Be careful, Griffin."

"I will." Glancing down at Mia, I place my hand on the top of her head, my large palm nearly covering her entire head. "You're going to have to let go sweetheart. I promise I'll be right back. Okay?"

"Fine." She pouts, pushing out her lower lip and releasing me with an exaggerated huff before she stomps dramatically over to the couch and climbs up, crossing her arms over her chest. "I'm gonna' wait right here. Hurry up."

My lips twitch in amusement, but I nod, knowing I need to deal with whatever just happened as quickly as possible. I walk out the door and reiterate, "Lock the door," before pulling it closed.

I step out on the porch and pause, listening before cautiously making my way around Mallory's house, checking behind every bush, tree, dark corner and thoroughly around the garage. Looking up and down the street and checking easy escape routes focusing on the opposite direction of my truck. Circling back towards the driveway where Olivia said she saw him, I assess where someone might've had a good view inside the house but I don't see anything, not even a little dirt out of place. Odd.

Retreating back to the house, I knock on the front door. "Hey, Mal, it's me. Will you unlock the door?"

"Coming." The click of the lock sounds just before she opens the door. "Everything okay?" she asks, a slight tremor apparent in her voice.

"Yeah, there was no sign of anyone or anything. It's all clear for little girls to get back in their beds."

"Thank you," Mallory mouths.

"Okay." I watch as Mia trudges over to her mom and gives her a hug. "Goodnight Mommy. I love you lots and lots."

"I love you baby girl, lots and lots and lots. I'll be right in to tuck you in." She lets her daughter go and Mia turns towards Olivia, wrapping her arms around her.

"Goodnight, 'Liv'a."

"Night Mia."

She spins and crashes into my legs once again, making me smile as my hand falls to her head. "Goodnight Mia."

"G'night."

I watch as she runs down the hall to her room as I hear Mallory ask, "Please don't say anything to Matt."

"Why the hell not?" I question. There's no way I'm staying quiet without Mia in the room.

Olivia's face pales. "Um…"

"Because he worries way too much and he'll have the house on guard twenty-four − seven. That would scare my kids. It's probably nothing."

"Don't you think your safety and your kids is a hell of a lot more important than taking a chance that it's *nothing*."

Planting her hands on her hips, she glares at me, seething. "My kids safety is the most important thing to me, Mr. Erickson. I've been doing a great job taking care of them by myself. I don't need you to come in here and…"

Another knock sounds at the door, taking us by surprise. "Mallory, it's me, Matt."

Our attention swings to Olivia and she shrugs sheepishly. "Sorry. I texted my sister when Griffin was outside and told her what happened. She must've told him."

Mallory grimaces, her shoulders sagging in defeat. Matt pounds again. "Mal, open the door."

I cross my arms over my chest and stand waiting as she crosses the room and lets him inside. "Hi, Matt. Are you here picking up Olivia?"

"Seriously?" he challenges, giving me a head nod. "You had some guy lurking around outside. Why didn't you call me?"

"I just found out a few minutes ago when we got back."

"That's a few minutes too many for not picking up the damn phone, Mal."

I huff a laugh as she focuses her glare on him. "Stop, we're fine."

He looks at me and asks, "Did you look around? See anything?"

I nod. "Yeah, I looked around, but didn't find anything. I'll check again when the sun comes up to make sure I didn't miss anything."

Mallory's eyebrows draw down in confusion as she looks back and forth between the two of us. "Wait, you trust him?" she asks Matt, making me flinch.

"What the hell?" I ask.

"Why wouldn't I?" Matt questions at the same time. He turns to me and glares. "Didn't you tell her?"

"Of course, I did."

Suddenly Mallory gasps, her eyes widening. "Wait, you were a cop in Waco. That's what Noah had said."

I shrug, not bothering to deny it. "I already told you I'm not going back to Waco."

"I know you guys are friends, but that's part of why you trust him."

She glances at Matt and he nods, assessing her reaction before looking back at me. "What's your plan?"

"We should talk to your guy that installs security cameras." He nods in agreement. "And I'm sleeping on the couch."

"What? No, you're not."

"Yeah, he is, Mal, unless you want me to call it in."

"I thought you were on my side."

"I'm always on your side," Matt proclaims, holding her gaze. "If he gets out of line, kick his ass and then call me and I'll finish the job for you."

"Why? I've been doing this on my own for a long time and me and the kids are just fine."

"You are, but with everything going on lately, I'm not willing to take a chance and you shouldn't be either." She flinches and I fucking hate it. I get that she wants her independence, but everyone needs to ask for help sometimes. It doesn't make you any less.

"Okay," she quietly concedes.

"Listen, if it's Griffin you don't want here. I'll take the couch."

My breath catches and I hold it waiting for her response.

"No, it's fine. He's fine. It's not him."

"All right. Then, Olivia and I are going to go."

She nods. "Okay. Thank you."

Matt looks at me and I give him a nod, letting him know without words I'll keep him posted.

Chapter Sixteen

♡ Mallory ♡

Quietly, I close the door to Mia's room and take my time, peeking in on Ollie and Tiegan, all three, sound asleep. Stopping at the hall closet, I pull out a blanket and pillow, wondering what I've gotten myself into. I knew Matt would be overprotective, but I wasn't prepared to have Griffin in the same mode. I should've known he was a cop, but he did say he's not going back. Does that only mean he's not going back to Waco or does it also mean he's not going back to being a cop? Honestly, I don't know if I want to know the answer.

Figures. I finally start dating again, and I'm in a situation I don't know if I want to be in and yet, getting out of it is the last thing I want. Griffin makes my heart race like no man has in a very long time. He's a man I could stare at for days. His hard body, his colorful ink, his lips…mmm. And I love the way he looks at me, his blue eyes sparking, giving me my confidence back even though I didn't realize I'd lost it. Or maybe it's because I didn't have this kind of need for my confidence the last couple years. It was never gone, just hibernating until I was ready for it to shine again.

The things he does for me are incredibly sweet, like the flowers. Walking through the flowers today talking about our favorites and telling him things about myself I'd all but forgotten gave me the giddy feeling inside making me practically bounce with each step; a feeling I didn't think I'd ever have again. I'm having fun getting to know him, learning the little things and some big ones. His family and friends are obviously important to him. He works hard and thrives outdoors. The way he makes me laugh and listens to what I have to say means everything to me. I love how he respects me, my wishes, and my kids.

Now that he's here, even if it's just for tonight, everything suddenly feels complicated and intense. Maybe it's my nerves or my doubts talking after learning what I should've already known. He's one of them. It's not a bad thing, but it might be for me. I've always been proud of Noah and all our friends at the station. They became our family and I love them all for it. If it weren't for them, I'm not sure I'd even be considering moving on, but getting into a relationship with another cop after everything we've been through… I shake my head and gulp down the lump in my throat, halting my thoughts.

But the question remains no matter how hard I try to shove it away. How do I know he would come back to me every day?

I'm getting too far ahead of myself. Tonight, was only our second actual date if I don't count our run-ins and I'm thinking like we have a future, but don't I need to think that way and consider all possibilities with my kids just steps away? I don't want them getting attached to someone who could so easily disappear.

Exhaling harshly, I trudge down the hallway, my steps faltering when I spot Griffin sitting on the end of the couch, his long legs stretched out in front of him with his boots off to the side. Seeing him relaxed in my house – my space – causes my chest to tighten, all my earlier hesitations instantly racing to vacate my thoughts.

Clearing my throat, I step into the room as he turns his head, focusing on me. "I brought you some things." I set the pillow and blanket down on the opposite end of the couch.

"Thank you."

"You're welcome."

"Sit with me?" he requests, patting a spot on the cushion.

"Okay." I lower myself, sitting right next to him, twisting my body so I can look at him.

"You all right?"

I nod. "Yeah. I'm just thinking."

"You know it could've been anyone outside. Maybe it had nothing to do with you or Olivia."

My face falls. How could I have already forgotten about that? I'm so fixated on Griffin that I brush past someone trespassing. "That doesn't make me feel any better."

"Noah taught you self-defense?"

"Yeah. I learned when I was in college."

"Good." He puts his arm out and urges, "Come here."

Without a word, I slide under his arm and curl my legs up underneath me, leaning into his side. My hand moves up and rests on his chest, mindlessly brushing up and down. "Thanks for staying." Lifting my head, I glance up at him. "I still don't think I need you here, but thanks for staying anyway."

His lips twitch in amusement. "I'm sure you could handle it. Doesn't mean I want you to deal with anything by yourself if you don't have to."

I feel myself flush and press my face into his chest, not wanting him to see my reaction. Inhaling deeply, the scent of the outdoors and a musky fragrance I attribute to him floods my senses. "Mm," I murmur softly.

His breath comes out slow, controlled, before he speaks his voice low and vibrating over my skin. "Careful there darlin'. Having you pressed up against me along with those sounds you're making will quickly drive me mad."

The knowledge only urges me on. I smirk and glance up at him from underneath my eyelashes. "Me?"

He chuckles, shaking me. "Unless that's what you're going for?"

Pushing off his chest, I look him in the eyes, hovering over his face. He licks his lips and stares at me, waiting to see what I'll do next. Mirroring him, my tongue juts out, wetting my lips. "Nah. When I want to do that, I'll just go for it."

I press my mouth to his, and he wraps his arms around me, kissing me back soft and slow. My tongue slips into his mouth, meeting his, licking, tangling, tasting as my hand slides up his hard chest, curving around his shoulder. I pull myself up and readjust, tugging my dress up just enough so I'm able to swing my leg over his lap and straddle him. My other hand curls around the back of his neck and I tilt my head kissing him deeper.

His large hands find my hips, brushing the top of my ass, while mine glide along his jawline, pulling him closer, my body arching into his with every stroke of his tongue, every part of me igniting with need for this man.

"Griff," I whimper.

A low growl erupts from his chest as he flips me onto my back in an instant, breaking our kiss as I bounce lightly on the cushion. His lips, his tongue begin trailing torturous kisses along my neck leaving goosebumps in his wake, while his hands start exploring. One hand squeezes my ass and remains there, an anchor, keeping his weight at bay. His other hand glides up my side, running over the side of my breast, my nipples jutting out and begging for attention.

His mouth works its way down my chest, his hand brushing over my nipple, my body arching towards him, my breasts aching begging for his touch. Heat pools low in my belly, my pussy wet and ready. He gently bites my nipple through my dress eliciting a desperate sound from my lips, the sensation slicing through me, dizzying. "Please," I cry without thought.

"Shh," he rasps, glancing towards the hallway before his lips cover mine in another heated kiss.

Right, I need to be quiet. Breaking our kiss, I gasp for breath. "I need…"

"I know what you need, Mal. Just tell me, can I please be the one to give it to you?"

My eyes fly open and I meet his hooded gaze as he waits, unmoving, staring at me with lust, need, anticipation. Without breaking eye contact, I nod and force out the words needing to be clear. "Please make me come."

His eyes widen and flare, darkening to a deeper blue. "My pleasure."

He grabs the blanket behind my head and shakes it out, covering us both as he lays back down. "Just in case." He nods towards the hallway, squeezing my heart and further igniting my desire for him.

"Thank you."

He smirks. "Don't thank me yet."

My mouth opens to retort, but the words exit my brain the moment his hand skims across bare skin, caressing my butt cheek over my panties. Gliding down my leg to my knee, he lifts it gently, my dress slipping further up. "Take them off."

Hooking the sides, he tugs them down, his fingers trailing along my skin making me bite my lower lip to keep quiet. "Damn, I want to see you." I shake my head, not ready for him to come to my room, but before I can say a word, he redirects as if reading my mind. "But not tonight."

He nips at my lower lip, watching me as his hand moves to the inside of my thigh, his fingers sliding across my sensitive skin and connecting with my wet folds. "Mm," I moan. His head dips down, his mouth licking and sucking a tender spot on my neck, shooting tingles throughout my body, every part of me fully aware of everything he's doing to me.

Pulling back, he watches me as he circles my clit with his thumb, my blood boiling, and my pussy swelling as he pushes one finger in, then two. My body squeezes his fingers as he slides them in and out, curling them in, towards my g-spot. I'm not able to remain quiet any longer. "Ahh…"

His lips crash into mine as he kisses me hard, continuing his ministrations with his fingers, slow and steady. Gradually, he picks up the pace as my body heats and swells, caving to his expert touch. My world spins around me as my vision flashes and my body begins to pulse, squeezing his fingers. I moan into his mouth, not able to catch my breath, but I don't give a damn as my pussy throbs around his fingers, as if he were inside me.

Finally, my body slows, and Griffin's movements follow the lead. My head falls back as he breaks the kiss and I gasp for breath. "Damn. That was the sexiest thing I've ever seen. You're absolutely gorgeous, Mallory."

My eyes flutter open as his fingers slip out from inside of me. Holding my gaze, he brings them right to his lips and closes his mouth around them. His eyes close and he moans, sucking my juices from his fingers. As he pulls his fingers out of his mouth, his eyes open, meeting my gaze. "So damn good. I can't wait for more."

My lips twitch in amusement and I dramatically glance down before returning to his eyes. "I'm sure you can't."

He chuckles softly and shakes his head, squeezing me tight as his hard length presses into my side. "I'll be just fine. Nothing more than that will happen in your living room with the kids down the hall. My respect for you will always win."

My face heats and I suddenly feel naked even with all my clothes on, well almost all. He moves back as I begin to scramble, tugging my dress down and looking around for my panties. "Can I have my underwear please?"

He arches his eyebrows and shakes his head. "One, no. I'm sure you have more in your room."

Narrowing my eyes, I fix him with a glare. "Griffin."

"Two, those lacy, skimpy, sexy as sin things cannot be called underwear. I wear underwear. You? Anything you put on your body has to have a better name than that."

"What?" I quirk a brow.

"Panties aren't bad, or lingerie. Or we can come up with a new word like mallies. You know, part your name…"

Rolling my eyes, I interrupt, "Are you trying to distract me from getting in my head?"

His lips twitch. "Is it working?"

I laugh and give him a chaste kiss. "It's working."

"Good."

"I think I should get to sleep. Kids will have me up early."

"Stay here with me a little longer," he requests, holding his arms out.

"Okay." I crawl into his arms, both of us getting comfortable. "But I am going to sleep in my room tonight. Alone."

"I know," he claims, his voice soft. "Just give me a little more time with you if you're willing."

How can I say no to that?

Chapter Seventeen

♡ Griffin ♡

My eyes blink open, squinting into the sunlight peeking through the front window, the warmth of Mallory's body missing. I was hoping she would come back, but I'm not that lucky or even a little surprised. Having her in my arms felt perfect. The way she kissed me and continued to touch me was maddening. Seeing her fall apart underneath me hit me like it was everything and nothing I've ever felt, but I wouldn't push knowing her kids could walk out at any moment. There's no way in hell I would put any of us in that situation. What we did was risky enough, but apparently we couldn't stop at making out. If we were truly alone, I'm afraid we would've jumped in too fast. I don't want her to have any regrets when it comes to me. It's likely been over two years since she's been with someone unless there's something she's not telling me, but I don't believe that for a second.

Being in her house for the first time hit me in more ways than one. Everything about it made it feel like a home. The soft tones, the comfortable furniture, the various sizes of discarded shoes by the front door and the pictures on the wall. Seeing pictures of her and Noah, as well as Noah with his kids was bittersweet. I hate that I never saw this piece of him in life. It's my fault I never did and seeing him happy in the pictures with his family only intensifies my guilt. I'm only here because he can't be. That doesn't sit well with me. He should be here.

I see movement out of the corner of my eye and slowly sit up, stretching my arms above my head as a soft gasp leaves Mia's lips the moment before she jumps into my lap. "You're still here," she shrieks, throwing her arms around my neck.

Chuckling softly, I wrap my arms around her tiny body, hugging her back. "I'm still here."

Tiegan trudges out of her bedroom, rubbing her eyes and yawning, halting the moment she spots me. "You're the guy from the farmers' market that mom hit with her car."

Laughter erupts before I can stop it. "That would be me."

"What are you doing here?"

I smirk, appreciating the apprehension. "It was too late to drive home last night so I slept on the couch."

"And he was protecting us from the man 'Liv'a saw outside," Mia proclaims, spinning around and plopping in my lap as she looks at her sister.

"What?" Tiegan shrieks, wide-eyed.

"It's nothing to worry about. The guy was probably just lost," I claim, waving my hand dismissively.

Her eyes narrow, but she doesn't respond, instead taking up residence on the other end of the couch as Ollie walks out, momentarily giving me a sense of deja-vu with his likeness to his father. He looks at me, then to both of his sisters. "Hi."

"Good morning, Ollie." I grin.

"Aren't you the guy from the farmers' market that found my sister?"

"Yes…"

"Did you bring any food? I'm hungry."

I laugh as Tiegan rolls her eyes. "You're always hungry."

"It's time for breakfast. I'm allowed to be hungry, Tiegan."

"I'm sorry. I didn't bring any food this time."

"Oh, okay." He frowns, and I fight to hold back my laugh as he ponders his choices, the same look on his face I remember Noah having when he was trying to make everyday decisions. "Maybe I'll go wake up mom."

"Why don't we let her sleep in a little bit? I can see what you guys have in the kitchen and make you something?"

"You cook?" Ollie asks wide-eyed.

"Of course. A man has got to eat."

"There's not much. We didn't go to the farmer's market yesterday and my mom said she would go grocery shopping today," Tiegan claims.

"Well, knowing your mom, there has to be something for breakfast," I say, lifting Mia off my lap and setting her down as I stand.

Suddenly, an idea pops into my head, one I hope Mallory will be okay with. Reaching for my phone, I type out a text to my mom.

Me: Good morning, Ma. Any chance I could bring a few extra bodies to breakfast this morning?

Mom: There's always room for more. But who's coming so I know what and how much I need to prepare?

Me: Mallory and her three kids.

Mom: Wonderful! We can't wait to see them! Asher and Mason will be happy to have other kids here.

Me: Thanks Ma.

Mom: Anytime. See you soon!

Me: Love you.

Mom: I love you too, Griffin.

I slip my phone in my pocket and glance at the kids, suddenly worried they won't be on board. "What if we go out to the farm and we can have breakfast there with my family?"

"How big is your family?"

"Well, there's my mom and dad. Plus, I have three brothers and two sisters. One of my brothers is married with twin boys."

"Asher and Mason?" Ollie asks, possibly the only twin boys he knows.

I nod, fighting my smile. "That would be my nephews."

"Awesome!"

All of them glance at one another as if asking permission, an array of expressions on their faces. "What about mom?" Tiegan asks warily.

"We'll bring her too." As long as she's willing.

"Awesome!" Ollie declares.

"Yay! We get to go to the farm with prince charming," Mia croons, hugging my legs.

Chuckling, my hand runs softly over her head. "How about you guys quietly go get ready and then come back out here. I'll go talk to your mom."

All three of them turn and go back to their rooms, as I make my way down the hall towards Mallory's room and knock softly. A responding groan reverberates through the door bringing a smile to my face. "Mallory, it's me, Griffin. Can I come in?"

I hear her soft gasp. "Griffin?"

"Yeah, can I come in?"

"Um, yeah, sure, come in."

I push the door open, finding a gorgeously rumpled Mallory standing next to her bed dressed in a pale purple tank top and gray pajama pants decorated with tiny purple flowers, her nipples drawing my attention. Clearing my throat, I lift my gaze, looking into her eyes as I pull the door shut behind me. "Good morning, beautiful."

A soft snort escapes her lips making me laugh. She blushes the color of a tomato, quickly covering her mouth as her eyes go wide. "I'm sorry."

"Don't be. It's cute." She arches her eyebrows in disbelief making me chuckle as I slowly close the distance between us. "And you do look beautiful, Mal. I just wish seeing you like this would've been the first view I saw this morning, but I'll take it anytime."

Giving me a crooked smile, she rolls her eyes, disbelieving. I stop in front of her and lean down, brushing my lips over hers before the kids start knocking on her door. "Mm…" she murmurs, making my cock twitch, craving her attention.

"Your kids are up and they're hungry." I force out the words before I forget why I'm here.

"Ugh," she groans. "Oh, no. I still have to go to the store."

"How about y'all come out to eat with me at the farm instead."

"Just you?" she questions, arching her eyebrows. "I thought you said you were having breakfast with your family?"

I shrug, admitting, "Well, it's Sunday and my siblings are all in town. Most of them are heading back to their other home today, but it will likely be the whole family unless there's something I don't know about."

Her eyes widen, her lips forming a perfect o, giving me thoughts on other things she could do with her mouth. "I'm not sure what the kids will think."

"They're all in."

"What?"

"Well, they told me about the groceries and we're having a big breakfast at the farm today anyway. It's Sunday, so it's no hassle."

"Are you sure? We're four people."

I chuckle. "My mom would feed the whole town if she could. Besides, my siblings are heading back so breakfast is mandatory for me. Asher and Mason will be thrilled to see more kids."

She frowns. "It seems like a lot."

"You're overthinking."

Ollie crashes into the room without knocking, dressed in blue jeans and a blue and white soccer t-shirt. "Mom, did you hear we're going to the farm for breakfast? You have to get ready so we can go," he urges, bouncing on his toes.

She heaves a sigh, looking at me out of the corner of her eye. "I guess I better get moving then."

"Yes!" His footsteps retreat down the hallway.

Mallory looks at me and crosses her arms over her chest.

I shrug, giving her an impish grin. "They're excited."

She sighs dramatically. "Yeah, I guess they are. So, we better not disappoint them."

"Yes," I mimic, giving her another chaste kiss. "I'm going to take a quick walk around the house while all of you get ready. I'll come back in to get all of y'all when I'm done. Sound good?"

"Yes, Mr. Erickson."

Chapter Eighteen

♡ Mallory ♡

Griffin parks the truck and Ollie immediately jumps out, spotting Asher and Mason running into the house. Tiegan helps Mia unbuckle as Griffin swings their door open, Tiegan jumping down and Griffin lifting Mia. When he goes to set her down, she hangs from his neck like a monkey, swinging her legs to get closer making him laugh.

He wraps his arm around her, holding her up as he looks down at her. "Do you want me to carry you darlin'?" She nods her head vigorously, pressing her face into his chest, squeezing my heart. "All right. I've got you, Mia."

I gulp down the sudden lump in my throat, overwhelmed with emotion, but quickly push it away. Griffin glances at me and steps closer, whispering, "Are you okay?"

"I'm good." I bite my lower lip and slowly release it. Griffin's eyes track the movement as he licks his lips in response.

"There's nothing to be nervous about, my family doesn't bite, although I might."

Mia pushes back and looks down at him, her eyes narrowed in warning. "A prince is not s'posed to bite."

He gives her a crooked grin. "It's only when I'm hungry." Then he pretends to take a bite out of her tummy and she squeals with gleeful delight.

The back door of their farmhouse swings open, and Griffin's mom stands in the doorway. "Are y'all comin' in? Ollie is already filling his plate and impatiently waiting for you to get inside."

We laugh and pick up our pace as Mia presses her face back into Griffin's chest. "Thank you so much for having us. I hope it wasn't too much trouble."

"Mallory, dear, it's wonderful to have you and the kids for breakfast. I've told you before, you're welcome here anytime." It may be true, but I thought it was something people said when they felt sorry for you as they watch you grieve from the outside. I should've known someone like Mrs. Erickson was genuine when she offered, but it's not something I could take anyone up on easily, especially when we were struggling with so much daily. She leans in pulling me into a hug, my hands going around her, missing the warm gesture from my own mother. "It's good to see you finally take us up on the offer and with one of my handsome boys, no less."

My face heats and I attempt to brush off her comment, smiling. "Ma," Griffin mumbles in warning. She purses her lips and waves him off.

"Thank you," Tiegan and I say in unison as she releases me.

Grabbing Griffin's elbow to gently halt his movement, I remind my youngest to do the same. "Mia, what do you say?"

I smile taking in the moment as she peeks at Mrs. Erickson, barely looking up from Griffin's shoulder. "Thank you," she whispers, quickly burying her face against him yet again. She has the best seat in the house. I wouldn't mind doing the same.

"You're welcome sweetie."

The moment we step inside, we're swarmed by his family. My eyes widen and I take a step back in self-preservation, bumping into Griffin as he puts his free hand protectively around me. "Back up, guys. Give us some space. They aren't a display."

Laughter erupts around the room, easy chatter soon filling the large country kitchen. An oak farmhouse table takes up half of it, giving us enough room for all of us to sit together. I like it. Barstools line a long tan, and white, granite countertop if they ever needed more room and with the size of their family, I'm sure it's common with company.

Tiegan bites her lower lip nervously, her eyes shifting from the ground to all the new faces and back again. Griffin's younger sister smiles brightly, giving us her attention. "Hi, I'm Harper."

"Hi, I'm…"

"I know who you are," she interrupts. "You're Mallory and that means you must be Tiegan."

Tiegan nods and shrugs as if she's not sure what to do. "Yeah."

"Do you like to read?"

Tiegan's eyebrows hit her hairline, glancing at me. "How did you know that?"

She smiles. "Just a guess. Reading is one of my favorite things to do. Do you want to come sit with me and maybe we can talk books? Or something else, if you'd like."

Tiegan glances back at me and I nod in encouragement, my heart warming. I appreciate how welcoming they're all being to me and my kids.

Everyone introduces themselves before his dad calls out from the end of the table. "I believe Griffin asked you to give them some room to breathe. Everyone find a seat at the table so we can enjoy breakfast together before y'all have to go."

I watch in wonderment as everyone quickly disperses, the respect they hold for their father obvious.

"I'm happy to see you're feeling better Mr. Erickson."

"Me too." He chuckles. "It's good to see you and have you and your kids joining us. As you can tell, we're used to a house full of a lot of love and chaos. It's just the way we like it."

"Well, thank you for having us."

"Mallory was Asher's favorite teacher," Robin claims, nodding towards me as if in approval.

"Who doesn't love their Kindergarten teacher?" Wyatt retorts, smirking, earning Griffin's heated glare.

"Well, Mason sure wanted to be in there with all the stories Asher told. He likely embellished a few of them, but I'm pretty sure you will be known as the favorite teacher in our house for a very long time," Colton adds, giving me a smile mirroring Griffin's.

I feel my cheeks heat. "Well, thank you."

"Sit by Sage and me," Robin requests, grabbing my hand. "I'd love to catch up and Sage has the best stories about Griffin."

"I'm pretty sure I have the best Griffin stories," Wyatt claims, sitting up straighter in his chair.

"True, but I'm more likely to be able to share my stories at the table without getting in trouble." Sage smirks, arching her eyebrows in challenge.

Wyatt raises his hands in surrender. "You win."

"Why does there need to be any stories about me?" Griffin argues, sitting down next to his brother, Wyatt with Mia still attached, and across from me.

"You got an extra appendage there, Griff," Wyatt teases.

Lifting her head, Mia glares at Wyatt. "I'm no 'pendage."

Wyatt's mouth drops open, feigning surprise.

"I'm pretty sure that's a princess," Beau claims, nodding at Mia as he sits on Griffin's other side.

Mia beams and pushes away from Griffin, looking at his youngest brother. "I am a princess."

Beau nods knowingly. "I can see that. It's an honor to sit and have breakfast with such a beautiful princess."

"Thanks. Did you know he's a prince?" she asks, patting Griffin's chest. "And that means you're a prince too since you're his brother."

"They're both my brothers, so, am I a prince too?" Wyatt questions.

Mia purses her lips, thinking hard before she shakes her head, answering matter of fact, "No." Griffin's head falls back as he and Beau laugh at their brother's expense and I attempt to stifle my giggle behind my hand.

Knowing my kids are comfortable, I feel myself relax and finally begin filling my plate along with everyone else. The huge spread of pancakes, eggs, bacon, sausage, home fries, fresh fruit, pastries, and breads smells fantastic. It's almost overwhelming looking at all the food being passed around the table.

"Colton, start us off," Mrs. Erickson requests.

Everyone sets their silverware down, some falling with a clatter, and I follow suit, glancing around the table as Colton begins a familiar prayer, the rest of the family joining in on autopilot.

"Dig in," his dad declares, just before taking his first bite of bacon.

"Dad, you're not supposed to eat that," Harper scolds.

I take a bite of my scrambled eggs and a satisfied moan leaves my lips. "Farm fresh food is so good, I don't know how we can eat it any other way."

"My mom's cooking likely has something to do with it," Sage chimes in. "She's amazing in the kitchen. I've tried to learn what I can from her just to do little things, but it's never the same."

"I understand that. I do okay, but since my kids eat mostly chicken fingers, hamburgers, pasta and an occasional cheese pizza, I don't really have to cook that much. The challenge is trying to find the vegetables that they like or at least will eat and unfortunately, it's different for all three of them."

Robin nods. "Yeah, the boys may be twins, but what they eat is definitely not the same. Asher is my picky one."

"Speaking of picky," Sage begins, "when we were little, I was really picky and Griffin would eat anything, so Wyatt and I used to sneak the food we didn't want onto Griff's plate when he wasn't looking. He was always so determined to finish what was on his plate he kept eating."

"Why are you telling this story?" Griffin groans and Wyatt laughs.

"Until we all decided it was a good idea to add all of our food to his plate to go outside to play. Griffin ended up sick and the rest of us grounded," Colton adds, chuckling.

"We can be a lot, but I promise, you get used to us," Griffin claims, sounding as if he's already planning our next visit.

"Do you have a big family?" Wyatt asks.

My face heats and I shake my head. "No, I was an only child, but Noah's sister has always treated me like we're sisters."

The room quiets, making my stomach turn, Sage quickly speaking up. "We all loved Noah like he was one of our brothers."

"Remember when Griff, Noah, Matt and Reid were jumping off the loft in the barn and y'all convinced me to do it?"

Griffin laughs. "Yeah, and you broke your leg while we all got in trouble. Wasn't our fault you couldn't jump."

I watch as all three of my kids slowly bring their attention to the conversation, realizing the stories include their dad.

"Or what about the time you guys stole a couple of our horses to go out on a date since you couldn't drive and one of the horses spooked from thunder. You guys walked back here soaked while I had to go with dad to find the horse," Colton complains.

The stories about Noah, Griffin and their friends, mostly including Matt and Reid continue, giving me a sense of peace, I thought I already had.

At the same time, it increases my curiosity, why haven't I met Griffin before? We really do need to talk about his ex. What was so bad that it would keep him away? Pushing my questions aside for now, I focus on the stories. Hearing things I never knew about him warms my heart. It's been a while since talking about him felt good. At the same time, I'm working out Griffin and Noah's connection in my head and heart, as if this is his way of letting me know it's okay.

It's not long before we're all done eating, breakfast is cleaned up and the kids are playing outside with Beau and Harper. "I'm going to go sit with dad," Griffin's mom announces, stopping in front of me and pulling me into another hug. "Mallory, we really hope you come back again soon. It will get pretty quiet today after everyone leaves."

"You'll still have me and Colton," Griffin adds, putting one arm around me and one around his mom.

"And my grandchildren, but the fact remains that it's much quieter. I have to admit, I'm thrilled Griffin is finally home to stay."

Me too. "Thank you again. Everything was delicious."

"Y'all are welcome anytime dear."

A soft smile touches my lips as we say the rest of our goodbyes and make our way to Griffin's truck. "Thank you for bringing us today."

"Thank you for coming."

"I can't believe you were so close with our dad," Tiegan mumbles, glancing at Griffin with a curiosity she didn't hold before making my stomach flip. "I like all the stories about all y'all," she says, referring to her dad, Griffin, Matt and Reid.

I'm in so much trouble with this man.

Chapter Nineteen

♡ Griffin ♡

With Wyatt and Sage back at work, while Harper and Beau returned to school, Colton and I have had our hands full along with the farmhands. Honestly, we spend half our time wrangling our dad. He's antsy to get outside and help, trying to sneak out more than once. Sure, I get that he likes getting his hands dirty, but we're here to help, so he can rest and get better; use it while you can. He takes worrying about him to a whole new level. I wouldn't want to be anywhere else. I'm glad I'm here to help, but fucking let me do it!

Normally I enjoy staying busy. When I was in Waco, I'd work out, work, go out once in a while, hook up and start all over again. But that's not working for me here when Mallory consumes my every thought. It's driving me crazy barely getting to see her. It's been a hell of a long time since that was the case for me but I don't give a shit. I'm not one to fake it for anything; she will know how I feel.

She's busy with her kids and end of the year stuff for school, but anytime I get a break, I send a text or call if it's after school. It's not even close to enough; I'm thirsting for more.

And with no sign of anyone sneaking around her house, or doing anything shady, she doesn't want to confuse her kids and have me on the couch every night. I get that, but it leaves me feeling uneasy. My only reprieve is knowing Matt, Reid and I have been taking turns stopping by to see her to make sure everything is alright and everyone at the station has been doing regular drive bys at her house on each shift. If it were anything less, I'd be camping on her front porch if she kicked me out, but I'm not about to scare the shit out of her for someone Olivia might have seen out the window. Although, I have no doubt it happened. I'm just hoping like hell it was a one-time thing, but it never hurts to be a little more aware or protective.

I'm packing up everything at the farmer's market with the help of Robin while Colton stayed at the farm getting things done. "Thanks, Robin."

She huffs a laugh. "You don't have to thank me, Griff. It's what you do for family. You know I'm here for all of it."

"Sure, but I appreciate it anyway."

"How's everything going with Mallory?"

I heave a sigh, falling back on my heels. "Fine. I'm gonna drop off some food and flowers for her and the kids after we're finished."

"Fine? Why just fine?"

"I've barely seen her this week. We watched a movie with the kids on Tuesday night and last night I stopped after they went to sleep and had maybe a good hour with her before Mia woke up and she kicked me out."

"What's a good hour?" My lips curve in a salacious grin making her grimace. "Forget I asked."

A soft chuckle escapes my lips. "For you, sure." Heaving a sigh, I shake my head. "But after spending nearly the entire weekend together last weekend, it feels like we took two steps back."

"Because of her kids?"

"Yeah." I grunt in frustration as I lift two crates into the truck.

"As a mom, I would've done the same."

"I know and it's likely the right thing to do, but it's been a helluva' long time since I've had this kind of interest in someone and not seeing her makes it damn hard to inch forward."

"That's what you want?"

"Hell, yeah, that's what I want."

She gives me a crooked smile. "Maybe it will change with summer."

Nodding, I agree. "Yeah, kindergarten graduation is on Tuesday, but her kids are in school all week. Well, everyone but Mia. Mal sounds like she's ready for summer vacation."

She laughs. "As a teacher, I'm sure she is. She's not teaching summer school?"

"Nah. She said since Noah passed, it's nearly impossible to teach over the summer, or at least not worth the costs of babysitting or childcare." I slide the last two crates into the back of the truck.

"Makes sense."

I feel her eyes on me and stop, turning to look at her. "What?"

She startles and shakes her head. "Nothing."

"Spit it out, Robin. What do you want to say to me?"

Heaving a sigh, she blurts out, "Have you talked to her?"

I wince. "Not yet."

"You need to do that before you get in too deep with Mallory."

"Yeah, I know."

"Why don't you take my car and I'll bring the farm truck back with everything. Colton can help me unload and I'll meet you back at the farm?"

"Your minivan?" I taunt hoping to lighten the sudden pressure surrounding us.

Her lips twitch as she narrows her eyes. "You know damn well it's an SUV."

I chuckle and we switch keys. "Thanks." I grab the crate I put aside for Mallory and switch it from one back seat to the other and wave as Robin drives away.

As I sit in the front seat, I tap Mallory's name on my cell, but she doesn't pick up. "Howdy, Mal. Just finished up at the farmer's market and I'm heading to your place with a few things. If you aren't home when I get there, I'll leave it by the back door."

I drop my cell in the cup holder and pull out, hoping she'll be home soon. Even if it's only for a few minutes, I need to see her smile. My thoughts drift to Robin's advice, knowing she's right. I've been putting it off for so long, it's become easier to avoid her and pretend it never happened. Even that doesn't make me forget. I think it's time to face her so I can move on. Maybe if I don't catch Mallory, I'll see if she's around. Although I have no idea how the hell to start that conversation. It doesn't matter how many years I've had to dwell on it.

As I pull along the curb at Mallory's house, finding the driveway empty and no missed calls or texts on my phone. With a heavy sigh, I climb out of Robin's car and pull on the crate I put together for Mallory with flowers, fruits, veggies, and some herbs and leave it by her back door. Picking up my phone, I hover over the contact I renamed *Bitch* the year I left

Piper Falls causing my stomach to churn in protest. Without connecting, I drop my cell back in the cup holder and pull away from the curb, making my way towards her house instead.

It doesn't take long before I park in front of her pale green ranch. She still lived at home when we were together, but she's lived here since she graduated college, a home I've driven by several times over the years, but never had the guts to even get this far. I gulp down the lump in my throat and take a deep breath, exhaling slowly as I remind myself, she can't get to me this time; never again. Taking another deep breath, I step out of the car and force myself to put one foot in front of the other, trudging towards the front door. Lifting my hand, I knock and close my eyes, waiting.

The sound of her laughter echoes as I hear her approaching the door. "Let me see who's here," she calls out to someone. Maybe I should've tried harder to call.

The door swings open and my gaze collides with her wide blue eyes as she gasps in shock, "Griffin."

With a nod, I offer her a tight smile. "Hi, Carla. How have you been?" She looks the same, but older. A light splattering of freckles covers the bridge of her nose, her strawberry blonde hair cascades around her shoulders in waves, and her curves are a little more full than I remember, all to her benefit. She's as gorgeous as ever.

"What are you doing here?"

"Thought it was time we finally talk. Don't you think?" I quirk a brow.

"Yeah, umm…" she trails off, appearing slightly stunned.

"I'm sorry about Noah," I tell her sincerely. I always hated that I was never able to give her my condolences.

She nods, gulping hard, her eyes suddenly teary. "Me too, Griffin."

"Hey, Carla, I can't find…"

My mouth drops open as Mallory steps up behind Carla and grins, her eyes lighting up. "Griffin. How did you know we were here?"

"Ah…"

"Oh, I texted him," Carla claims, jumping in, glancing between us. She shrugs. "I hope that's okay."

Opening my mouth to refute, I shake my head, but nothing comes out. The last thing I want to do is lie to Mallory, but I don't have a fucking clue what to say. I wanted to talk to Carla so we can move on from the past, the best we can, before I tell Mallory about everything that happened with us, especially considering their relationship. It's the right thing to do.

"Of course, it's okay." Mallory grins and steps towards me, giving me a kiss on the corner of my mouth. Momentarily, I stand frozen in Carla's doorway, Mallory's sweet gesture only succeeding in turning my face red at the awkward situation.

"Um, I left you a message."

She frowns and runs her hands through her hair. "Yeah, I left my phone in my car when Carla picked us up."

I give my head a slight shake, attempting to clear the fogginess and focus on Mallory. "You left it in your car?"

"Yeah, but Carla called the garage and it should be ready soon."

"Wait. What happened to your car?"

Mallory glances at Carla. "Umm…"

"She didn't tell me," I interrupt. "What happened to your car?"

She waves me off and spins on her heel, about to walk away. "Oh, it was nothing. I just had a couple of flats."

Reaching for her, I gently grab her arm. "A couple? How did you get a couple of flats? Where were you driving?"

Her body reacts to my question, flinching. "I wasn't. It must've been from when I was driving home last night."

"You got a couple flats while your car was sitting in your driveway?" Her eyes widen as I step closer, my heart hammering with the possibilities.

"Yes," she responds, holding my stare, her eyes defiant, daring me to throw down a challenge.

"Mal…"

"Mommy…" Mia's sweet soft voice interrupts causing me to release my hold on Mal as we all turn towards her.

Her eyes widen the moment she spots me and she shrieks with glee. "Ah! Prince Charming is here." Charging me, she crashes into my legs just above the knees and wraps her small arms around me, one of my hands falling to the back of her head. "Are you here to make pizzas with us?"

A low chuckle escapes my lips. "I can't darlin'. But I'm glad you guys are okay." Her face falls, and she juts her lower lip out dramatically making me laugh. "How about we catch up later? After pizzas?"

Grinning, she nods emphatically and twirls back towards the kitchen. "Yay!"

"Wow, she really loves you," Carla mumbles, reminding me where I am and why I'm here. Carla frowns, a flash of what I think is jealousy appears in her eyes.

"She does. Since the day we were at the farmer's market and he found her, she talks about him constantly," Mallory reveals, grinning.

"She does?" I question, my eyes widening in surprise.

Mallory blushes and nods, making my chest tighten and my dick twitch. Fuck, I need to get out of here. "Well, I'm glad you're okay. Let me know if you need help with anything."

She smiles. "Thanks, Griffin. Carla will give us a ride back to the garage after we eat. The car should be ready by then."

I nod. "Great, say hello to Austin for me."

Her brow furrows. "Austin?"

"Yeah, Austin Bauer, like the garage? He's likely the one changing your tires. It's his family garage and he's my cousin on my moms' side."

"Oh, okay."

"Let me know when y'all are home. I left food from the farmer's market by the back door."

"Oh, wow, thank you." She smiles, squeezing my heart in the palm of her hand as Carla stands by, watching us, putting me on edge.

Pulling out my phone, I glance at the screen and slip it back in my pocket. "I gotta' go. I'll see you later. Nice seeing you." I nod at Carla, everything about the moment feeling awkward as fuck as I spin on my heel, forcing myself not to run back to Robin's car.

The moment I slide behind the wheel, my phone beeps with a text. I pull it out and glance at the screen.

Bitch: You could've warned me.

Me: We haven't talked in years.

Bitch: Still. You obviously didn't forget about me, and Mallory is my sister-in-law.

I huff a humorless laugh. Of course, I didn't fucking forget about you. How could I? I want to say something, but I don't. It's not worth it.

Me: I know. We do need to talk.

Bitch: Yeah, Griff. We do. What works?

Me: Lunch.

Bitch: I'll make some time this week and let you know.

I don't respond. Why bother? Groaning in frustration, I run my hand down my face and drop it on the steering wheel. It's time to get this bullshit over with. I hope after I do, Mallory will still give me a chance.

Chapter Twenty

♡ Mallory ♡

My teeth run over my lower lip as I bite down nervously. I can't believe Carla texted him. How did she even know he was the guy I've been dating? I didn't even know they were friends. She's never said anything to me. This town is known to gossip, but I'm surprised she didn't ask me before doing something like that. It's not like her at all. Why was it any of his business?

Maybe that's why she didn't really tell him what happened. I was hoping to avoid that confession all together, knowing it would only make him worry, but I had to forget my phone. Did she tell him the woman he's dating is at her house with her kids if you want to check on them? It doesn't make sense.

Are Griffin and I dating?

I huff a laugh and roll my eyes at myself feeling more like my nine-year-old, but I can't stop myself. I'm confused why he knows anything at all. But now that he knows about my car, I know I'm in trouble. He was protective when he thought Olivia saw someone out the window. What will he do knowing my tires were slashed while sitting in my driveway?

"Mommy, Mommy, prince charming is here," Mia shrieks, her face plastered to the front window.

"He has a name, Mia," Tiegan retorts, rolling her eyes. "What are we supposed to call him, Mom?"

My lips twitch in amusement. "Why don't you ask him."

She frowns, scrunching up her face as if I just suggested she go swimming in a pool of mud. "I'm not doing that."

He rings the doorbell and the chimes echo throughout the living room. Closing my eyes for a moment I take a deep breath and exhale slowly.

"Mommy, let him in," Mia demands.

My lips twitch as I pull the door open and paste a smile on my face. He stands on my front porch in boots, faded blue jeans and a navy-blue t-shirt, giving me the perfect view of his colorful ink and his firm biceps, my body heating and my fingers twitching to reach out. I lift my gaze to his, finding his blue eyes sparkling as he aims his sexy grin at me. Licking my lips, I force out a greeting. "Hey."

His eyes quickly move up and down my body, taking in my white cotton shorts and light blue tank top. "Howdy Mal."

All three kids surround him, Mia squeezing his legs while his hand gently falls to her head. "You're here!"

He chuckles softly, "I'm here, darlin'."

"Do you watch soccer? Who's your favorite team? What about your favorite player? Did you ever play? Will you play with me? We could turn on the light and play in the backyard." Ollie starts shooting questions at him rapid fire.

"Whoa, slow down Ollie. Give me a chance to answer." He laughs.

"And no, you're not going outside right now. It's late," I remind him.

"But, Mom." He frowns and dramatically stomps over to the couch, flopping down making me bite the inside of my cheek to stop myself from laughing.

"That's okay, Ollie. I'll play with you another time."

Ollie's face lights up. "Really?"

Griffin nods. "Promise and an Erickson promise is as good as gold."

"Is that what we're s'posed to call you? Mr. Erickson?" Tiegan asks, looking up at him, giving him a tentative smile. It's the first I've seen from her in quite a while making my breath catch in my throat and my stomach twist into knots.

"Why don't y'all call me Griff?"

"Okay, Griff," she repeats, testing out his name and sucking her lower lip into her mouth as she turns away from him, walking towards the coffee table and sitting down on the floor, her knees pulled up to her chest.

"How was your pizza?"

"It was so good," Mia raves, finally releasing his legs and looking up at him, her lips pursed. "We ate it all. There's none left for you."

He gives her a crooked grin. "Next time."

Mia looks up at him with an innocence and adoration I don't know if I remember seeing on her little face. "Wanna play a game with us?"

"I'd love to."

"I'm…" a wave of emotion slams into me and I clench my fist, steeling myself.

Turning towards me, he gives me a pointed look reminding me the real reason he's here. "How are you doin'?"

Instead of answering I step back and wave him inside, attempting to pull myself together. "Come on in."

The door clicks closed behind him. "I see you got your car fixed."

My heart drops into my stomach. Yup, that'll do it. "It's as good as new." Pushing my shoulders back and standing tall with a confidence I don't yet feel, I grin and stride towards the kitchen, my bare feet slapping against the wood floors. "Anyone thirsty? I'm going to grab a glass of water."

"Why don't you guys pick the game and get it set up for us? I'm going to grab some water and talk to your mom for a minute," Griffin states trailing after me as they all surprisingly listen to him.

I stand at the sink, filling a glass of water and feel the warmth of his body as he moves in behind me, placing his hand on each side. "I understand you don't want me to stay because of the kids, but after today, I need that to change. Hell, I'll sleep in my truck in front of your house if I have to."

"Griffin…"

"This is not about us, Mal. Yeah, I want you to want me here, but I'm telling you this is only about you and your kids. You have no idea who did this or why."

"Probably just some kids doing something stupid." I'm not sure if I believe him, but it's the one thing that doesn't stress me out.

His body tenses behind me before relaxing, leaning slightly closer. His voice comes out low, his hot breath brushing against my ear, making it difficult to breathe. "I don't give a damn. Did you report it?"

I flinch, setting the glass down and grabbing another one to fill to keep my hands busy. "Umm…" Of course, I didn't report it. If I did, I'd have the entire Piper Falls Station 28 police department breathing down my neck.

He exhales slow and steady; controlled. "Why the hell not? What did you tell Bauer's Garage?"

"It's fine, Griff. I can take care of myself." I've been doing it for two years and even before then. It took me a long time to regain my confidence after losing Noah like we did. "I'm not letting another man, especially one who used to be a cop try to take over my life."

His eyes widen and he nods, pursing his lips. "That's not what I'm trying to do, Mal. I promise."

I glance at him out of the corner of my eye. "That's not what I meant."

He shakes his head, letting me know to forget about it. "Let me stay for me. I won't be able to sleep if I'm down the road. I'll crash on the couch like last time. Just let me stay, please. I need to know that y'all are okay." I bite my lower lip in hesitation. "I'll have to leave to help Colton around four-thirty anyway, so the kids will never know I stayed."

"Four-thirty?" I echo, my eyes widening in surprise.

"Yeah, I'll let him start without me."

"Without you? But that's early."

"Yeah, the animals are up early."

He kisses me on the spot behind my ear that never fails to drive me crazy, eliciting a soft moan from my lips, my body arching towards him without my consent, wanting to melt into his. Panting, I mumble, "Okay, fine. You can stay, but on the couch."

"You got it."

Needing to breathe before I walk back out to my kids, I push off the sink, forcing him to take a step back, leaving goosebumps in his wake. I clench my jaw and stride back to the living room without ever taking a sip of water. A moment later Griffin follows behind with two glasses of water in his hand. "You forgot this." He smirks, handing me a glass, his fingers lightly brushing mine.

"Thanks," I grumble, setting it down on the end table. Taking another deep breath, I force myself to focus on my kids. "Okay, what are we playing tonight?

"Uno," the three answer in unison as Griffin settles next to Ollie on the couch and I sit between my two girls on the floor, curling my legs up underneath me.

"That's my favorite game," Griffin announces, wide-eyed, earning genuine smiles from all four of us.

My heart squeezes, as if restarting. I've craved this feeling for so long. I practically forgot what it feels like, but it's there. He fits in so easily. Maybe it's too easy. Having him here almost doesn't seem right. Ironically, it feels exactly right. I think that's what scares the crap out of me.

Chapter Twenty One

♡ Griffin ♡

Leaning back against the couch, I stare at the ceiling, waiting for Mallory to return from checking on the kids, making sure they're asleep. I'm grateful she's not kicking me out, but I wasn't kidding about sleeping in my truck. I get why she doesn't want me to sleep here, but between what happened with Olivia last week and then having her tires slashed in her own driveway, I'm not comfortable walking away, even if it's just for the night. My gut is telling me it has something to do with her whether she wants to believe it or not. Maybe me being around will deter whoever is doing this, but there's no way in hell I'm taking a chance; not when it comes to her – to them.

My phone pings with a text. Reaching for it, I glance at the screen, my body going rigid the moment I see who it's from.

Bitch: Lunch on Wednesday?

I close my eyes, huffing out a breath. This is what I need to do, but it's the last thing I want. The thought of dealing with her, with our past still turns my stomach. The one thing that will get me through is the sooner I get it over with, the sooner I can confess it all to Mallory.

Me: Sure. Noon?

Bitch: My place okay?

Me: Yup. I'll bring Papi's. Let me know what you want.

Bitch: Thank you. Anything. You know what I like.

What the hell, Carla? You know what I like? You always have to push the line, but I'm not playing games. Fuck this. I turn off my notifications and drop my phone on the coffee table, running my hand through my hair and back down my face in frustration. Attempting to clear my head, I close my eyes and focus on my breathing.

"You look comfortable."

The sound of her voice slows my heart rate and calms me down. Opening my eyes, I lift my head and smile at the simple beauty standing in front of me. "A little, but…" I trail off and readjust, my dick already swelling with anticipation.

Her eyebrows draw down in concern. "What's wrong?"

"Nothin a little bit of you can't fix."

She rolls her eyes and laughs, the sweet sound making my dick twitch. "Smooth, Mr. Erickson, real smooth."

I give her a cocky smile. "Is it working?"

"Maybe."

"Are the kids asleep?"

"They are." She nods, staring into my eyes.

"Good." Reaching for her hand, I give it a light tug. She stumbles forward and sits on the edge of the cushion, pressed against my side. "That's not good enough." Sitting up, I give her hand another tug, my arm wrapping around her back as I pull her against me. Not willing to wait another moment, I press my lips to hers, my tongue sweeping inside seeking its mate. A groan of satisfaction leaves my lips as her body melts into mine.

One hand slides up to the back of her head, holding her close. I tilt my head, deepening our kiss, our tongues licking, twisting together, fighting for dominance as I get drunk on her sweet taste, the touch of her lips, the feel of her body pressed against mine. My hand slides down her back, following the curve of her ass, before slipping underneath her short white shorts. Squeezing her butt cheek, I pull her closer, groaning as she rubs against me, my dick instantly as hard as granite.

Her hands slide up my arms, over my shoulders and hook around the back of my neck, holding on tight as she kisses me back with all the pent-up energy since the last time our lips connected. She's like a drug; my drug. I can't get enough and I feel like I've barely had a taste. I'm desperate to explore every part of her, but I need her ready too and she's not there, not if she still has me pinned to her couch with the kids down the hall instead of behind her locked bedroom door.

She pulls back, gasping for breath, resting her forehead on mine. "I've wanted to do that all day."

"You can do that anytime you want darlin'."

She laughs. "Sure, I can."

"I'm sure as hell not going to be the one who stops you."

"Griff…"

"Come a little closer and let me show you how much I don't mind."

A salacious smile tugs at her lips. She reaches for the blanket over the back of the couch and pulls it up over us as she collapses against my chest. Her lips brush across my neck, followed by her tongue. "I want to lick every line of your tattoos."

An involuntary groan leaves my lips. "Fuck, I want that. You don't even have to ask, I'm all in."

Her body shakes slightly as she giggles. "They're so beautiful," she murmurs, her admiration clear, making my heart skip a beat. "Do you have reasons for them or do you just like the designs?" She glances up at me from underneath her long eyelashes, biting her lower lip and driving me crazy.

"Every one of them has a reason; some big and some small."

"Would you tell me?"

My chest tightens. "That would absolutely be my pleasure, but I have better ideas for this mouth at the moment."

Cradling her face in my hands, I cover her mouth with mine, moving together with her in a perfect rhythm. Our kiss remains soft, luscious, controlled, my tongue poking out to explore, to taste.

"Griff…" my name comes out a soft whimper.

My lips brush down her neck, stopping to kiss her sensitive spot and watch the goosebumps breakout across her skin. Cupping her breast, my thumb skims across her nipple, causing her body to arch towards me, searching for more. "You drive me to the brink and throw me to the wolves. I'm dying to touch you, taste you, be inside you."

"Yes," she pants, "I want that, Griff, please. I'm so wet."

I kiss her again, as her hands slip underneath my shirt, her fingertips running over my muscles, her soft touch leaving goosebumps in its wake. My head falls back as her hand glides over my hard length eliciting a groan. "Fuck, Mal."

"Oh wow," she mumbles under her breath, as she slips her hand underneath my waistline, barely grazing me.

"Mom!" Tiegan calls from her bedroom. Startling us both, Mallory swiftly jerks away from me.

With a soft sigh, I urge, "Go."

Quickly, she pulls herself together and rushes down the hall to tend to her daughter. Tonight is just not our night. I close my eyes and wait, relaxing as the sound of her footsteps approaches.

She sits down next to me with a heavy sigh. Opening my eyes, I arch my eyebrows in concern. "She okay?"

Nodding, she explains, "She had a bad dream about Noah. Tiegan remembers a lot about him and things before he died." She shrugs. "I'm both grateful and sad about that. It will be a good thing one day, but I think it's hardest on her sometimes and I hate that for her. She used to get bad dreams all the time, but they're coming less and less all the time." She frowns and bites her lower lip, looking away.

"That's okay, Mal. It doesn't mean she's forgetting him."

Her eyes widen in surprise as she gasps, looking at me with shock and wonder causing my heart to skip a beat. "How did you..." Her voice catches and she gulps down the lump in her throat.

I reach up, brushing her hair away from her face and tucking the loose strands behind her ears. "I'm just paying attention. I care about all of you."

She looks into my eyes, her own filling with tears. Her eyelids flutter as she blinks rapidly, attempting to keep the tears at bay. I pull her to me and wrap my arms around her, kissing her on her forehead, her nose, and her soft, full lips. Laying back, I keep her close as her hand slides over my chest.

"We need to stop making out on the couch like a couple of horny teenagers." She giggles, successfully lightening the mood and making my dick twitch once again.

"Well, that's not going to happen until you're ready to invite me into your room, you come home with me, or we find somewhere else to go."

She laughs louder, pressing her face into my chest to muffle the sweet sound. "Sorry, I don't know why I can't. Soon. It's just..."

"You don't have to explain anything to me, darlin'. I understand," I whisper, pressing another sweet kiss to her lips and giving her a comforting squeeze. "We'll get there when you're ready; when we're ready."

"I am ready."

"Make sure all parts of you are on the same page. I'm looking for this thing between us to hold steady. I don't need you to jump ahead for me."

"Maybe I'm doing it for me," she retorts defensively.

"If that's the case, Mal, we'll be there soon. Just make sure you're ready to jump in the deep end with me."

Chapter Twenty Two

♡ Mallory ♡

The last two days of school go by without incident. "Tanner, thank you so much for helping me with everything for the kindergarten graduation. I couldn't have done it without you."

He blushes adorably and turns away. "It was no problem, Mallory. You did all the hard work, I just rescued you with my computer skills." A low chuckle slips through his lips. "You know I'm always here for you."

"Yes, I do. Thank you."

"You want to grab some dinner with the kids and celebrate another year over?" he asks, stuffing his hands into his pockets as he rocks back on his heels.

"I'm sorry, but I promised Griffin he could come over for dinner tonight. It's taco Tuesday. You're welcome to join us."

He shifts uncomfortably. "I don't know. I don't want to intrude."

"You wouldn't be. You know we would love to have you."

"Thanks, Mallory." He shakes his head. "So, have you agreed to any of these other dates? Or have the single dads stopped asking you out?"

Shaking my head, I huff a laugh. "Let's just say, I've been doing a better job of avoiding them lately."

He chuckles. "You always have turned a lot of heads."

"No, you're exaggerating."

"Believe what you want, but I think we both know the truth. Most of the guys in our high school class asked you out at one time or another and a couple of the girls."

I roll my eyes. "A few maybe, but it didn't matter, I had a boyfriend for most of junior and senior year."

"Yeah, but he turned out to be an asshole."

"True, but at least I found out he cheated on me, thanks to you."

He shakes his head. "It wasn't just me. The idiot was making out with her in the hallway at a party. What did he think would happen?"

"True but thank you. By the way, how's Carolina anyway? You haven't mentioned her recently."

Frowning, he turns away. "She ah, she cheated on me."

"Oh, my gosh, Tanner. I'm so sorry. I had no idea." I wrap my arms around him, giving him a hug before pushing back and playfully swatting him on the arm. "Why didn't you tell me?"

He shakes his head and shrugs. "I didn't think it would be fair for me to complain about a woman who cheated on me when you just started dating again. I didn't want you to feel bad and think you had to stop talking to me about it."

"I don't care about that. You can always talk to me. You two have been together for three years. I guess it's lucky she kept pushing off your wedding date."

He laughs humorlessly. "Yeah, lucky. I guess now we know why."

"Forget about her. You're too good for someone like Carolina. I never liked her anyway and now I know why." He laughs at my lame attempt to make him feel better. "Tanner, please come over tonight. It will be fun."

"Maybe next time."

Pausing, I narrow my eyes at him before conceding. "Ugh, fine."

"How's it going with Griffin anyway? You've been on several dates now."

A smile tugs at the corners of my lips as Griffin floods my thoughts. "Yeah, we have. I almost can't believe it. It's been going really well, Tanner. We have so much fun. He makes me laugh and he really listens to me. It's like he has a way of making me feel special, like whatever I have to say is the most important thing in the world." I blush, shrugging. "I know it probably sounds silly to you."

"No, Mal. I think it's great. You deserve the best."

My smile widens. "You know, he's incredible with the kids too. Even Tiegan seems to be warming up to him and you know she doesn't do that with many people, especially in the last couple years. There's just something about him that pulls you in and makes you want to relish in everything about him. I think I really like him." A dreamy sigh escapes my lips and my face heats in response.

Glancing at me, he grins. "That's great, Mal. I'm glad you're happy. You know that's all I want for you."

"Thanks." Pausing, I reach out, giving his hand an appreciative squeeze before letting go as he nods in acknowledgement. "Will you help me with a couple of these boxes? I want to get a few of my things out to my car to store for the summer before I pick the kids up from after care. It's going to take me several trips back and forth from home, so the sooner I get started the better."

"Of course, but you know I can always come over with a load of your things in my truck. I'm sure I could get almost everything in."

"It's okay. I want to go through things as I put them in the boxes so I can sort it. I'm sure it will take me a couple days to do that anyway."

"Okay, so which ones do you want me to grab now?"

I point to the boxes by my desk and he picks two up, while I swing a tote bag over my shoulder. "Ready?" I ask, heading towards the door.

"Yup." We walk out of my classroom and exit the school side by side, both of us with our hands full.

As we get to the car, I set my box down on the ground and pop the trunk. Tanner sets both of his boxes inside and picks up mine doing the same. "Thank you."

"You're welcome."

Pausing, I pull my front door open and set my tote bag on the floor by the passenger seat, catching something on my windshield out of the corner of my eye. "What's this?" I mumble, reaching for an envelope tucked underneath my windshield wiper. I glance at the front, my name written in simple block lettering giving me a sense of deja-vu and making my stomach churn.

Tanner steps up behind me, glancing over my shoulder, and voicing my concern. "That looks just like the other letter you got, the one you wouldn't report."

"Yeah."

"Open it," he commands, his hand falling to my back in silent support.

My heart pounds, I hold my breath and my hands shake as I open the envelope and unfold the letter. At first glance, I find this one shorter and I'm able to focus on the words.

Darlin' Mallory,

You sure ain't makin' this easy. It's our turn to be together. I'm getting impatient. School is out and I can't wait to make you mine.

"Mallory, are you okay?" I don't answer, I can't. "You have to report this Mallory. This is too far; way too far."

I shake my head and watch as he reaches for his phone, unlocking the screen, prompting me to respond. "Who are you calling?"

"The police."

Reaching out, I put my hand over his, halting his movements. "No, they can't do anything at this point."

He freezes, begging me with his eyes. "You can't ignore it."

"I'm not. I promise I'm taking it seriously, but there's no reason to call the police. This doesn't say anything; not really." It's creepy as fuck, but there's nothing here.

"But there's two of these and what if it happens again, or something worse?" he challenges, pulling away from me and crossing his arms over his chest.

"Let's make a deal," I prod, anxiously running my teeth over my lower lip.

He frowns. "What kind of deal?"

"If it happens again, I'll bring all three letters to the police."

Shaking his head, he huffs a humorless laugh. "That's not a deal. What if something happens in the meantime? That would fucking kill me, Mal. I'd never forgive myself."

Heaving a sigh, I relent. "Fine, I'll tell someone, just please let me do it my way because of the kids?"

He arches his eyebrows in challenge. "Bringing in the kids, Mal? You're not playing fair."

I shrug. "I'm a single mom, I don't have to play fair."

He narrows his eyes on me, stepping closer as he drops his hands to his sides. "Maybe I will come over for dinner tonight."

"Maybe you're no longer invited."

He laughs.

Chapter Twenty Three

♡ Mallory ♡

"Mom, may I be excused?" Tiegan requests.

"Me too, please?" Mia adds.

"Looks like you ate enough. Just bring your dishes to the sink please, girls."

"Okay," they chime in unison.

"Mind if I have seconds?" Griffin asks, giving me a crooked smile.

"Go for it," I offer, holding out my hand.

"Me too," Ollie announces as he jumps off his chair, following behind Griffin and garnering my attention.

I watch as Griffin shows Ollie how he makes his taco and folds it over at the ends so nothing spills out, my son watching closely and mimicking his every move, even adding black beans which he always claimed were gross. The two tap their tacos together and take a bite, most of the filling remaining inside the wrap. My chest tightens and I blink back the tears in my eyes, overwhelmed with emotion.

Griffin lifts his gaze, meeting mine and grins, holding up his taco in a toast making me laugh.

"I see what you mean," Tanner comments, nudging me gently. "He's good with the kids and it's obvious he likes you."

"You think so?"

He huffs a laugh, arching his eyebrow. "You're kidding, right?" Blushing, I shrug. "You know he does, Mal. It's good to see you dating again."

"Thanks. It's strange, but I think I'm finally ready."

"You've been taking things at your pace which is what you should do. And it looks to me like you're doing just fine. But I think you should tell him what's been going on."

Griffin steps up behind me, his hand falling to my shoulder and my body tenses. "What's he talking about? What's been going on?"

My eyes widen before narrowing, glaring at Tanner. He did that on purpose. "Oh, it's nothing. Just something that's been happening at school."

"Nothing?" Griffin questions, clenching his jaw. It's obvious I'm lying, but I'm not doing this in front of my kids.

I shake my head and mumble. "Can we talk about this later? Now's not really a good time," I claim, my gaze sweeping to my kids.

He gives me a slight nod and walks over to Tiegan, sitting on the couch, reading a book. He flops down next to her and she looks up, smiling. Her whole face lights up as she talks animatedly about something.

"Ollie and Mia why don't you two go get ready for bed," I suggest, giving both a pointed look.

"Then can we watch a movie?" Mia whines.

"If you can all agree, maybe. Let's see how long it takes you to get ready for bed. You were a little slow coming to dinner tonight, so it's a little later than normal and Ollie and Tiegan still have school tomorrow."

"Ugh, why do I have to go?" Ollie whines. "I want to help Griffin at the farm."

"You're almost done. Maybe when you are finished, I'll take y'all back over to the Erickson's farm."

"Awesome!" Ollie and Mia run down the hall to get ready for bed as I walk over to Tiegan, asking her to do the same and she does without giving me any pushback, taking me by surprise.

"What did you say to her?" I laugh, grinning at Griffin.

"We were just talking about books. What do you need to tell me? What's been happening at school?"

"Umm…" My heart drops like a lead balloon into my stomach and I shake my head. "I know how this conversation goes and I'm not doing it."

"You do?" Griffin questions, arching his eyebrow.

"I can deal with this myself."

"I'm sure you can, but you don't need to when there are other people around who care about you, who can help. And it's obvious Tanner thinks I should know."

I turn my glare on Tanner again. "Maybe I should go," he mumbles, backing towards the door.

I point at him in warning. "You started this."

His eyes widen and his mouth drops open as he shakes his head. "I did not start anything like this, Mal."

Wincing, I scrunch up my nose with regret. "That's not what I meant, Tanner." I shake my head. "Forget it, I'm sorry."

He nods, glances at Griffin and back at me. "Give him a chance Mallory. Someone besides me needs to know."

Sighing, my shoulders sag in defeat. "Fine. I'll talk to him."

"Great, now that we've got that settled, don't you think it's time to fill me in?" Griffin crosses his arms over his chest, his arms bulging. He looks down at me, brooding, giving me goosebumps, the kind I would normally welcome if I weren't so worried about what he's going to say.

"Say goodbye to the kids for me. I'll see you tomorrow." Tanner backs away from me and waves towards Griffin. "Nice meeting you."

"You too," Griffin grunts, keeping his eyes on me.

Tanner walks out and I lock the door behind him, slowly turning around, ill-prepared to face Griffin. "So…"

He's suddenly in my space, his fingertips gently tilting my head up to meet his gaze. "Mallory, what's going on? Please let me in. You don't have to do everything alone. I want to be here for you."

Closing my eyes, I exhale slowly and steel myself as I open them. Looking him in the eye, I confess, "I have been getting asked out by some of the single dads, which isn't a big deal, I dealt with it. But I may have gotten a letter that seemed a little…off."

He frowns. "Off? Off how?"

"I don't know it was kind of like a creepy love letter or something, but shorter," I say, trying to play it off like it's not a big deal.

"Let me see the letter," he murmurs, his voice deadly quiet making my heart skip a beat. If I didn't know better, I'd think he was pissed at me.

"What?"

"I'm ready." Ollie announces, followed by Tiegan and Mia attempting to pull her head through the sleeve of her pajamas.

"Mommy, I'm stuck."

I giggle, grateful for the reprieve and help. "There she is." I smile as her head pops through.

"Thank you," she mumbles, giving me a hug, followed by one for Griffin before grabbing his hand and dragging him to the couch. "Come on! We're watching a movie."

"It's my turn to pick," Ollie announces.

I sit down on the couch, glancing over my daughter to look at Griffin as the kids argue about what movie we're watching. He mouths the words I expect, "We will finish this later."

Pasting a smile on my face, I nod. I guess there's no going back now.

Thanks a lot Tanner.

Chapter Twenty Four

♡ Griffin ♡

"Would you have ever told me about this if Tanner didn't say something?" I question, looking down at Mallory, a defiant spark in her eyes.

"Of course I would, but in my time and my way. I don't want to disrupt the kids' lives because someone's dad got it in their head that he's going to date me."

"That's not what this is. This isn't normal."

She plants her hands on her hips, glaring up at me. "I know that Griffin. Don't talk to me like I'm clueless."

Sighing heavily, I stare at the ceiling, trying to get my emotions under control before responding. "I'm sorry. That's not what I want to do. I'm just trying to understand why you wouldn't want to report something like this."

"Why? Because I know what it's like to be a cop's wife and have the entire Piper Falls police station hovering over you while my kids just try to be normal. It doesn't work. I don't want them to have to worry about some idiot."

"And you think not saying anything or ignoring him will make this guy stop? 'Cause from the sound of this, I don't think he will."

She winces before quickly schooling her features. "No, that's not what I think, but he could be harmless."

"And what if he's not? What if this is related to the other shit that's been happening to you?" I challenge, leaning towards her.

She shakes her head, dismissing my comment like it's no big deal. "It's fine, Griff, I can take care of myself. I've been doing just fine on my own."

"I know you have darlin'. Believe me, I don't doubt that for a second. It's one of the reasons I can't stop thinking about you."

Her head snaps up and her eyes widen. "What?"

A soft chuckle leaves my lips. "You know what I said." Her pretty mouth presses into a thin line. "Look, why don't we just figure out what to do now."

"Fine," she grunts, making my lips twitch in amusement. Damn. She looks sexy as hell when she's pissed.

"What if you and the kids come stay out at the farm?"

She sulks, crossing her arms over her chest, pushing up her breasts and narrowing her eyes as I force myself to keep my focus on her face. "Do you not understand what I just said? No! I'm not going anywhere." Huffing in frustration she drops one hand to her side as she points down the hall, still glaring. "This is their home, the only one they've ever known. It's their connection to their dad. I'm not leaving, Griffin. No one will scare me away from anything when it comes to my family."

Not able to hide my reaction, I flinch before quickly covering it up. She's right. This is Noah's family and I'm the outsider who craves to find a way inside. Slowly, I nod my head in acknowledgment.

Sighing heavily, she looks at me with pity or regret, I'm not sure. But that's the last fucking thing I want. "Griffin—"

My jaw clenches and I shake my head to stop her. "Don't Mal. You don't owe me an explanation."

"But—"

Interrupting, I continue. "I don't ever want to replace Noah. He was a good man, one of my best friends. Hell, I loved him like I do my brothers and I would give anything to have him back, but that's impossible."

Tears well in the corners of her eyes prompting me to reach up and gently wipe them away. "I didn't mean for this to happen with us. Hell, I didn't even know who you were when I first met you. But this is happening, Mal and I'm not fightin' it. I don't want to." Pausing, I cradle her face in my hands, staring into her eyes my own stripped bare. "I'm already starting to fall for you darlin' and there's no way in hell I'm backin' down because his ghosts are lingering. He'll always be watching out for you and the kids and that's the way it should be. But I know Noah would sure as hell want you to keep living and move on because he would want the best for you; for all of you. He will always be your family, Mal, but that doesn't mean you can't make room for someone else; for me. Let me know when you're ready."

Tipping my head down, I brush my lips across hers, the soft kiss shooting tingles throughout my body. I pull back and look down before I let go and step back. Needing a few minutes, I tell her, "I'm going to go out to my truck for a few." I stride for the door when her soft touch on my forearm stops me in my tracks.

"Don't go."

"I'm not leaving."

"No." She steps closer, her body heat seeping into my skin and spreading like wildfire. "I don't want you to walk out the door right now Griffin."

Turning, I look at her, finally meeting her heated gaze making my dick twitch. "Mallory?" I question, arching my eyebrow, needing clarification on what she wants.

Glancing at me, she puts her pointer finger to her lips as she backs down the hallway. She stops at each of her kids' doors and cautiously peeks inside, likely to confirm they're sleeping. The moment Ollie's door clicks shut, she turns her focus back on me. Her searing gaze shoots heat straight to my groin. A sexy grin tugs at her lips. Her tongue juts out to wet them, freezing me in place, my eyes glued to her body.

Moving with confidence, she slides her hand down my arm, weaving her fingers through mine, and holding on tight. She gives my hand a gentle tug, leading me back down the hallway and stops in front of her bedroom door, her hand grasping the handle.

My free hand falls to her shoulder and I lean down, kissing her behind her ear and watching goosebumps erupt across her skin. Whispering, I ask, "Are you sure about this, darlin'?"

Looking me in the eyes, she nods, my heart thundering at her conviction. "I'm positive." Then she pushes the door open and pulls me across the threshold, letting me into her world as I quietly close the door behind us and lock it.

My eyes remain glued to her as she pushes up on her tiptoes and pulls my head down to hers, kissing me hard before falling back on her heels. I cover her mouth with mine, lifting her, her legs wrapping around my back and holding me close as I walk her back to the bed, barely registering my surroundings, too consumed with her.

She falls back with a giggle as I bump the edge of the bed. Climbing over her, I kiss her, my tongue, licking the seam of her lips, begging for entrance she willingly gives. Our tongues collide, dancing, licking and tasting until we're both out of breath.

Pulling back, I make my way down her body, along her jawline, to her neck, then her collarbone. Leaning back, I tug at the hem of her tank top. She sits up and pulls it over her head, my eyes going wide at the sight of her in a silky, demi-cut, pink bra, her chest heaving as she attempts to catch her breath. "Fuck, Mal. You're so damn beautiful."

Reaching for me, she grabs my shirt, pulling it over my head as she falls back on the bed. Kissing her again, I moan into her mouth, relishing the feel of my skin on hers as her hands roam my chest, my arms and my back. Moving down her body again, I push her bra strap to the side, pressing my lips underneath. My hand slips underneath her bra, cupping her breast, my mouth inching towards its destination. Holding the material back, my tongue licks her skin, circling her nipple before sucking it into my mouth, her salty-sweet taste already addicting. Flicking her nipple with my tongue, I release her slowly, grazing her with my teeth.

She whimpers, arching her back towards me and pulling me close as I let go with a soft pop. "Griff."

I look down at her, her hair a beautifully tangled mess, her lips swollen and her skin flushed. She sits up, pressing her lips against my chest. Her tongue slips out, licking and kissing me along the lines of a fire tattoo, my breathing picking up its pace. Reaching around her back, I flick the hook of her bra. She leans back and tosses it to the floor, attempting to return her attention to my chest, but I lightly nudge her back, giving her a salacious grin. "I have some work to do."

She arches her eyebrows in question, eliciting a low chuckle from my lips as I kiss her stomach, my hands on the edges of her shorts as I request, "May I?"

"Please."

I tug her shorts and panties down in one swift move, dropping them to the floor. My mouth instantly finds her inner thigh, kissing as I lift her leg. Inhaling her scent, I moan, my mouth watering. "You smell so damn good. I need to taste you."

"Oh, God."

My mouth closes on the inside of her other thigh, my teeth grazing the sensitive skin as I lift her other leg. Exhaling slowly over her neatly trimmed pussy, I watch her body reacting to me, twitching, heating, prickling, my dick becoming impossibly harder. My tongue juts out, licking her from back to front, both of us moaning with pleasure. Repeating the movement, I pause at her clit, circling it with my tongue and sucking it into my mouth, humming in satisfaction, as my tongue presses flat, putting more pressure on her folds.

"Ah," she grunts, grabbing a pillow and shoving her face into the stuffing, hoping to muffle the sounds she can't hold back. One, then two fingers slip inside her slick pussy, my mouth and tongue going to work on her clit in slow, deliberate movements with just the right amount of pressure. Her fingers weave into my hair, grasping the ends and tugging lightly as I lick, suck, and move in and out, curling my fingers slightly inside. It doesn't take long before I feel her becoming hotter, wetter and tighter, squeezing my fingers as I flatten my tongue against her. Her insides begin to pulse, squeezing me as she moans, tugging harder on my hair and urging me on.

The vibrations of my groan glide over her as I enjoy her scent, her taste, her muted sounds, her reactions, and most of all knowing I'm the one that's pushing her over the edge and making her fall apart. Keeping my mouth on her and my fingers sliding in and out, I lift my gaze watching her as her body convulses around me.

As she collapses against the mattress her hold on my hair relaxes. As I give her a kiss, I remove my fingers, licking them clean. Her eyes flutter open and she meets my gaze, her eyes widening as I pull my fingers out of my mouth. "Mm," I mumble, giving her a wicked grin. "You're absofuckinglutely delicious darlin'."

Chapter Twenty Five

♡ *Mallory* ♡

The things this man can do with his tongue could likely kill me. I don't remember the last time I had an orgasm like that; one that thoroughly rocked my body. My insides are still vibrating with aftershocks, only making sure I'm primed and ready for more. And I'm sure as hell willing. I didn't even realize I was holding back until he called me on it. His sweet confession succeeded in making my heart race, my breath catch and my body ignite, impossibly making me want him more.

"My turn," I announce, grinning back at him.

"You don't have to do that."

"Oh, Griffin. Believe me, I know I don't." I get up on my knees and make my way over to the side of the bed, kissing him on the lips and tasting myself on him. Pulling back, I put my fingertips in his waistband and look him in the eyes. "So maybe you should shut up and let me do what I want."

He chuckles that low sexy sound spreading goosebumps all over my body. "Mallory, you can do anything you want, darlin'. You've got full reign on me."

I smirk, kissing him again before leaning back, unbuttoning his jeans and pulling the zipper down. "A little help here?" Arching my eyebrows, I bite my lower lip as I look up at him from underneath my eyelashes, waiting for his help.

His eyes flash causing my heart to skip a beat as he leans down, sucking my lower lip out from between my teeth, and pressing a tender kiss to my lips. "I can do that," he mumbles, kissing me once again.

Giggling, I fall back on my heels, watching him as he slips out of his jeans, leaving them on the floor. Satisfied, I lay on my side and pat the spot on the bed next to me, not bothering to cover myself, loving the way his eyes flare when they sweep over my body. "You coming?" I taunt, keeping my voice playful when I just want to jump him.

"Oh, I will, I'm just getting myself under control."

"That's the last thing you need."

He laughs as he sits on the bed, his boxer briefs still on. "See, that's where you're wrong, my sweet Mallory."

"Oh, yeah?" I rasp as he inches closer, stopping as one hand falls to my hip and the other props his head up so he can look at me.

"Definitely. I love that you don't bother to cover yourself." Reflexively, I move and he gently grabs my wrist, stopping me. "I mean it. Your confidence is sexy as sin." He brushes his lips over mine. "Between that and watching you come apart as I worked your sweet pussy with my mouth, my tongue and my hand–" He moans, kissing me again as he holds me close, his hard length pressing into my stomach. "You, my darlin' Mal, are everything I could ever want and it won't take much to toss me into the ravine." He groans, pressing his lips to mine, our mouths quickly moving in a perfect rhythm.

A soft whimper escapes without my consent bringing me back to the present. Planting my hands on his firm chest, I push back, looking down at him as I catch my breath. "Then, give me a chance to explore, Griff. I want to know what you like, what makes you squirm, makes you happy…"

"You do."

I narrow my eyes and lean forward, nipping at a spot on his neck. "Hey." He laughs. "Okay, do with me what you want. I'm all yours." He grins, his eyes sparkling.

Draping myself across his chest, I kiss him hard, one hand gliding up and down his arm and the other roaming over the rigid muscles of his abs. Tearing my lips away from his, I kiss him along the scruff of his jaw, down his neck, along his collarbone, and across his chest as my hand slips under the elastic of his boxer-briefs. Without hesitation I reach down, running my hand over his hard length, wondering if I will be able to fit him in my mouth as his chest rumbles with his low moan.

My lips tingle as I kiss his chest, licking the lines of his tattoos as I explore each one. A familiar blue American flag stands out, torn at the end and drawing my attention. I continue kissing him, methodically working my way down his hard chest. Snagging my fingers in the sides of his underwear, I tug, sliding them down his thick thighs and tossing them on the floor. Gripping him, I wrap my fingers around his hard length and squeeze him from base to tip. My hand slides down, cupping his balls as my tongue flicks out, starting at my hand and slowly licking to the top, circling him and sucking him into my mouth. His salty taste hits my tongue, eliciting a low growl from him.

In an instant I'm on my back, staring up at him wide-eyed. His lips come crashing down on mine, kissing me hard. I moan as his tongue licks my lips and slips inside my mouth. Our tongues tangle together, licking, twisting, moving in an erratic rhythm, not able to get enough. "I want you so bad, Mal. I need you to tell me what you want."

"I want this. Griffin, I want you. I want to feel you moving inside me. Do you have a condom?"

"Yeah." He nods, kissing me tenderly. "Don't move, darlin'." Griffin climbs off the bed and reaches into the pocket of his jeans, grabbing his wallet, pulling out two square foil packets and tossing one on the nightstand. As he climbs back on the bed, he hands me the condom, kissing my lips, my chin, the spot behind my ear.

"Griff," I moan.

"I love every little sound you make." He licks the same spot and kisses it again, igniting me further, my insides heating, swelling, pooling, making me feel like I'm about to combust.

I hand him back the condom, watching as he rips it open with his teeth, slides it out and rolls it over his thick cock. Looking down at me, he asks, "Are you sure, Mal? We can stop at any time, but I need you to be sure."

Licking my lips with anticipation, I nod my head as I stare into his eyes. "It's been over two years, Griffin. I promise, I'm ready."

He nods, his Adam's apple bobbing up and down as he gulps hard. "I'm going to start slow. Talk to me, tell me what you need. I want to know if you need to stop, to slow down, to move a different way; anything you need, Mal. Got me?"

My chest tightens and I nod. "I got you."

He hovers over me, pausing at my entrance. Leaning down, he kisses my lips until my body relaxes, focusing only on him. Lifting my right leg, I hook it around his back and he pushes inside, pausing to look at me. "You okay?" I nod and he pushes in further, finally thrusting all the way inside me making me gasp.

"Ah." Stopping, he kisses me, waiting for my body to adjust to his size. "I feel so full." Taking a couple deep breaths, I relax, urging him on, "Keep going, Griffin. I'm okay."

Doing as I request, he begins to move, slow, but confident, deliberate thrusts, shocks shooting through me as he hits the right spot deep inside me over and over again. "You're so tight, darlin'. You feel so damn good."

His hand covers my breast, pinching my nipples and gently rolling, adding to my desire as he kisses me. Heat floods me, and he soon moves easier, and steadily picks up his pace, the sound of our breaths and our bodies coming together echoing in my bedroom.

My arms wrap around him and I drag my fingers down his back, squeezing his firm butt, attempting to pull him closer. My breathing picks up and my body heats. Struggling for breath, my head falls back, a soft moan coming from my lips as he picks up the pace and I arch my back and hips matching his every move.

His mouth moves down, covering my other nipple as he sucks it gently into his mouth, his tongue swirling around and flicking it before he releases it with a soft pop. Going back for more, he runs his teeth over my nipple, grazing it as he continues moving in and out of me at a steady pace making it difficult to breathe.

"Griff," I whimper, my fingers digging into his back. My vision starts to blur and I'm unable to catch my breath. I'm hot, sweaty and swollen, my insides ready to explode. "More, faster, please."

Obeying, he quickens his pace. He grasps my hip with one hand, holding me in place as he pumps into me. "I can't hold on much longer, Mal. Please. I need you to come."

As if on command, a tingling ignites deep in my core, overheating and exploding as he pushes me over the edge. "Ahh." My insides clench around him, my entire body throbbing, squeezing him again and again.

Just as I start to come down, his fingers grip me a little tighter, his moves becoming erratic. I try to hold on, prying my eyes open and focusing on him, wanting to watch his release as he falls. He thrusts deep inside me and holds himself there at his climax. It feels as if he's everywhere inside and around me.

With a soft groan, he collapses, holding himself just above me so he doesn't crush me. I relax into the mattress, a smile pulling at the corners of my lips. "Mm," I mumble, brushing my lips against his chest, now slick with sweat. "I almost forgot how much fun that is."

He chuckles, slowly pulling out of me and rolling to his side, keeping his hand on my hip. "You're okay?"

"I'm fantastic, Mr. Erickson."

He groans, a sexy smile tugging at his lips. "You won't get much of a break if you keep calling me that, darlin'."

I arch my eyebrows in surprise. "Really?"

"There's just something about the way it rolls off your tongue that's sexy as fuck."

"Huh."

Leaning on his elbow, he brushes his lips against mine and gently pats my hip. "Let me clean up." He stands and looks around while I shamelessly stare at him in all his glory. Damn the man is hot. "No bathroom without getting dressed?"

Smirking, I shake my head. "Nope."

"Okay."

I watch as he grabs his jeans before stopping him. "Wait. I have baby wipes in my nightstand."

He arches his eyebrows in question, making me blush. "Baby wipes?"

"Yeah, they clean really well. I'm a single mom who hasn't had sex or even fooled around with a man in over two years before now."

Griffin's eyes flare and his voice comes out a low rumble as he asks. "What else you got in that drawer of yours?"

"Something I don't need if I have you," I declare boldly, my entire body heating.

"You got that right, darlin'."

Chapter Twenty Six

Griffin

After a fantastic night with Mallory, a morning working hard at my parents' farm, and a quick run, the last thing I want to do is have lunch with my ex. If it were up to me, I'd never have to see Carla again. Unfortunately, I'm not that lucky. If I want this to work with Mal, and I sure as hell do, it's time to get this nightmare over with, so we can all move on, without having to avoid important life events like everyone assumed I had done. I don't blame them since that's what I wanted everyone to believe. In reality, I did miss Noah's wedding and I held so much regret over it. I could never ask Mallory or her kids to do something like that, especially when I wouldn't want them to concede.

Noah was one of the few who knew our whole story. I can imagine it wasn't easy in his position: his sister and one of his best friends. He always told me he understood, but more than once he told me to grow some balls and face it. I guess it's time.

With a heavy sigh, I grab the paper bag filled with food from Papi's and climb out of my truck. Stepping up to her door, I straighten, pushing my shoulders back and exhaling slowly, attempting to calm my sudden anxiety. The muffled sound of the doorbell ringing makes my body tense, waiting as Carla pulls the door open, pasting a smile on her face. "Hi, Griffin. Come on in."

I give her a stiff nod, stepping inside. "Hey, Carla."

Her eyes quickly sweep over me from head to toe before she looks away without a word. Clearing her throat, she asks, "You want to eat in the kitchen?" Spinning on her heel, she wanders towards the kitchen without waiting for a response and I reluctantly follow. "What did ya' get?"

"I don't know," I grumble, setting the bag on the table. "A few things. I'm sure there's something you will like in there."

"Thanks for bringing all this. I'm sure you still know what I like."

Refusing to entertain her innuendos, I roll my shoulders to release some stress. "You're welcome. Figured it was better than going out somewhere."

"Why? Don't want to be seen with me?"

I arch my eyebrows in challenge and narrow my eyes, waiting for her to answer her own question.

"All right, fine. You win."

"This isn't a fucking game, Carla. And I sure as hell didn't win anything. That's part of the damn problem. It was never a damn game for me."

She scoffs. "You think this was a game for me?" She narrows her eyes, glaring at me, as she crosses her arms over her chest in both defiance and defense.

Heaving a sigh, I put my hand up, begging her to stop as we both sit down at the square pine table in the corner of her small kitchen. "Can we just start over? We haven't even started and we're already fighting."

Grimacing, she nods in agreement. "Yeah, we were always good at that. But it sure made the making up part a helluva' lot of fun with you." She quirks a brow and licks her lips, watching me close for my reaction.

Ignoring her, I focus on the food. Pulling it out, I hope to give us both a chance to gather our thoughts knowing nothing about this is easy. I hand her a burger and put a mixture of fries and onion rings in the middle of the table, the simple gesture familiar. She looks up at me and smiles, her eyes soft. "Thanks."

I nod stiffly. Grabbing a burger of my own, I unwrap it, taking a bite and swallowing before returning my gaze to her. "Look, I know you don't give a shit about me—"

She shakes her head, interrupting me. "That's not true. I still care about you, Griff. I don't know if I ever stopped loving you."

Instinctively, I flinch. "Carla, cut the shit. We haven't seen each other in years and we didn't exactly end things on good terms."

"We didn't really end things at all."

Heaving a sigh, I set my burger down and look her in the eyes. "At least out of respect for Mallory, can you not say things like that?"

She snorts and tosses a fry in her mouth. "Really, Griff? What about you? Why don't you show some respect for Noah? You know the guy we lost two years ago?"

Planting my hands on the table with a bang, I glare at her. "Don't you fucking dare use Noah as leverage for anything. He'd be pissed you even suggested it."

At least she has the decency to look embarrassed, her cheeks turning red as she breaks my stare. "You're right. I'm sorry."

For a few moments, we sit, eating in silence. "I was at the funeral."

"What?" Her eyebrows draw down in confusion as she stares at me. "Hiding in plain sight?"

"Something like that." I nod.

"I know you were mad at me Griffin, but I would've given anything to know you were there. I really needed you." Her eyes well, tears spilling over onto her cheeks.

My chest tightens. "I'm sorry."

"I know. Me too, Griff." She reaches over and grabs my hand, squeezing as I pull away.

Before I have a chance to second guess myself, I blurt out the question I've been wanting to ask for years. "Why'd you do it, Carla? I know we were kids and it probably wouldn't have worked out anyway, but why the fuck did you do it? We were good together once upon a time."

She nods, giving me a sweet smile. "Yeah, Griff, we were really good together." Taking a deep breath, she tilts her head to the side assessing me. "It's no excuse, but it had nothing to do with you, not really. I was always Noah's little sister or Griffin's girlfriend. I didn't have an identity of my own anymore and I hated it. Then you started talking about leaving, going away to college, and leaving me behind."

"But I wasn't leaving you."

She looks me in the eyes, her own pleading. "That's really hard to believe no matter how much you love someone when you have the whole town gossiping and treating you like you're naïve and don't have a clue about life. I loved you, but I was seventeen and vulnerable, Griffin."

I huff a laugh. "You know that didn't matter to me. I always thought I would come back to Piper Falls and to you."

"Until I cheated on you."

I huff a humorless laugh. "Yeah, that fucking broke me, but that isn't exactly what did me in." Her eyes widen in surprise. "Do you remember the night you told me you were pregnant?"

She nods, turning her head, wiping away her tears. "Yeah."

"I was so fucking happy. You know I always wanted kids, so it just happened a little earlier for us. I knew it would be hard, but I thought we would figure it out because I believed we would tackle it together." Pausing, I gulp down the sudden lump in my throat, fighting to keep my emotions at bay. "I thought the look on your face was because you were scared, but that weekend, I caught you making out with Derek Peters. That's when you told me you didn't know if the baby was mine or his." I feel the punch in the gut all over again and pause, taking a deep breath. "Then you had a miscarriage, and we never found out the truth."

"I'm sorry," she whispers, wiping away more tears.

Ignoring her, I clench my fist and continue. "Damn, Carla, I felt like I lost everything when you lost the baby." She glances at me, her confusion obvious. Unclenching my fist, I tic off each item on my fingers, one by one. "My girlfriend, our future, my friends, and even Piper Falls, the only place I had ever known as home."

"That doesn't even make sense, Griffin. I'm sorry I cheated on you, but the miscarriage hit all of us," she cries as if she's the only victim.

"Exactly!"

"What does that even mean?"

I scoff. "After three years together, you were the one who cheated, but Noah was *your* brother. You were the one who had the miscarriage, so it didn't matter if the baby was mine or Derek's, or how much I felt the loss because you were suffering. You were in pain. You were depressed. You were going into your senior year of high school and couldn't escape. I couldn't look at you for what you did to us, what you gave up without a second thought and what we lost. I was grieving all of it by myself."

"Griff, I didn't want that for you. I wanted you with me, but I knew I messed up and I didn't think you could ever forgive me. But Noah knew. You didn't have to do anything alone."

I shake my head. "Yeah, he knew you had a miscarriage and that we broke up, but he didn't know about the rest. I didn't want him or anyone else, but especially him, to look at you any different." She winces. "He fucking adored you, Carla. I get it. You're his sister; that's how it should be. I wasn't going to hurt him by telling him any different. But me?" I point to myself. "I was disposable."

Her eyes widen and she shakes her head vehemently. "Griff–"

Narrowing my eyes, I interrupt, "It was highly doubtful I'd get a job here anyway. I could leave, but that wasn't an option for you."

Her gaze drops to the table. "You didn't have to do that."

"Yeah, I did, Carla. My only regret is letting it interfere with the people and things I should've been here for. But everything I thought my life would become disappeared in an instant and I was struggling to start over. I thought I needed to find something and somewhere new. Although we never lost touch because Noah acted as the glue that kept us all together, but even my best friends, the guys that I went through everything with and would take a bullet for, became the background in my life because of it."

"I'm so sorry, Griffin. I didn't realize." She shakes her head as tears stream down her cheeks.

Heaving a sigh, I try to let go of my anger, a past I cannot change, and remind myself how young we were. We should've talked about this years ago, but I was too much of a fucking coward. Standing up, I walk around the table to her, pulling her out of her seat and into my arms. She holds on tight, clinging to me, crying. "I'm so sorry."

"Don't do that, Carla. I'm not telling you this for you to feel guilty. Those things were my choices because seeing you was something I couldn't deal with. I'm telling you because I think it's time we finally clear the air for several reasons."

She winces in my arms and pushes back just enough to see my face. "Reasons like Mallory?" She arches her eyebrows in question.

I nod, the corners of my lips tugging upwards at the thought of her. "Yeah, reasons exactly like Mallory."

Untangling herself from my arms she steps back, wiping her eyes. "You really like her, don't you?"

"First woman I've had any real interest in since you."

She flinches at my admission. "I'm sorry."

"It was my choice."

"Still, I am sorry, Griffin. I promise, I really did love you."

Pressing my lips together, I give her a firm nod, accepting her apology likely for the first time. "Thanks. I'm sorry for the way I handled everything." Her eyes widen in surprise and I clarify, "I'm sorry for disappearing."

She gives me the first genuine smile I've seen from her in years. "Thanks. I didn't realize I needed to hear that."

I nod, walking back to my seat and taking another bite of my burger.

"My nieces and nephew are pretty incredible too, aren't they?"

I grin. "They really are great kids."

"How do you think Mal will take me and you having a past?"

My stomach twists into knots and I look away, shaking my head. "I honestly don't know, but I hope like hell she'll give me a chance to explain when I tell her."

"You know, I always hoped you'd be part of our family, but not this way." I narrow my eyes, remaining silent and she giggles, waving me off. "I'll vouch for you."

"Please don't. I don't think that would do me any good."

"Fuck you, Griffin." She throws a handful of fries at my head.

Chuckling, I shrug non-apologetic. "I thought it was only right that we have the conversation before I talk to her, but I'm telling you now, I plan on confessing everything to Mallory. I won't hold anything back."

"I'd expect nothing less from you." She scrunches her nose up in displeasure. "It's weird seeing you with them more than anything when it should be Noah."

"That's something we can agree on."

"But Griffin?" She waits for me to meet her gaze, her eyes sad. "I think he would love knowing it's you when it can't be him."

Nodding, I wonder and hope that she's speaking the truth. I wish he could give me a sign or something, letting me know it's okay or at least that he forgives me for wanting what used to be his. I don't want to take his place, but I would move the world for all four of them. That's what he'd want. Right? A familiar weight settles over my shoulders, desperate for him to know my truth.

Chapter Twenty Seven

♡ Mallory ♡

Standing in front of my desk, I look around my nearly empty classroom, minus a few remaining boxes, the moment bittersweet. I love my job, and I'm ready for summer after a busy year with my students, but I'm sad knowing they'll all be in another class next year, starting over with a new teacher and a different mix of kids. It's the same thing I feel like I've been doing constantly since Noah has been gone, starting over and it's never easy. It took us a long time to find a new normal, but this year, we finally found our place and now we seem to be doing it again with Griffin around more all the time.

"Any more boxes for me?" Tanner asks as he steps into my classroom.

"I just have these last few, but I have to go and pick up Mia from dance in a few minutes and then I have to get back here to grab Tiegan and Ollie."

"Why don't I get your last couple boxes and get Tiegan and Ollie after school's out and meet you at your house? Otherwise, you're probably cutting it too close."

"Are you sure?"

"Yeah, I'm positive. You know I'm here anyway and there's a reason I'm on the list to pick up your kids."

"True."

"How about I pick something up for dinner tonight too? The kids can help me pick something out."

"That's really nice of you Tanner, but I think I need a quiet night with the kids tonight. We've all been so busy with the end of the year," I ramble, more exhausted from my night with Griffin than anything, but I'm not about to tell Tanner that.

"So, no Griffin tonight?"

I shrug. "I don't think so. He was helping his family earlier and then he said he had something to take care of this afternoon."

He stops, arching his eyebrows in question. "Huh. I wonder what he had to take care of at Carla's house."

My eyes widen. "What? He was at Carla's house?"

He waves it off like it's no big deal. "Yeah, I was driving by her house at lunchtime because I had to run home to grab something for Mr. Silvan and I saw Griffin go inside Carla's with a bag from Papi's. Maybe it has something to do with you."

Griffin would have no reason to be at Carla's on my behalf. I bite my lower lip in thought, my stomach suddenly churning.

"I'm sure it's nothing. From what I've heard the two of them don't really get along anymore, so it could be good they're trying to smooth things out."

My eyebrows draw down in confusion. "What do you mean? Why don't they get along?"

Tanner turns beet red and swiftly takes a step back, talking fast, like word vomit. "Oh, um, nothing. I'm sorry, I didn't mean to say anything. I just assumed you knew. It's no big deal. I'm sure it's fine now. It's been a long time and…"

"Tanner, stop." I step towards him, grabbing his hands in hopes of calming him down as my own heart begins hammering inside my chest, waiting for the inevitable. "What are you talking about?"

He opens and closes his mouth like a fish. "I really shouldn't be the one to tell you this. Why don't you ask Griffin when you talk to him? Or even Carla?"

"Because I've known you longer than I've known either of them and I trust you, so I'm asking you."

With a heavy sigh, he shakes his head in defeat. "Okay, fine. You know I can't hide anything from you. I guess the two of them used to date in high school. I'm sorry."

My heart drops into the pit of my stomach. What does he mean they used to date? "Griffin and Carla used to date? Like they were boyfriend and girlfriend?"

He winces and nods his head. "That's usually what that means." I narrow my eyes, glaring at him. "I'm sorry. I thought you knew, especially knowing how much time you two have been spending together. Or I at least thought it might be something Noah or Carla might've mentioned."

I shake my head and shrug, confused. "Nope. No one has said anything; at least not to me." And why the hell not? Doesn't he think that would be some useful information? Doesn't Carla? She knows how hard it has been for me to even think about dating again. Why wouldn't she tell me? I don't understand.

"Are you okay, Mal?" he asks, giving my hands a squeeze, reminding me I'm still holding his.

Taking a deep breath, I swiftly pull myself out of my haze and let go of Tanner. Pasting a smile on my face I nod. "Oh, yeah, I'm fine. It's not a big deal. Griffin mentioned he wanted to talk to me about his ex, but the kids interrupted us. I'm sure that was the conversation he was talking about." I frown, hating my half-truth. Why didn't he tell me yet? I feel like a fool not knowing something like this until now. Shouldn't that be something I already know?

"Okay," Tanner says, dragging out the word.

"Really, I'm good. I've got to go pick up Mia at dance. I'm going to be late. Thank you for getting Tiegan and Ollie for me and the last of my boxes. I'll meet you at my house in a little while."

"You're welcome. I'll see you in about an hour."

Grabbing my purse, I wave as I walk out the door, desperate for some space to think without his look of concern, even if it's only for the two minutes it takes to drive to the dance studio up the street.

Why wouldn't he tell me? Were they serious? I feel a little stunned going from such a great night last night to being so confused. I understand why Noah or Carla never told me, it's not like we ever talked about her ex-boyfriends beyond the guy she was in love with and Griffin didn't live here anymore once I did, so why would they tell me? Is she the reason Griffin never came around? He said it had to do with his ex. My stomach twists into knots, suddenly anxious, wondering what could have happened between them to make him stay away? Was he the high school boyfriend she was in love with? I feel like I'm going to throw up.

As I park my car in front of Swing Bridge Dance Studio, my phone rings, Griffin's name lighting up the screen and for the first time since I almost hit him with my car. The sight makes me frown and leaves me feeling uneasy. My hand hovers over the answer button, but I decline the call and quickly hop out of the car, rushing inside the studio.

"Mommy!" Mia calls the moment I step through the door. She spins towards me in her pink tutu and crashes into my legs, hugging me tight and making me laugh.

"Hi, sweetie. I'm so sorry I'm late, Miss Jami." I glance at her new teacher, giving her a look of apology.

"That's okay, it happens and I actually have a short break before I have another class, so it worked out."

"Thank you, anyway. I really do appreciate it."

She nods. "Mia did a great job today."

"Wonderful. Did you say thank you to Miss Jami?"

"Thank you." She grins.

"You're welcome. I'll see you next week, Mia."

Grabbing Mia's hand and her pink sling dance bag, I ask. "Are your shoes in here?"

"Yes, I have my other shoes on now. See?" She points her toes at me.

I nod my head, smiling. "Good girl. Let's go." We wave and walk out the door. I buckle Mia into her seat and pull out, driving towards home.

"Dance was so much fun, Mommy. My friend Violet and I got to be partners today and we had so much fun together. I can't wait to see her again." Mia jabbers, practically bouncing in her seat as she talks about dance and her friends, bringing a smile back to my face.

When I pull into the driveway a few minutes later, I'm feeling a little better, just as my phone beeps alerting me of a text. I glance at my phone, seeing a message from Griffin.

Griffin: Hope you got your classroom packed up. Left a voicemail earlier, I'm having dinner with my dad, then I'll be over.

Me: That's okay. The kids and I are good tonight.
Griffin: Glad to hear it. I'll see you soon.
Me: I don't think tonight works for me. I'll talk to you tomorrow.
Griffin: That's not an option sweetheart.
Me: Too bad Griffin.
Griffin: Sounds to me like you're pissed off about something. I promise I can make it better.
Me: No thanks.
Griffin: Ouch.

I wait a moment, glaring at the screen, but nothing else comes through. Apparently he doesn't care that much. Looks like he gave up.

"Mommy, can we go inside? I'm hungry. Where are Tiegan and Ollie?"

"Yes, Mia, we're going in now. I was just reading a message. Sorry." I drop my phone in my purse and hop out of the car before helping Mia out. "And Mr. Pratt is bringing your brother and sister home from school today."

"Is he gonna' stay for dinner tonight?"

"I'm not sure."

She purses her pretty little lips as we walk inside, and she sets her bag down. She looks up at me, tilting her head to the side. "What about Griff?" she asks, dragging out the f. "Will he come over to have dinner with us tonight too? I want to show him the new dance Miss Jami was teaching us today." She puts her arms out then up, turning in a circle.

My stomach drops. "Um, I don't think he can make it tonight, Mia. I'm sorry."

"Oh, okay." Her sweet face falls, along with her voice, squeezing my heart.

Apparently Griffin not only has me wrapped around his finger but my sweet angels. This isn't good.

Chapter Twenty Eight

♡ Griffin ♡

Sometimes living in a small town is the bane of my existence, but I'm not letting small town gossip get in the way of my relationship with Mallory. There's no assurance that's what's holding her back, but I can almost guarantee someone said something to her. Maybe someone from Papi's told her I bought lunch for two, or maybe one of Carla's neighbors saw me at her house, or Carla could have told someone.

Most of the town knows we have a past. At least anyone who knew us or our families at the time sure as hell does. Someone could've mentioned it to her or at least something about how Carla and I used to date. But we broke up thirteen years ago. I think that's long enough that it shouldn't be a deal breaker. I told her part of the reason I've stayed away is because of my ex, admitting the situation is complicated.

I'm so fucked.

I shake my head in frustration. It doesn't matter. I'm not letting her push me away, not even for one night. I'd been planning on telling her the truth about my past tonight anyway now that I've cleared the air with Carla. Mallory thinks she can block me from coming over? Not going to happen, especially when she seems to have some kind of stalker.

Knowing texting or calling her at this point will get me nowhere, I pull up in front of her house and park, my eyes narrowing at the sight of Tanner Pratt's truck in the driveway. What the fuck is he doing here? Again…

I grab the flowers off the passenger seat and make my way to the front door, ringing the doorbell. The door swings open and Tanner stands in the doorway, his smile faltering. "Oh, hi Griffin. Mallory said you weren't coming tonight."

Forcing a grin, I grit through my teeth. "Well, she was wrong. Maybe she got the days mixed up."

He opens his mouth to argue when a sweet, soft voice squeals with glee like music to my ears. "Griff is here! You came!" Mia runs and crashes into me as I sweep her up in my arms and step past Tanner without another word.

"Hi Princess. Of course, I came."

"Mommy said you weren't comin'."

I grind my teeth and focus on the girl in my arms. "Well, I'm here. I wanted to hear all about the dance class you had today."

"You 'membered!" She beams.

"Griffin?" Mallory squeaks, gasping as she comes from down the hallway. "What are you doing here?"

My eyes drift down her body, covered with a simple dark blue tank top and light blue cotton shorts, her hair pulled up in a high ponytail, the heat making it curl at the ends as if calling me to her. Damn. I see movement out of the corner of my eye, and glance at Tanner, his eyes narrowed on me, like he has every right. Fuck that.

I grin. "I brought flowers from the farm for my girls." Shifting the flowers, I hold a small bouquet out to Mia.

"You brought me flowers? Yay!" Taking the flowers, she squirms out of my arms and runs to her mom, holding them up with pride.

"Those are beautiful, Mia," Mallory murmurs, a small smile tugging at her lips.

With my hands free, I walk over to the couch, where Tiegan sits curled up and hold a second bouquet out for her. "These are for you."

Her eyes widen. "For me?"

Nodding, I affirm, "For you."

"Th-thank you."

I glance at Mallory, closing the distance between us with her eyes glued to me. Giving her a crooked smile, I hold up the largest bouquet. "This is for you."

"Thank you, Griffin. This doesn't help your cause."

"The only cause I'm fighting for is you, darlin'."

She huffs a laugh and rolls her eyes, but thankfully doesn't ask me to leave. "Okay, fine."

"Did you bring anything for me?" Ollie asks.

"Something your dad and I would always say is the men in the house need to do things to make the women in the house feel special. It's our job. As long as you keep doing that, you'll always have something extraordinary."

"So, you didn't get me anything?"

I laugh, shaking a mint into his hand from the tin in my pocket. "How about this?"

He pinches his lips together, forcing a smile. "Thank you."

I hold out my hand, giving him a fist bump. "Next time you help me pick the flowers."

He nods emphatically. "Okay."

"Okay, it's bedtime y'all." Mallory nods towards the hallway.

"But Griffin just got here," Ollie whines, his shoulders sagging.

"Sorry, but he got here late and you and Tiegan have school in the morning."

"It's our last day!" Ollie grins, bouncing on his toes, attempting to hold in his excitement.

"Bedtime," Mallory repeats, arching her eyebrows in challenge.

"Listen to your mom. I'll see all of you tomorrow."

"Don't make promises you can't keep," Mallory mutters under her breath before giving me a sickeningly sweet smile.

"Fine," Ollie grumbles.

"Okay," Mia says.

"Mom, will you put my flowers in water for me?" Tiegan asks.

Mallory nods. "Of course. I'll find a vase for both you and Mia."

"Thank you. Goodnight, Mom."

I don't react as all three kids give me hugs and wave to Tanner before disappearing into their rooms down the hall.

"I'll be in to tuck y'all in soon," Mallory calls after them.

She smiles as she steps up to Tanner and gives him a hug. "Thanks for all your help this week and for coming over."

"You know I'm always here for you." I bite my tongue so I don't say something stupid. I'm sure he is. "Are you sure you don't need me to stay?"

"I'm sure. Thank you, Tanner." She follows him to the door and locks it behind him. With barely a glance in my direction, she goes back down the hall, slipping into each of her kids rooms one at a time before disappearing behind her own door.

Kicking my shoes off, I leave them by the front door, knocking quietly on Mallory's bedroom door. I hear her heavy sigh on the other side before she responds. "Goodnight Griffin."

"I want to talk to you, Mallory."

"We all want things, Griff. I'm processing some things I learned today. Give me some time to do that."

"I figured as much. Likely the same things I was planning on talking to you about tonight."

She laughs humorlessly. "Isn't that convenient."

"I don't want to wake your kids, Mal."

"Then go to sleep. Don't you have to be up in a few hours? We'll talk tomorrow."

"Not gonna' happen." I grit my teeth and stalk out to the kitchen, digging through the junk drawer for something to help me with the lock. Spotting a mini screwdriver, I grab it and stride back to Mallory's room.

"Mallory, are you decent?"

"What?"

"Are you decent?"

"Why?"

"Because I'm not letting you shut me out for some bullshit town gossip. I'm coming in and we are talking. I'm too old for games."

"I'm not playing games, Griffin."

"You're locking me out. If this isn't a game, you're whistling up the wind."

She heaves a sigh. "Griff…"

"I'm coming in, Mal." With a quick flip of my wrist, I unlock and open the door. Stepping inside, I close the door behind me.

"Griffin!"

"Sit down, lay down, whatever you need to do, but I'm asking you to listen to what I have to say and I believe you want to hear it."

"Ugh, fine." She flops down on the bed and scoots back against the headboard. "You're ridiculous."

"No, I don't want you in your head with things that aren't true. If you're going to hate me, hate me for the truth, but don't push me away when you have questions. Ask me. I will answer truthfully no matter how much I don't want to."

She purses her lips, staring at me, but I see the moment she concedes. "Fine. Is it true? Is Carla your ex-girlfriend?"

I nod, watching every movement, every expression, every emotion in her eyes. "We dated in high school for three years."

She gasps, her eyes going wide. "Three years?" I nod in confirmation as I cautiously approach the bed. "That's a long time. Why'd you break up?"

I huff a humorless laugh and shake my head. "Quite a few reasons. The biggest problem was that she was pregnant, but she cheated on me, so she didn't know who the father was. Then she had a miscarriage and none of us ever found out."

"Oh, my God, Griffin." She inches closer to me and pushes up on her knees, one hand falling to my back and the other to my forearm, my body calming instantly.

Sighing, I sit down on the edge of the bed, Mallory sitting next to me. "Carla and I talked about everything today. I wanted to talk to her before I told you. It was the right thing to do with everything that happened between us and your relationship with her."

"This is so fucked up, but you're right. I'm glad you talked to her before me because I need you to be one hundred percent honest and I'm afraid you would've held back otherwise."

"That's the problem. I knew I wouldn't hold back anything from you. If you pushed the other night when it came up, before I spoke to her, you still would've known everything. I'm too old to play games."

Her lips twitch. "I'm glad to hear it, but you're not that old."

I huff a laugh, appreciating her attempt at lightening the mood. "Carla was just about to start her senior year of high school and I was leaving for college. At the time I couldn't stay and after everything, I couldn't come back. I couldn't see her. She was the one who cheated but I felt like I lost everything because of it. My friends, being able to come home to Piper Falls, my girlfriend, my future, and my past." I pause, shaking my head. "Noah–

he knew what happened, except for her cheating, and he didn't let me go. He said he understood why I couldn't be around. He was the one who held us all together. Me, him, Matt, Reid."

"Is that what the torn blue flag stands for on your chest? The one with the one bright blue line and the thread?"

"You noticed that, huh?"

She nods. "It's hard to miss. I saw 101 written on the string."

"Noah's badge number," I affirm.

"I love that."

A lump forms in my throat. "Fuck, I miss him."

"Me too," she whispers, her voice catching.

Turning, I pull her into my arms and hold her tight. My eyes well with tears, a couple spilling over as I hold her and she squeezes me as if her life depends on it. Together we mourn our pasts, our shared and separate histories and what could've been in the comfort of each other's arms as if we need each other to survive and in this moment, it may be true.

I'm not sure how much time passes until we both calm. I press a kiss to the top of her head and she loosens her hold, lifting her head and looking me in the eyes, her own giving away everything she's feeling. "Can we do this? Us?"

Nodding, I hold her gaze, needing her to see the same truth reflecting back in my eyes. "I sure as hell hope so because I don't want anyone or anything else."

She presses her lips to mine. Shifting, I cradle her face in my hands as we kiss soft and slow. My heart pounds harder with each brush of her lips, my skin burns with her sweet touch, and my breath comes faster as every moment the thought of her, of us makes my body come alive with anticipation.

"I just want you."

Chapter Twenty Nine

♡ Mallory ♡

There's something about this moment that feels both surreal and pivotal. Overwhelmed with our shared grief and passion, I feel an intense need to be as close as possible to this man. He pulls his shirt off and tosses it to the floor as I do the same, sitting my pale pink lace bra and shorts. He looks at me, his chest heaving and eyes flaring.

Moving to my knees I grab his shoulders, holding him for support as I straddle his lap. He clenches his jaw, as I shift, my pussy settling over his hard length, now twitching beneath me. My breathing picks up its pace as I look down at this man, his gaze making me feel confident in every move I make. My lips brush his before moving across the stubble on his jaw, lightly scratching them and making them tingle. Tracing an invisible path with my mouth, I move towards his neck, his throat, his collarbone and down his chest. My tongue slips out and licks his tattoo, followed by a kiss.

"Mal," he groans, his fingers snagging my chin and gently tilting it up to meet his hooded gaze. "I need you."

Without a word, I cover his lips with mine. His fingers tangle into my hair, holding my head in his hands as we kiss; everything about it all-consuming. We move together, our mouths fusing as his tongue slips inside, colliding with its mate. I moan, the soft vibrations fueling us as we kiss.

Our movements quickly become more desperate. I kiss him harder, bruising our lips, our tongues dancing as our hands begin to wander. My palms slide over his shoulders and down his rigid chest, relishing in the feel of his body's reaction to my touch. His hands slide down my sides, over my ass and up my back, leaving goosebumps in his wake. Gliding his hands across my skin, over my sides and underneath my breasts.

One hand slides to my back, unhooking my bra and sliding it off my arms, and to the floor before I register it's gone. His hand returns to my front, caressing the skin around my breasts, and lighting me on fire. My breathing becomes erratic and my head falls back, gasping for breath as his thumbs brush over my already pert nipples, straining to get closer.

His head falls to the crook of my neck, licking and gently sucking. Taking one breast in each hand, he pinches my nipples between his thumb and forefinger, rolling it. I arch my back, and move my pelvis over his, desperate for the friction as my body tingles with growing desire.

"Griffin," I whimper.

His mouth replaces one hand, sucking my breast into his mouth, his tongue circling, flicking and sucking again before releasing it and giving the same care and attention to the other side. I grind into him harder, one hand sliding into his hair and holding his head to my chest as he licks, sucks and nibbles, exploring my body. Barely breathing, I bite the inside of my cheek, trying not to scream as my body gives in, throbbing. I can't do anything but hold on tight, riding it out.

My body slowly comes down from its high. Griffin pulls me close, kissing me again as he rolls me over, laying me on my back. He tugs my shorts and underwear down and tosses them to the floor before removing his own.

Lifting my hooded gaze, I watch him as he crawls towards me, laying down beside me and reaching for me. His hand skims across my stomach, his lips following his movement. "You're so beautiful," he whispers over my skin, giving me goosebumps once again. My chest tightens, feeling the sincerity in his statement.

Sliding down my body, he licks and kisses me again and again, leaving me panting for more all over. He presses a kiss to my core, his tongue jutting out and licking the seam before his teeth graze me. "Griff, please," I pant, tugging on his hair to get him to look at me. "Please come here."

He lifts his head, a salacious smirk on his lips just before he licks them. "Where do you want me darlin'?"

"I want your cock inside me, now."

His eyes widen, obviously surprised by my demand. "How the hell do I say no to something like that?"

"You don't."

He chuckles, the deep sound giving me chills. "Let me grab a condom."

"There's a box in my nightstand. I stopped at the store this morning."

He reaches over and grabs the box, ripping it open and pulling out a square packet. My eyes remain glued to him as he moves towards me, my heart racing with anticipation as he rolls the condom on his engorged cock. Bracing himself on his elbows, he hovers over me, lining up at my entrance. Lifting my head, I press my lips to his, my tongue sneaking out to taste him as it meets his in a slow dance.

My body heats as my hands roam his firm body. His sweet taste elicits a soft moan from my lips. Goosebumps erupt over my slick, heated skin at the slightest touch of his hand, his lips, his tongue, and having his body pressed to mine. "Fuck, Mal, you're so damn sexy." The deep timbre of his voice rumbles over my skin making my juices pool. His musky smell, mixed with sweat and sex has my senses going into overload. I'm surrounded with everything Griffin and I wouldn't want to be anywhere else.

"Please, Griff. I want you."

"I'm damn sure I want you, too, darlin'." He kisses me again. Pulling back, he looks down at me. "Are you ready for me?"

I nod and he thrusts inside in one swift movement. "Ah."

His lips crash into mine, and he kisses me, silencing me as he slowly begins to move inside me. I whimper, my hips arching to meet him. Grasping my hips, he sets the pace, slow and steady, making sure to push the last little bit to hit my g-spot, which will quickly push me over the edge.

My breathing picks up again and I tear my lips away from his, gasping for breath. My body goes on full alert as his tongue sweeps out licking the crook of my neck before he nibbles and sucks. My nails dig into his back, urging him to go faster, needing more of him, harder.

Reaching down, he hooks my leg behind my knee and lifts it, slipping it over his shoulder, and readjusting his angle. "Oh my God, Griffin," I mutter as he moves. Every time he thrusts inside, my vision blurs, a flash of white starting to take over. His cock pushes inside me sending shockwaves throughout my body as it starts to quiver from the inside out, building me up, preparing for my release.

"I need you to come baby," he murmurs against my neck, licking and sucking the same spot, urging me on as he drives inside my pussy.

"Yes." He pushes inside again, and again, harder and faster.

"You feel so damn good. I'm about to lose control, darlin'," he proclaims, barely holding back as he plunges inside, hitting my spot deep inside my pussy."

After one more thrust, I feel my swollen and soaked insides start to give, every part of my body tingling as he hits the spot again, pushing me over the edge.

"I'm coming," I mumble, my insides exploding, my pussy throbbing from my core, sending shockwaves throughout my entire body again and again. Griffin's frame goes rigid as he steels his body over me, but he doesn't move like I expect. As I feel myself relax into the mattress and I try to catch my breath, my eyes flutter open, looking up at him.

"You okay?" I grin, nodding my head and he gives me his sexy crooked smile in return as he wipes my hair out of my eyes. "Good. I'm not going to last, but I'm getting one more orgasm out of you first." My eyes widen. "This time, Mal, keep your eyes on me when you come."

"I don't know if I can," I rasp, still trying to catch my breath and not sure if that statement has more than one meaning.

He nods. "I know, but why don't we try?" He kisses me softly and licks his lips. "The thought of your caramel eyes on me, when they're boiling with that heat and desire brings me to the brink alone, but I know seeing it will be on a whole different level. I want to look at you and watch you come apart in my arms."

My heart gets stuck in my throat and I'm not able to do anything but nod. I want that; I want that with him. My entire body already feels like jelly, yet he has my pussy wet and ready to come again after only a few simple words.

Griffin licks my lips, his tongue sweeping inside and tangling with mine. He starts to move again and pulls back looking down at me. I bite my lower lip and release it slowly as I stare into his deep blue eyes, open only for me, the colors changing as if our souls are speaking, connecting, thriving. My heart hammers and my blood rushes through my veins, igniting every part of me.

Our hips thrust together, his movements reflecting mine, his exhale becoming my inhale, and his heartbeat matching my own. Soon, it's just us. I only see him. Letting go, I open myself wide for him, allowing him to see inside and hoping we can both survive everything laid before us together.

Holding my gaze, he drives into me until the feeling deep in my core has completely consumed me and my body relents, convulsing around him, milking him as his own movements become erratic. Grasping my hips, he thrusts so deep inside me that I grab his head and yank him to me, desperate to kiss him, my own guttural moan muffled as it goes in, and escapes through his mouth.

His lips fall away, but his forehead remains stuck to mine as we slow our movements, coming down from a high I'm not sure I ever experienced. The moment he stops, my head falls into the crook of his neck, needing a moment to catch my breath, pull myself together and process the moments between us.

Taking a deep breath, I exhale slowly, his hand falls to my back. Slowly, he runs his hand up and down, the movement comforting. "Are you okay, Mal?" Griffin asks, nudging my head with his.

"Uh," I grunt in response, not yet able to form words.

He chuckles, leaning back further and nudging me again. "Just need to know you're okay."

Nodding, I close my eyes. "Good."

"That's good." I feel his smile as he kisses my forehead. "Let me get rid of this." The bed moves as he climbs off, returning moments later.

"Can I take care of you?"

My eyes fly open colliding with Griffin's now lighter blue gaze. "What?"

He chuckles. "I grabbed the baby wipes from your drawer. I just want to help clean you up."

"Oh, okay."

I close my eyes, my body twitching as he wipes gently between my legs, placing a soft kiss on my belly when he's done. A content sigh escapes my lips as he pulls me into his arms, the simple movement squeezing my heart. At first glance, this man looks anything but gentle, but the sweet things he does are the things that could make me fall in love before I'm ready.

Chapter Thirty

◯ Mallory ◯

"Ouch," I grumble as I sit down at the dining room table. My entire body hurts, aching from last night with Griffin, while at the same time thanking me. I knew it had been a long time, but I guess I forgot my body would remember that too. Almost makes me feel like a born-again virgin. If it weren't for my three kids being living proof, I may believe it myself, but every moment of it was well worth it. My body hummed with pleasure at every little thing that man did to me with his tongue, his fingers, his body…my body clenches, making me wince again and try to push the images of a naked Griffin out of my head, although just temporarily.

As I dig through my boxes, attempting to put them in some kind of order so it's away and I'm prepared for next year, my mind drifts to everything Griffin confessed. My heart hurts for what he's been through and what he's lost. It almost feels like he's talking about someone else sometimes, when I know it's Noah, but I guess it feels like our memories of him are so different that it makes it difficult to connect. Ironically, I feel closer to Griffin after everything last night than I could've ever imagined. I hope he feels the same. At least I think that's what I want.

The thought of losing someone else I lo… care about terrifies me. If I give him my heart and lose him, I don't know if I could ever recover. But more important than me are my kids. I couldn't handle watching them endure anything close to what they had to with Noah ever again. I need to be careful. Sometimes I think it might already be too late for any trepidation.

A knock at the door pulls me out of my Griffin induced thoughts. I glance through the front window, spotting Tanner and pull the door open. "Hi, Tanner. What are you doing here? Shouldn't you be at school for the kids' last day?"

He laughs and shrugs his shoulders. "Why do you think I had to get out of there? The kids are already in summer vacation mode."

I laugh, waving him inside and watching as he leans down picking up a box from the ground. "Believe me, I understand. Mia is at a friend's house while I finish organizing everything from my classroom."

"A friend's house?" he questions, arching his eyebrows.

I shrug. "Yeah, actually Harper, Griffin's sister came home for the weekend and she offered to watch her at the farm."

"Oh, that was nice of her. Why not Carla?"

I grimace and look away, sitting down at the table going back to the box I was organizing. "I'm sure she's working." And I have no idea how to talk to her after everything Griffin told me.

"Huh," he mumbles, arching his eyebrows in question.

I ignore his comment, hoping he won't push. I'm not about to tell anyone secrets that aren't mine. "So, what's in the box?"

"Oh, It's a box of your things I missed the other day without realizing it. I figured it gave me an excuse to escape. You had a stack of mail in your inbox in the office, so I put all of that on top in case there's something you need." He sets it down on one of the kitchen chairs and shakes out his hands.

"Thank you, Tanner."

"No problem. Sorry I missed it."

"So, you and Griffin," he begins, bending his fingers back, stretching them one by one.

"Yes?" I prod, dragging out the word.

He gulps hard, his Adam's apple bobbing up and down. "Things are getting serious between you two?"

I shrug, working my way through the box. "I don't know. Maybe. We haven't really talked about it, but I love spending time with him."

"Well, that's obvious."

My eyebrows draw down in confusion. "What do you mean? Why would you say that?"

He winces, his cheeks flushing as he looks around uncomfortably. Stepping forward, he rips the tape off the top of the box he just brought in, looking as if he just needs something to do with his hands. "I um, well, you ah, have an um…"

"What Tanner?"

He scrunches up his nose in displeasure and shakes his head, pointing. I look down, trying to figure out what he's pointing to when he huffs in frustration and steps closer. Cautiously, he reaches up, pushing my shirt back just slightly, his fingers running over a mark left by Griffin's mouth without either of us realizing.

My body heats at the memory. "Oh."

He smirks, and clears his throat, stepping back as his hand drops to the side. "Yeah, oh. It's hard to miss with your hair pulled up."

"I thought I covered them up. But why does that bother you so much? Haven't you ever marked a woman before?"

His eyes go wide as he runs his hand through his perfectly styled hair and drops it to his side. "Sure, I guess, but this is about you Mallory. I don't want your kids seeing those marks and worrying about you."

"Thanks for your concern Tanner, but you know better than anyone that I can take care of myself."

He frowns. "Yeah, sorry I overstepped. You know it's because I care about you and without Noah or your parents–I just feel better watching out for you and knowing you and the kids are okay."

"Join the club," I grumble, lifting the mail out of the box he just brought and dropping it on the table.

"I'm sorry, Mal. I should go. I'll see you later."

His shoulders sag as he trudges towards the door. "It's fine. I know you didn't mean anything by it. Thanks for bringing the box over."

He nods. "You're welcome. I guess I've just been worried between the letters and the guy looking in your windows and I know a lot of men started paying more attention to you once you went out with Griffin, thinking that made you fair game. The comments I've heard…" trailing off he clenches his jaw and his fist. "I just get so pissed at the thought of something happening to you or the kids because of some asshole."

I heave a sigh and move closer to him. "Thank you for watching out for me. Since I was a kid, you've always been there for me and I appreciate it more than you know, but I'm okay. I already promised I would let the cops know if anything else happened."

"True."

"I'm okay," I emphasize, giving him a hug and stepping back.

"I should go but keep it that way."

Nodding, I wave as he walks out the door. "Bye Tanner."

Walking back to the table, I sift through the mail Tanner brought from school, most of it unnecessary. Suddenly, my heart stops and I gasp as my eyes land on a letter, my name written in black block lettering, just like the other unidentified ones. My hands shake as I open the letter, hoping it's not what I think, but needing to know.

Darlin' Mallory,

I missed seeing you this past week after school. Why did you disappear on me? I had been hoping to see you and do this in person, but since I don't have your number, I'm left with this letter or showing up at your doorstep. I figured this would be the better option. Now that the school year is over, your rules no longer apply and we can be together.

I was thinking we could go to dinner at Tangled Knots or Mia can come over to play with Topher while we have our own playdate. My number is below. I'll be waiting.

Frank Borato

Is this the same writing? It looks almost the same. Maybe he was trying to make it look a little different. He definitely creeped me out at school. Was it him? If it is, it worries me that something could happen to Mia. But what if it's not?

You can't think like that Mal. I need to tell someone.

With a heavy sigh, I grab my phone, but instead of picking it up, I start tapping out a text.

Mallory: Hey, Matt. How are you?

Matt: Good. All okay?

Mallory: I may need your help with something.

Instead of a text, my phone rings, making me groan. Heaving a sigh, I answer, trying to keep my voice cheerful. "Hi Matt."

"Everything okay? What do you need, Mal?"

"I just want to know if you can take a look at something for me. It's not a big deal."

"What is it? And if it's not a big deal, why did you call me instead of asking Griff for help?"

"I didn't call you."

"Another good point."

I huff in frustration. "Are you going to help me or not?"

"You know I am, but you need to tell me what's going on."

"Okay. Well, some things have been happening."

"What kind of things? Does Griffin know?"

"Not everything," I concede, wincing. "But he's been sleeping on the couch anyway."

"Since the guy Olivia saw outside?"

"Yeah."

"So again, what kind of things have been happening? Is it more of what happened with Olivia?"

"No. The other day it was my tires and I've gotten some letters."

"I'm on my way and I want to see those letters."

"Okay."

"Oh, and Mal?"

"Yeah?"

"Call Griffin."

Damn.

Chapter Thirty One

Griffin

Standing with my arms crossed over my chest and my jaw clenched, I watch as Mallory closes the door behind Matt, pausing before she turns slowly around to face me, her body stiff. "Well, hopefully giving all of that to Matt solves everything and you won't have to sleep on the couch anymore."

"I won't be anyway."

"What?" Her eyes widen as she stares at me in surprise.

I shake my head. "I won't be on the couch, Mal, and you know it as well as I do. I'm going to be in whatever bed you're sleeping in."

She plants her hands on her hips and stands a little taller, looking defiant. "What gives you the right?"

"You do. You are welcome to have the station take over if that's what you want. But I wouldn't be there without your permission."

"Griffin."

"Are we together, Mal?"

"What?"

"You seem to be having trouble hearing me tonight." I step closer to her and look down at her, still pissed I didn't know. This was the third fucking letter and she didn't tell me. I knew about one. What the fuck? Is she ever going to let me in or is this going to be a constant battle that I'll never win and never recover from?

"Are we together, Mal? Because my answer to that is yes, I'm dating Mallory, or yes, Mallory is my woman, or my girlfriend, or whatever the hell you want to call yourself. I don't really give a damn as long as I can say you're mine. As for you, I sure as hell expect you to say you have a boyfriend and if that's not the case, I'm either doing something wrong or I shouldn't be here." I take another step closer, stopping right in front of her. "Now, I need you to tell me, are we together?"

"Griff…" her voice cracks as she utters my name.

I shake my head, my heart pounding and my hands sweaty, not wanting another excuse, only needing her response. "The answer is quite simple, Mal. Do you want to be with me? Yes or no."

She gulps hard and nods, my body instantly relaxing as I'm flooded with relief. "Yes, Mr. Erickson, I want to be with you. We are together."

I arch my eyebrows in surprise. "Back to Mr. Erickson? Sounds like you either need to be punished or you're trying to make me forget about what's going on with you."

"Maybe it's both?" She shrugs, taunting me, biting her lower lip, a move she knows drives me wild.

"You're definitely fucking with me woman." I step into her space and back her into the wall, caging her in. "If that's the case Mal, don't shut me out. I need to know about this shit so I can protect you."

"I can take care of myself."

"I got it! I have no doubt about that, but everyone can use a little help sometimes and when it comes to you and your three kids, I want it to be me who's there for you. I don't want to get a message from my best friend telling me to drop what I'm doing and haul ass to your house because that statement alone scared the shit out of me."

Her face falls, and I know instantly that she understands where I'm coming from, making me feel like an ass for saying it. "I'm sorry Griffin. I should've called you and I should've told you everything before."

"I'm not asking a lot. Just talk to me. You knew what you told me wasn't everything. I'm sure you were holding back so I didn't worry, but you know that's not enough. I need you safe. If I don't know what's going on, how am I supposed to help?"

"Griffin, I get it, and I'm sorry."

I nod, pressing my lips to hers, kissing her soft and slow before pulling back and looking into her eyes. "Thank you."

"How about I make it up to you?" She reaches down, rubbing my length through my jeans, my cock standing at attention almost instantly.

"Fuck yes, but we're almost out of time before you have to pick up the kids from school."

She grins, her hands sliding up my chest. "I love that you know my schedule, but that's all about to change for the summer. You'll be seeing a lot more of all of us. Mia has dance a couple days a week, Ollie has soccer camp and Tiegan signed up for a few programs at the library."

"Good. Maybe y'all can spend more time out at the farm with me." I brush my lips across hers and will my heart to slow.

"We would all love that. The kids have been asking to go back since we were there. They loved it and they want to see more."

"Then that's what we'll do."

She smiles at me, the vision so bright it squeezes my chest. "You're so damn beautiful, Mal."

She blushes. "Thank you, Griff. I think you're pretty handsome yourself."

My lips curve up, giving her a crooked grin. "I'm glad you think so." I cradle her face in my hands and tilt my head, pressing my lips to hers, moving with her in a perfect rhythm. My tongue flicks out for a taste, knowing it won't be enough, but it will help me get through until I can kiss her like I want to again. Slowing our kiss, I pull back, looking down at her and giving her one more chaste kiss before I let her go.

Taking a deep breath, I prepare myself for how she'll handle my next question. "So, you okay with me moving in?" I'm positive she won't allow this to be simple, but I won't be letting this go until she agrees.

Her eyes widen as she echoes, "Moving in?"

I nod, kissing her on her forehead. "Yeah, Mal, moving in. How could I not with everything that's happened? Unless you and the kids want to come stay at the farm, but you said before that wasn't an option. I understand why and I didn't think anything had changed."

She shakes her head. "It hasn't, but that doesn't mean you can move in."

"I get that this feels faster than you expected, but this isn't about us, it's about protecting you and the kids. I'm not looking to fight with you, Mal, although we sure could have a lot of fun once we get to the making up part." I smirk, attempting to lighten the mood.

"Griffin." She narrows her eyes, glaring at me.

I chuckle, loving how sexy she looks when she's pissed off, but I know this isn't the time to play with fire. "Look, the kids haven't even realized I've been staying here all week. We can keep it from them as long as possible."

"Until one of them wakes up with a nightmare."

I shrug. "Maybe not even then, but we'll figure it out either way. There's just no way I'm leaving you alone."

She shakes her head. "I'm not alone and I can take care..."

"Yeah, I know you can take care of yourself, darlin'. But the letters, the guy outside your windows, the tires; it's a lot for anyone. For my own damn sanity, I need to be here, and you know Matt and the rest of the station will be patrolling or coming by a lot more often now that they know what's going on."

She sighs heavily, her shoulders sagging. "Yeah, I know."

"I'm honestly glad you called Matt and told him everything."

She winces, swiftly shrugging it off. "Griff, I'm sorry I didn't tell you it was more than one letter. I just didn't want you to worry."

"Forget about it, but please talk to me. I'm going to worry no matter what, but I need to know what's happening to be there for you how I should be. Hopefully this is the guy, but what if it's not?" I step closer.

"It has to be."

"I know." I nod and pull her into my arms, holding her close, my hand rubbing up and down her back in support. There's no point in arguing until Matt finds out more and knowing him, he'll move fast on this one.

"I wish we could stay here like this all day."

"Oh, sweetheart, I sure as hell wish the same, but," I pause glancing at my phone, "isn't it time to go pick up the kids from school?"

"Yeah." Leaning back, she pushes up on her tiptoes, giving me a sweet kiss and falling back on her heels. "Do you want to come with me?"

"I do, but maybe you should pick up the kids and I'll grab a few things from the farm to leave in my truck and some things to make dinner tonight. Since Mia is with Harper, I'll put her car seat in my truck and bring her back here with me."

"That sounds good. Thank you, Griff and thank Harper for me too."

"You don't have to thank me and Harper was excited to do it. Good timing that she came home last night. As for me, I'm here for you and the kids with anything you need. There's no other option for me."

She smiles and kisses me again before grabbing her purse and keys. "Then, let's go," she announces before I follow her out the door. I get in my truck and watch as she pulls out, heading towards the elementary school before I start my truck and make a U-turn heading back to my parents.

Hopefully she's right and this is over, but looking at the letters, I have my doubts. Similar is not the same.

Chapter Thirty Two

♡ *Mallory* ♡

With me and the kids off for the summer, we fall into an easy rhythm, Griffin quickly a permanent fixture. Although the kids still don't realize he sleeps here every night and leaves before they wake up, they are quickly falling in love with him, even Tiegan. How can I blame them when my heart is doing the same? It scares the crap out of me, but it doesn't make it any less real.

When we found out the letters had different inflections in the writing, and Frank Borato had an alibi for the other instances, my heart sank, but things have seemed to calm down since then. I'm not sure if the attention has slowed because Griffin is around all the time or if it's because whoever it was lost interest and moved on, but I'm grateful either way. Although, I wish we would've found out who it was, it's been over a month since anything has happened, so maybe it's over.

I glance down at the picture from the Fourth of July carnival last week of me, Griffin, and the kids and set it on the mantel. It's the first picture of the five of us together and I don't want it to be the last. We had so much fun going on the rides and playing games. Mia was so tired at the end of the day, she fell asleep in Griffin's arms during the fireworks. The memory brings a smile to my face and squeezes my heart.

Admittedly, everything about that day made it feel like we were a family. That's what I want to have again, a whole family. I'm sick of being broken, but is Griffin the right fit for us? It feels like he is with everything inside me. But what if something were to happen to him? Would I survive it? Would we?

The front door opens, startling me and I spin around with my hand over my racing heart. "Griffin," I whimper, my eyes colliding with his.

"I'm sorry, sweetheart. I didn't mean to scare you." He drops his bag by the front door and saunters towards me. His fingers weave into my hair and he tilts my face towards his. "How was your day?" he asks, brushing his lips across mine.

"Mm," I murmur in response, making him chuckle. The low rumble sends shivers down my spine. I love that sound.

"That good?" He smirks.

"The kids and I spent the morning at the library and the afternoon at the sports complex, so they were exhausted. I put them to bed about thirty minutes ago."

"I'm sorry I missed them, but I'm glad for the time with you." He kisses me again, keeping the kiss soft and slow, igniting the fire inside me, but I hold my hand firmly on his chest, maintaining some distance. He pulls back, arching his eyebrow in question. "Everything okay, Mal?"

"Yeah, I just wanted to know how your dad's follow-up visit at the doctor went."

He grins. "It went great. He got the all-clear to go back to work."

"That's fantastic."

"Yeah, of course my mom wasn't happy, but Colton, Robin and I will still help him as much as we can, so it will alleviate some of the work. Colton has been behind on everything at his job, so this is good timing for him. He really needs to catch up."

"And what does that mean for you?" I question, afraid of the answer, but knowing I need to ask.

He moves back, assessing me. "It means my dad is better. It means things might be getting back to normal, whatever that is, at my parents farm. It means that I can go back to work, but I'll tell you now, I'm not going back to Waco, no matter the circumstances."

"You're not?" I question, a lump forming in my throat.

"Hell, no. I'm not going anywhere without you darlin'." He presses his lips to mine as a tear escapes out of the corner of my eye. "I wouldn't make it without you or your three kids with me to keep it interesting."

I laugh as he wipes my tears away. "Good."

"I do need to work though."

"You'll figure it out."

I push up on my tiptoes and kiss him again. "Are you hungry? We had spaghetti and meatballs for dinner."

"I grabbed something at my parents', but I need to grab a glass of water before I feast on you," he declares, licking his lips.

"Griffin…"

"I'm not going to consider apologizing so don't bother."

My voice comes out breathy as I respond, "I'm not going to stand in the way of a hungry man."

He leans down, his tongue diving into my mouth as he scoops me and I wrap my legs around his back.

When we reach the kitchen he sets me on the counter and steps back, breaking our kiss. His thumbs run along my inner thigh, inching towards my core, my pussy already throbbing with need. "Maybe I'll just take you right here."

"Damn I want that, but we can't with the kids."

"I know darlin'. I wouldn't take the chance." He presses his lips to mine again before he turns around, grabbing a glass and filling it with water.

He nods towards the long stem red roses. "Nice flowers."

"Thanks."

"Where did you get the roses from, Mal?"

"Oh, I'm sorry. I guess I forgot to say thank you. The kids got me sidetracked today after they came." Planting my hand on his chest, I push up on my tiptoes, and press a kiss to his lips, wanting to melt into him.

His eyebrows draw in confusion as he pulls back, looking down at me with a shake of his head. "Mal I…"

A shriek comes from down the hall interrupting us. "Mommy," Tiegan cries.

Spinning on my heel, I charge towards my daughter's room with my heart in my throat and Griffin on my heels.

I drop down onto my daughter's bed and pull her into my arms. "Sweetheart, what's wrong?"

"I had a bad dream about daddy." My heart drops into my gut as I glance up at Griffin. It's been a long time since any of us have had a nightmare like that. "I miss him so much, Mom," she whimpers, my heart squeezing, aching for my daughter's pain.

"I know sweetie, I miss him too."

Her head lifts off my shoulder and I know she's looking at Griffin before I even hear his voice. "It's okay to miss him. I miss him too."

"You do?"

"Every single day, sweetheart." He sits behind me and takes both of us into his arms, squeezing us both causing my own tears to spill over.

"Griff?" Tiegan asks, looking at him with watery eyes.

"Yeah, darlin'?"

"You won't let anything happen, right? You'll always come home to us?"

My chest tightens with her words making it impossible to breathe.

He grasps the back of her head and looks her in the eyes with me still pressed between them. "Your dad would've given anything to come home to you. He died way too soon, but he died protecting you. He was one of the bravest men I've ever known and I know he loved you, your mom and your brother and sister more than anything else in this world."

She nods, tears slipping out of the corners of her eyes as she looks up at Griffin. "Do you love us, Griff?"

I hear Griffin's quick intake of breath in my ear, his voice catching as he speaks. "Of course I love you, Tiegan. I love all of you so much and I carry that with me everywhere I go."

"Does that mean we're going to lose you too?" she questions in a much softer voice as if she's afraid of the answer.

"Oh, sweetheart. I'm going to do everything in my power to stay here with you for as long as God will let me. I promise. I bet your dad is watching over you too and I'm sure he'll do what he can to help."

"I love you, Griff," my daughter cries, scrambling over me to hug Griffin tighter. "I don't want you to go."

"Shh," he soothes, rubbing her back and holding her close. "It's okay. I'm right here, Tiegan. It's okay."

I scoot over, my tears silent as I sit watching Griffin and my daughter have a beautiful and heartbreaking moment I'm not sure how to take. Everything about it feels overwhelming. He said all the right things, but were they the right things for us? Does he really love us? Is he in love with me? I don't know and the uncertainty makes my whole body hurt.

Nearly an hour passes before Griffin and I find ourselves in my room, with me cuddled in his arms, my head resting on his chest as he rubs comforting circles on my back. "Are you okay, Mal?"

"Yeah," I rasp, gulping down the lump in my throat. "What about you? That's a lot to take on from a nine, almost ten-year-old."

"My heart fucking broke for her. I felt so helpless. I can't even imagine what it was like for you when you lost him."

"Yeah, it sucked."

He huffs a humorless laugh and kisses me on the top of the head. "I watched y'all at the funeral. The kids seemed so small. You had Mia on one side and Ollie on the other, while Tiegan was glued to Matt."

I shake my head. "I couldn't pry Tiegan away from Matt. It was like he was her connection to her dad and she was terrified if he walked away he wouldn't come home. Carla and Noah's mom and dad were a big help, but they were a mess too. They had each other, but me and the kids all really leaned on Matt. Amber and Reid were there supporting us too. I'm sure the rest of the town was there in the sea of people, but I don't remember it. I couldn't really look at anyone else besides those sitting with us. The entire funeral was like a blur. I kept praying I would wake up and Noah would be there, sitting next to me."

Griffin kisses the top of my head. "I'm so sorry."

As Griffin holds me, I cling to him, my mind drifting, putting me in the time and place of my worst nightmare, the day I wish I could reverse. "The funeral was bad, but I'll never forget the day we lost Noah." I zone out, talking, while everything I'm feeling and seeing makes me feel like I'm watching myself live the tragedy all over again.

The kids were playing in their playroom and I was making dinner. Noah was working so I wasn't expecting him to be home until sometime after seven. When the doorbell rang, I turned the stove off and went to answer it. Matt and Reid stood on the doorstep, both had looks on their faces I couldn't quite decipher, but I tried to ignore it.

"Right on time for dinner. You know I always make extra. Must've planned it this way, didn't you?" I laughed. I stepped back from the doorway to let them in, but neither moved. "Y'all going to come in or not?"

"Mal…" Matt began his voice cracking.

"Mallory, we need to talk to you," Reid finished.

My heart dropped into the pit of my stomach and I reached for the wall for support, finally registering their demeanor. Both men took a step inside, coming to my aid and escorting me to the couch. My legs shake as they lowered me, sitting on each side.

"Wh-what happened? Where's Noah?" My breath picked up its pace and my heart raced, the silence dragging the seconds into hours. I already knew what was coming but I refused to believe it.

"Where are the kids?" Reid asked. I point down the hall, not able to speak.

"I'm so sorry, Mal, but Noah was shot today and he didn't make it." Matt's confession gutted me. My body sagged into the couch and blood rushed in my ears. The crushing sensation on my chest was too much.

Noah.

"Noah pulled a van over for speeding and when he was approaching, the suspect shot him. I was dispatched, but he was gone before I got there. I'm so sorry, Mal," Reid informed me.

I'm just glad the kids keep me so busy that most of the time I'd stay off social media and I refused to listen to the police scanner Noah kept at home. I didn't want to assume the worst with every report. A lot of good it did me.

They stayed, helping me tell our kids that their dad was gone. We all broke, but Tiegan yelled at Reid. "Why didn't you save my daddy?" She cried, hitting him in the chest and he took it. She has been clinging to Matt ever since.

Two grown men held us together with tears in their eyes as we all fell apart.

Chapter Thirty Three

♡ Griffin ♡

I stand in front of the reception desk at Station 28, Miss Caroline Parsons hanging up with Chief Carmichael. "I let the chief know you're here, Mr. Erickson. He's finishing up on another call, so he said he'll be a few minutes."

"Thank you." Piper Falls is a small town, but it's big enough that there's a decent size team. Of course, in comparison to the station I worked at in Waco, this is miniscule, but I want this, knowing the team here is already like family. Bill Camden is the lieutenant retiring from one of the patrol shifts. Admittedly, I'm not thrilled it's the night shift, but I'll take it to be here if they'll have me, now I just need to get the job.

"Griffin Erickson, what the hell are you doing here?" Lieutenant Caden Andrews asks, grinning as he walks through the door. He reaches out, shaking my hand as we give each other a firm pat on the back with our free hand.

"Caden, it's good to see you. I heard Lieutenant Camden is retiring, and I'm hoping to transfer in." His eyes widen in surprise. "How are you, man?"

"That's great news. I'm good. I believe Matt and Matteo are in the back. Come say hello." He glances at Miss Parsons. "I've got him."

We walk into the bullpen, just as Matt lifts his gaze. "Look what the cat dragged in," Matt drawls, grinning wide as he leans back in his chair, his focus on me.

"Hey, man." I wave.

"Finally, here to apply?"

"I already did and my chief in Waco gave me a good reference. I'm just here to talk to Chief Carmichael for my official transfer interview."

"About damn, time." He stands shaking my hand.

"Hey, Matteo, it's good to see you." I nod, shaking his hand.

"Hey man. I heard you were back. How's your dad?" Matteo asks.

I force a smile. "Better, thanks for asking."

"Good to hear."

"Hey, Matt, if you have a minute, I actually have something for you on one of your cases," I inform him.

"Something new?"

I nod. "Yup."

He cracks his knuckles and leans forward as Matteo grabs his phone, taking a call with a wave.

"I have to get to work anyway. I'll catch you later," Caden states, turning and heading to his office.

Matt arches his eyebrows in question. "What's up, Griff?"

"Someone sent Mallory roses yesterday, but there was no card and no indication where they came from."

He shrugs. "So? What the fuck am I supposed to do with that?"

"I think it's the guy who's been stalking her."

"What makes you say that?"

"Something about it is off, she doesn't get flowers from anyone but me or at least from the farm."

"Now you just sound like a jealous boyfriend."

I huff in frustration. "Look, you know me, Matt. Something is off. This wasn't a parent thanking her or even someone asking her out or there would've been a fucking card. The guy that was stalking her disappeared after that last letter, and it was reported to you. Now suddenly, after over a month of silence, she gets flowers. I only give her flowers from the farm, but she seemed to think they were from me."

"Okay, first, didn't you tell her?"

"I was going to, but then Tiegan…" I shake my head, trailing off. That's not something I'm confessing, not even to him.

"So now some guy is interested in her and you think he's a stalker."

"Fuck yes, but you know that's not why. That guy is still out there."

"You're right, he is out there, but you can't accuse every asshole who asks her out or sends her flowers for stalking."

"I know but someone sent her roses and it sure as hell wasn't me. I'm just asking you to keep your fucking ears and eyes open."

"You know I already do, but I appreciate the heads up." I grunt in response. "You're a cop, Griff. Think like one."

I nod, knowing he's right, but when it comes to Mallory and the kids, it's almost too personal to think straight and there's no way in hell I'm taking any chances when it comes to them. I guess that makes it good he's involved. "I know."

Matt's phone rings and he holds his hand up, indicating for me to wait and picks it up. "Detective Bradley." Glancing at me, he nods. "Yes, Chief." Matt disconnects the call and points to a door behind me with the chief's name on a plaque. "Chief Carmichael is ready for you, Griff. He said you can go right in."

"Thanks, wish me luck."

"You've got this."

It's not long before I'm walking out of the station with an offer for the job once the paperwork is finalized. As I climb in my truck, I reach for my phone, my finger hovering over Mallory's name, wanting to share the news with her first, but something holds me back. This is probably a conversation I should have with her in person. Instead, I press my mom's number and hold the phone to my ear.

"Hello?"

"Hey, Ma."

"Griffin. How'd it go at the station? Did you have your interview yet?"

"Yeah, I did. I got the job. Looks like I'm staying in Piper Falls."

"Oh, that's fantastic! I can't wait to tell everyone."

I chuckle. "Would you mind sharing it with the family? You'll likely talk to everyone before I do." She loves being able to share the big news and I hate having to call around to everyone. Besides, it gives her a reason to call all her kids to check on them when I know she wants to do that anyway.

"Of course, I will. Is Mallory happy?"

"I haven't told her yet. I literally just walked out of the station and besides, I want to tell her in person."

"Good idea."

I heave a sigh, my stomach churning at the thought of telling her about the job. For some reason, we haven't talked about this. It wasn't intentional, but I sure as hell hope it doesn't feel that way to her. "Honestly, Ma, I hope she'll be okay with it. I'm worried about how she'll react knowing what happened to Noah."

"I understand, but your job is different than Noah's was, you won't be patrolling as much as he did."

"Yeah, I hope she sees it that way, but it's not like I wouldn't be patrolling at all. Afterall, I will be the lieutenant for patrol. I love my job though and I think being home and working at Station 28 will be something I'll love even more than I did working in Waco. I tried so hard to get away from here after everything that happened with Carla. Now all I want to do is come home and do what I love but I want to do it with Mallory by my side and the kids too."

"I've never heard you talk with so much confidence about your future Griff. Hell, you haven't brought a woman home since Carla."

I shrug even though she can't see me and make my declaration as if the reason is obvious. "I haven't wanted to bring anyone home before, but when it comes to Mallory…" I pause, gulping down the lump in my throat, suddenly overwhelmed. "I love her, Ma. And I love Tiegan, Ollie and Mia too. They're incredible kids."

She laughs. "Yeah, they are. I'm proud of you, Griff."

"Thanks, Ma. Even at my age, you can never hear that too much."

"Oh," she huffs, waving me off, "you say that like you're old, but that would mean you're saying your Mom is old and I know you would never say that."

"Never." I chuckle. "I love you, Ma."

"I love you too, Griffin. Go talk to Mallory and bring her flowers. You're going to need all the help you can get."

I laugh, knowing she's right and hoping it will do me some good. There's no way I want to lose her. "Thanks a lot. I'm probably going to head out to the fields now to pick flowers before I drive back to Mallory's."

"Good luck."

"Thanks, Ma." I disconnect the call and drop my phone in the cup holder before starting my truck.

Hopefully she won't let this get in the way of us because I don't think I will ever be able to let her go, at least not where it counts. On my way out to the farm to pick some flowers for my girls, I drive by the cemetery, feeling something pulling me. I haven't been to his grave yet, but I don't know if I'm ready.

Chapter Thirty Four

♡ Mallory ♡

Griffin walks in the door with his arms full of colorful flowers, along with a couple bags. I walk up to him and push up on my tiptoes, giving him a kiss. "Hi. I'm glad you're here. What is all of this?"

"I brought some things for all of you."

"Griffin, you don't have to do that all the time." I laugh. "Besides, you just bought me flowers."

He stops in front of me and shakes his head. "I don't buy flowers, Mal. I'll pick them and cut them in the fields, but I don't buy flowers."

My heart stops, and I look at him with wide eyes, wondering how I didn't realize this sooner. "You didn't get me roses yesterday?"

He shakes his head. "No. And if I did decide to buy you flowers, it wouldn't be to buy you something you don't really care for. If I'm buying, I'd look for the unique flowers, the ones that are hard to come by when you live in Texas, ones we don't grow in our fields."

My voice shakes as I continue. "Griffin, that sounds great and all, but don't play games with me; not about this."

"You know I don't care for games, Mal, not when it comes to you, the kids or us."

"But there was no card, no name, no nothing." He nods his head. "Then, who got me the flowers?"

"I don't know, but…"

"You think it's him, don't you?"

My breathing picks up its pace and my heart hammers in my chest, my stomach suddenly queasy. Focusing on Griffin, I watch as he sets the flowers and bags down on the coffee table and steps over to me, cradling my face in his hands. "I don't know, sweetheart, but I don't like it and I don't think it's just my jealousy on this one. Unfortunately, I'm going to need you to quiet down so you don't scare the kids."

"Griff…"

"Mom, what is all of this?" Tiegan asks as she walks into the room, followed by Ollie and Mia.

Griffin presses his lips to my forehead before he steps away and walks over to the table, pasting a smile on his face for the kids. "I brought flowers for all my girls and I stopped at the bookstore for you and…"

"You went to the bookstore?" she shrieks making me laugh and shaking my nerves loose enough to focus on the now.

"Yeah, I found a new YA fantasy book I thought you might like to try. Well, it was recommended to me." He hands her the bag. We watch as she pulls out a book and instantly jumps up and down with excitement.

"Griffin, this is fantastic! I've been wanting to read this. Thank you so much!" She throws her arms around him and hugs him tight, his arms falling to her back as he grins, enjoying her enthusiasm.

"Is there something for me?" Ollie asks.

"Actually, I got you something a little different Ollie. I got us tickets for the minor league indoor soccer game in a couple weeks."

"All of us?"

I nod. "Yeah, I thought it would be fun for all of us to go to the game together, but we could go just us if you want to."

"No, I want to go together, all of us as a family," Ollie declares, making me gasp and Griff's eyes widen. "It will be so much fun. Thanks, Griff."

Ollie gives Griffin a hug and Griffin's eyes well, but he quickly blinks it away, clearing his throat. "You're welcome."

"What about me? It's my turn!" Mia announces, jumping up and down in excitement and bringing another smile to my face.

He chuckles as he swipes something off the table. "I got you this, princess." He holds out a small gift bag, and she quickly latches on to both the bag and his hand. I arch my eyebrows in question feeling like this is a lot but loving every single moment with him and each of my kids. He's sure spoiling all of us.

Mia pushes Griffin towards the couch with her free hand and commands, "Well sit down already, mister, so I can open it."

"Okay, okay." Laughing, I watch as he sits and she lets go of him to climb into his lap. She opens the bag, throwing tissue paper on the floor and pulling out a small glazed wooden box with hand painted pink flowers on the top. As she lifts the lid, soft music plays while a small ballerina, wearing a pink tutu and a crown, spins in a circle.

"She's a pretty ballerina, just like me. I love it so much."

"I'm glad sweetheart."

"Thank you," she mumbles, wrapping her arms around Griffin's neck and hugging him tight once again.

As the kids settle and eventually go to sleep, I cuddle into Griffin's arms on the couch, my palm lying flat on his chest, the feel of his heartbeat against my hand calming. "That was really sweet of you to do all those things for me and the kids. Although, you didn't have to, you know."

"I know, I wanted to. I like doing things for all of you."

"Well, thank you."

"Besides, I had a reason to celebrate."

My eyebrows draw together in confusion and I lift my head, looking up at him. "What are you celebrating?"

He looks into my eyes, holding my gaze. "Being able to stay in Piper Falls, being able to stay here with you."

I smile, my heart skipping a beat. "Sounds like a good reason for us to celebrate." Leaning forward, I brush my lips over his.

"Mal…"

"Hmm…" I kiss him again, my tongue flicking out, licking the seam of his lips, begging for entrance. He obliges, my tongue plunging inside as our mouths seal together. I kiss him harder as my hand begins to roam.

Stopping me, he grabs my wrist, sliding it behind his neck as he sweeps me into his arms and stalks towards the bedroom, still kissing me with ferocity. Our teeth clash, tongues collide, and lips bruise as I moan into his mouth desperate for more, my body already tingling in anticipation.

He tosses me on the bed, breaking our kiss. Both of us breathing heavily, he looks down at me, his eyes hooded and licks his lips. With one hand he pulls his shirt over his head and drops it on the floor. Maintaining his eye contact with me, his pants go next, pooling at his feet.

I bite my lower lip in anticipation as I stare at the man in front of me, letting it slide through my teeth. I pull my own shirt over my head just before he crawls over me, sucking my lip out from between my teeth. The simple action makes me wet. "I want you Mr. Erickson," I mumble breathlessly.

His eyes flare and reaching for me, he tugs my shorts off in one swift move, leaving me in my light blue bra and panties with my nipples aching, desperate for his touch, the material of my bra almost too much. Leaning up, I unhook my bra, throwing it behind me, my legs rubbing together hoping to relieve the ache between my legs as his eyes slowly drag over my body. "Mr. Erickson?" he questions, his tone tight, heated as his hand runs over his rigid cock.

"Yes, Mr. Erickson," I whimper. "I want you to suck my nipples, I want you to lick my pussy and I want you to fuck me until I can't see straight."

He drops his boxer briefs to the floor and strokes it again. I can't take anymore and slip my hand into my panties, slipping my finger inside my opening, moaning at the contact.

"Fuck, Mal." My panties are gone in an instant, followed by my hands, now pinned above my head as his tongue sweeps inside my pussy, his hands reaching up and pinching my nipples as my back arches towards him.

"Ah, I'm gonna' come," I rasp, barely breathing, my body swollen, sensitive, wet and ready.

His teeth graze my clit as he rolls my nipples between his fingers, pinching hard. When suddenly he stops, leaving me aching. Lifting my head, I find him looking at me, licking his lips. "I want you on your stomach with your hands above your head and your ass in the air."

Nodding, I do as instructed, his palm caressing the curve of my ass. He kneels behind me, his tongue jutting out and licking me again, making me whimper and desperate to reach for him. His hand comes down on my ass, a light sting before his mouth connects with my pussy once more as his hand runs over the tender skin. He does it again, my body beginning to lose control as his tongue connects with my swollen core, pushing me over the edge. My body pulses, his tongue cleaning up my juices.

As I come down, my body relaxes and I try to catch my breath. He pulls my ass right back up. "Stay here for me baby, I'm gonna' make you come again."

I hear the condom wrapper just before I feel him at my entrance. He grabs my hips and thrusts inside, hitting a spot so deep I didn't know it existed. My body is still swollen, already primed as he pulls back and plunges in again and again, harder and faster. My body easily hits the wall, convulsing, squeezing his cock, milking him as he pounds into me, seeking his own release. His movements quickly become erratic as his own release ensues and we both gasp for breath as our bodies start to recover.

He pulls out, but I close my eyes, not able to move. He chuckles behind me, and carefully cleans me up. Gently rolling me over, he climbs up next to me, looking down at me with his sexy grin. "You okay?"

"I'm fantastic."

He chuckles, wiping my hair off my face. "Every single time you called me Mr. Erickson since I met you, I saw that vision of you in my head with your gorgeous ass up in the air and ready for me."

My eyes widen. "You did?" he nods. My lips twitch as I ask, "So was it as good as you imagined?"

He laughs "Better darlin'. So damn much better. And the things that have been coming out of your mouth lately might have something to do with it."

My cheeks heat as I curl into him with a small smile on my face, my eyes already closing without my consent, heavy with sleep. The roses rush back into my mind just as I drift off to sleep.

Chapter Thirty Five

♡ Griffin ♡

"Do you think I should tell Matt about the roses?"

"Already done. I ran into him and mentioned it."

"Oh. Thanks."

Guilt weighs heavily on my chest as I think about my conversation with Mallory this morning. I didn't just run into him, I saw him at the station, the same station I'll be working at in just a couple weeks. I need to tell her and deal with the consequences now. If she were to find out without me even mentioning it, I don't know how we could recover from that and I can't lose her.

I started to tell her last night and then her mouth had other ideas. It doesn't take much for her to put me in that same mindset. But I need to keep my focus and let her know. I drive by the cemetery, the urge to pull in strong. Parking near Noah's grave, I hop out, making my way over to his headstone, sitting down on the matching bench nearby. Taking a deep breath, I lift my head, reading his headstone.

Noah Dolan
Beloved son, husband, father, and brother in blue.

My chest tightens and my eyes well. "Why the hell did it have to be you, man?" Everything suddenly feels like too much. Overwhelmed with grief and uncertainty, I drop my head in my hands and let my tears fall for all that was lost the day he was taken from all of us.

When I pull myself together, I take a deep breath, and exhale slowly as I lift my head, looking at his gravestone once again, wondering what he would think of me being with Mallory; me with his family. "Matt seems to think you would be okay knowing I'm with Mallory now that you're gone. I sure as hell hope he's right because that's the only place I want to be. I promise I'll take good care of them. At least if she'll still have me after I tell her I'm going back to work. If only you could give me a sign."

Mallory's car pulls up and parks behind mine, making me tense. This isn't exactly the place I want to have a conversation about us. It feels like Noah's watching. Not the kind of sign I'm looking for. I watch as she gets out of the car and strides towards me. She looks up at me and forces a smile. "Hi. What are you doing here?"

I arch my eyebrow in question, knowing the answer is obvious. "Hey."

She sits down next to me on the bench, leaving space between us and looks at Noah's headstone. "Do you come here often?"

Chuckling, I shake my head. "Man, that really does sound like a bad pickup line."

She giggles, nodding. "You are right about that, especially here."

"But the answer is no. I've been wanting to, but…" I shake my head and look away, tears returning to my eyes.

"It's okay."

Blinking them away, I look back at her and question, "Is it?" I need her to understand what I'm asking. This isn't about him being gone anymore, this is about us and our future; if we have one at all.

She presses her lips firmly together, pausing before she finally nods. "Yeah, it is. You've said it yourself, Noah really was a good man. "

"Yeah, and he loved you and the kids." I gulp down the lump in my throat. "I meant it when I said I'm not looking to replace him, but sometimes I wonder if I'm enough for all of you."

"Griffin…"

"I fuck up, I make mistakes."

"We all do."

I nod pursing my lips. "True, but are mine too much? Am I too much?"

She licks her lips, dragging her lower lip through her teeth in thought making it difficult to breathe. "You won't know if you don't tell me what's going through your head. No games, just like you said, right?"

Turning on the bench, I grab her hands, running my thumb over the backs as I look her in the eyes, begging her to believe in me, in us. "No games."

She nods, urging me to speak. Her phone rings, swiftly breaking the moment. She pulls her hand away and grabs her phone, glancing at the screen. "I'm sorry, Griffin, I have to get this."

"Go ahead." I nod and drop her other hand.

"Tanner? Is everything okay?" She pauses, her mouth dropping open. "He what?" Instantly alert, I look back at her, my eyes wide. "I'm on my way." She disconnects the call with a huff and jumps up.

"What's wrong? Is Ollie okay?" I stand, following as she walks backwards.

"Yeah, it will be, but I gotta' go." She points behind her, gesturing to her car. "Ollie fell on the soccer field and lost a couple teeth. Tanner has him and he's on the way to the dentist right now. I could hear him crying in the background."

"I'm going with you. Tanner has him?"

"Yeah, he's one of the coaches at Ollie's soccer camp this week."

"Huh. I didn't realize. Leave your car and I'll drive you. That way when we bring him home, you can sit with him."

She glances at her own car before beelining for the passenger side of my truck and jumping in. I start my truck and pull out, racing towards the dentist, at least it will only take two minutes to get there. Out of the corner of my eye, I see Mallory sucking her lower lip into her mouth and running her teeth over it. Keeping my eyes on the road I reach over, giving her knee a squeeze in support. "He's going to be okay."

She nods emphatically, gulping down the lump in her throat. "I know."

I pull up to the Piper Falls Family Dentist office, and park next to Tanner's truck, Mallory jumping out the moment I shift into park.

We rush inside, the receptionist pointing towards the back. "He's in room three." I move to follow Mallory and the receptionist calls to stop me. "Excuse me, Sir, you can't go back there."

Not bothering to stop, Mallory grabs my hand and pulls me along as she rushes to find Ollie. "He's with me."

Mallory gasps as we step in the room, her wide eyes on Ollie, covered in blood and his lip cut and fat. The tears in his eyes spill over the second he sees her. "Mommy, I lost my teeth," he stammers, the words coming out slurred.

"Oh, honey." She rushes to his side, opposite Tanner and grabs his hand as Dr. Leeann Klotz leans back looking at Mallory.

"I know there's a lot of blood, but he's okay. Luckily the teeth he lost are baby teeth, so I didn't need to do anything except help him stop the bleeding. His adult teeth will come in eventually and in the meantime, he'll just have a gap. He has some swelling in his mouth, lips and cheek, but ice and children's Tylenol should do the trick."

Mallory breathes a sigh of relief. "Thank you."

She nods in acknowledgement. "He also may have trouble with regular foods the next few days. Liquids and soft foods will be best."

"Like ice cream?" Ollie asks, his eyes a little brighter.

We all laugh and Dr. Klotz nods. "Yes, like ice cream. Popsicles or ices are even better because ice cream can add to the phlegm, but some is okay." She pushes her chair back, throwing her gloves and mask in the garbage can before washing her hands and turning back to Ollie. "We'll see you in a couple weeks just to make sure you're healing properly. Okay?" He nods. Giving her what I think might be a smile. "You did great Ollie. Don't forget to grab a couple prizes from the treasure chest on your way out and put your teeth under your pillow for the tooth fairy."

"Can I get something for my sisters too?"

Dr. Klotz grins. "Of course. You're such a sweet brother."

"Griff told me the men in the house need to do things to make the women in the house feel special. It's our job."

My lips curve up in a smile as I look down at Ollie, my chest tightening with pride. I nod. "That's right, Ollie."

He smiles and winces, swiftly frowning.

Dr. Klotz glances at me, swiftly dragging her eyes over me from head to toe. "Smart man," she mumbles and waves to Ollie as she walks out of the room.

Mallory looks at me, her eyebrows drawn down as she wraps her arm around Ollie, helping him up.

"Looks like you did awesome at soccer camp today," I proclaim, giving Ollie a crooked smile.

He grins, showing off the gap in his teeth. "I scored right before that guy tripped me. He was mad he got beat by someone smaller than him."

"What kid?" Mallory asks, looking at Tanner.

"It's taken care of, Mal. We'll talk about it later," he responds, glancing at Ollie.

She nods and lets go of Ollie, stepping over to him. "Thank you so much for bringing him."

His eyes widen, appearing slightly offended. "Of course, I'm gonna' bring him, Mal. I love him like he's my own."

"I know." She nods, reaching her arms out.

"I'm covered in blood, Mal."

"I don't care, it's partly my DNA." She hugs him and he pulls her close, his lips curving up.

I don't like it. Clearing my throat, I hold out my hand, asking Ollie, "Ready to go home?"

"Yeah."

"Let's go find some gold in Dr. Klotz's treasure chest."

He rolls his eyes dramatically, reminding me of Tiegan. "She doesn't have real gold in there."

"She doesn't?"

"No, it's like cool toys and games and superballs and stuff."

"It sounds better than gold to me."

He nods, tugging me towards reception, Mallory and Tanner following right behind.

Chapter Thirty Six

♡ Mallory ♡

While I'm getting the girls to bed and Ollie comfortable enough to go to sleep, Griffin walks to the cemetery and returns with my car. Exhausted, I sigh, collapsing on the couch next to him. "You doin' okay?" he asks, draping his arm over the back of the couch.

I nod. "As good as I can be. All that blood." I shake my head. "I'm happy I didn't pass out or throw up."

He chuckles. "Well, I think you did good," he proclaims as if I were the patient.

"After Dr. Klotz said he was okay, I just tried to focus on that." Remembering the way the doctor looked Griffin up and down makes my stomach turn. "She sure seemed impressed with you today."

He smirks, pushing my hair behind my ear. "Is that jealousy I hear?"

"Did you not see the way she looked at you? It was pretty rude with me standing right there."

"Yeah, right there next to Tanner. How would Dr. Klotz even know we were together?"

I brush him off. "We came in holding hands and besides, Tanner and I are friends. I've known him most of my life."

"And she would know that how?" he echoes, his lips twitching in amusement.

"You're not jealous of Tanner, are you?"

He shakes his head. "No, but I don't like how he looks at you, Mal. The looks he gives you are far more than friendly."

"That's not true." I shake my head in denial.

"Yeah, it is. I can guarantee he wants to fuck you darlin' and he absolutely hates me knowing I do."

"No, he doesn't."

"He does because he wants you and I have you."

"Do you, though, Mr. Erickson?" I challenge, narrowing my eyes and crossing my arms over my chest in defiance.

"Mal…" he says my name in warning, although I'm not sure if it's because of our argument or because I'm blatantly taunting him. I know I'm pushing but I can't help it. Tanner is harmless and I hate that he's even accusing him. "Did you at least ask him if he sent you the flowers? The roses?"

I frown, searching through my memory. "I don't think I asked. I guess he could've, but all I have to do is ask him and he'll tell me. That doesn't mean anything."

"Because he's such a great guy," he mutters, sarcasm thick on his tongue.

"Griffin…"

"What about that rose heart thing that was left on your doorstep? Did you ever ask him if he gave you that? Because he was one of the people you mentioned as a possibility of leaving it for you."

"You mean the rose quartz heart?"

"Yeah, that thing. Maybe he has a thing for roses of any kind, even if they aren't your thing."

"Yeah, I asked him and Carla and they both said no, remember?" He frowns, nodding. "Maybe I should accuse Matt because he's been there for me. Or how about Carla? You guys were together for three years and I was married to her brother."

"Now you're being ridiculous."

"But Griff, that's my point. We can come up with a reason, for almost anyone. Tanner could've asked me out years ago. I've known him since we were kids, and he's never asked me out before, not once, but he's always been a good friend to me. He was there when I was bullied as a kid, he was a friend when my parents abandoned me when I was pregnant, and he was there anytime I needed help. He's been there when no one else was and that's saying something in my book."

He winces but keeps pushing. "Well, maybe things changed, but he absolutely wants you and I don't like it. Maybe he's the one that's been stalking you."

I laugh. "Tanner isn't stalking me, Griffin. He has absolutely no reason to. He can come over anytime, we hang out, he gives me and the kids presents and we buy things for him, I know his family, hell he's been our emergency contact next to Carla since Noah died."

He scoffs. "Really?"

"Yes, of course because I trust him," I emphasize, glaring at him.

"Well, I don't."

Throwing up my hands in frustration, I mutter, "Great, but he didn't do anything to me. Did you know he was the one that insisted I call the cops when I started getting the letters? Why would he do that if he was the one who did it? And he was at his parents the night Olivia saw someone looking in the windows."

"What about when your tires were slashed?" he challenges, not even bothering to respond to my defense.

I stand up, not able to sit still, Griffin mirroring my movement. "He wanted me to call the cops. Tanner always pushed me to report everything that happened because he was worried about me and the kids. There's no way he did any of it. Please, lay off him."

We momentarily stare at one another, both of us holding our glare before he concedes with a grunt. "Fine." With a heavy sigh, he runs his hand through his hair in frustration. "Let's agree to disagree. But I still don't trust him and I'm begging you to just be aware that the man has a serious thing for you."

"Whatever, Griff." I huff, rolling my eyes. This is ridiculous.

He plants his hands low on his hips. "You know I'm not playing games, Mal."

"I'm well aware. Let's just drop it. I hear you, Griffin and I know what you think of Tanner."

"It's more than that. It's—"

I hold my hand up, begging him to stop. "I understand what you think. I promise." He nods, his movements rigid. "But remember, if anything were to happen with anyone, I can take care of myself."

"Yeah, yeah, I know and I'm grateful for it." He frowns. "I don't like fighting with you, Mal."

"Is that what we're doing?" I question, arching my eyebrow.

"Smartass." He chuckles, stepping towards me.

"Didn't you tell me making up could be a lot of fun?" I taunt, letting my eyes drag over his body.

His lips twitch in amusement and he arches his eyebrows in challenge. "I know we could have a lot more than fun making up. You up for the challenge?"

"Always with you."

"Mommy." Griffin and I spin around finding Ollie staring at us, rubbing his eyes. "My mouth hurts."

"Oh, sweetie." I rush over to Ollie, guiding him back to his room. "Let me get you something to help it feel better."

Griffin's accusations run through my head, but everything about them seems outrageous. Tanner has alibis. Besides, I know Tanner better than anyone and it's definitely not him.

Sighing, I lay down with Ollie, as my phone pings with a text. I glance at my screen and frown.

Carla: Hey, Mal. I'm sure Griffin told you that he's my ex and about what happened between us. I've been afraid to reach out, but we're still family, and I miss you and the kids.

Carla: I was young, in love and scared. I made some stupid decisions that I regret. I'm sorry. I can't lose all of you, too. Please forgive me.

I heave a sigh. I hate that they were ever together, and for so long. It's even worse that she cheated on Griffin, and he suffered a loss that he didn't even know if it was his to lose, they all did. But she's right, she was young and she didn't do anything to me or the kids. Now that I've had time to process everything, I know I can't let what happened between her and Griffin impact her relationship with us. She's our family no matter what. And besides, if Griffin can move on from it, I sure as hell can.

Me: I believe you live and learn. I'm sorry for what you all went through. I know it couldn't be easy. I'm glad you had Noah.

Carla: Thank you Mallory. I love you.

Me: I love you, too, Carla.

Carla: Can I see you and the kids? Or maybe I can take the kids this week for a day? And you can hang out some. or do what you need to do?
Me: Sure. Let's figure out a day. Thank you.
Carla: Thank you!

I wrap my arm around Ollie and press my lips to the top of his head. I can't imagine miscarrying a baby like that at any age. I'm thankful for my three kids every single day. I close my eyes for a few minutes, hoping my boy feels better soon.

♡ Griffin ♡

I watch Mallory walk down the hallway with Ollie and reach for my phone, pulling up Matt's name.

Me: What do you think about Tanner Pratt?
Matt: He's a stuffy asshole. Why?
Me: He has a thing for Mal.
Matt: You sure about that?
Me: Positive. I don't trust him at all.
Matt: Not really surprised. I'll look into it.
Me: Thanks.
Matt: Knowing you won't be able to be around as much, I'd get Prestige Guardians Security to get her system in place ASAP.
Me: On it. She won't be happy.
Matt: Good luck.
Me: Thanks.

I put my phone down and close my eyes, waiting for Mal to come back, but I fall asleep on the couch without her in my arms.

Before I leave for my parents to help out at the farm while I still can, I go in search of her. I'm almost thankful when I find her room empty, knowing it's not our argument about Tanner that stopped her from coming back.

Quietly, I push Ollie's bedroom door open, finding her sound asleep in his twin bed next to him bringing a smile to my face and squeezing my heart. I press a kiss to both of their foreheads and sneak out of the room. Making my way down the hall, I check on Tiegan and Mia giving them both a kiss on the forehead before locking them all safely inside as I slip out the front door, what I feel for them only growing stronger.

Chapter Thirty Seven

♡ Mallory ♡

Although it's been a few days since my fight with Griffin and everything seems to be back to the way it was before, I still feel on edge, like I'm waiting for the inevitable end. I'm not sure if it's because of our argument about Tanner or if it's because I feel like there's something he's holding back or not telling me, but it sits there in my gut, in my chest, in my head eating at me all the same.

Frowning, I glance over at Ashton Davidson from Prestige Guardians Security as he's taking out the necessary equipment to install security cameras around my house. It's not his fault Griffin paid him when I said I didn't need them. Honestly, it was more about not wanting to put the money into something I don't believe I need. Obviously Griffin didn't agree.

"I promise the cameras aren't meant to be intrusive. They are really only here to protect you and your kids," he comments, reassuring me again.

"Thank you, Ashton. I do appreciate your help. Are you going to be working for a little while?"

"Yeah, it will take me a bit to get everything hooked up and running."

"Would it be okay if I ran a quick errand? I have something I want to get done while the kids are out."

"No problem. I'm already online and I have your number if I need it."

"Thank you. I'll be back soon."

I grab my purse and keys, and a large cookie tin the kids and I made this morning, waving to him as I walk out the door. I stride towards the station needing the fresh air, hoping it will help me get my head straight. This is the same path I used to walk often on the days I had free, dropping something off for Noah and the men and women who became family to us both.

I haven't had the courage to walk through the doors in a long time, but I want to talk to Matt to see if he knows anything new on my case. I want this over with so I can move on and not have to think about it anymore. As I approach the station, I start to wonder what's been holding me back from going inside for so long, the feeling of trepidation has almost completely dissipated.

I pull the door open and step up to the front desk, smiling at the familiar face. "Hi Linda."

"Mallory, dear, it's so good to see you. How are you? How are the kids? You have to bring them in so we can see them."

I laugh. "I will. They're actually with Carla today. But I'll stop when we have time. Is Matt in?"

"Yes, Detective Bradley is in the back."

The door swings open and Matt walks out with Griffin by his side, both of their eyes wide as they land on me.

"Mal," Griffin murmurs my name.

Matt walks over to me with a wide smile. "Mal, you're here," he declares, knowing how long it's been.

I nod. "I am. I brought these for you and everyone," I gesture towards the back as I hand him the tin. "The kids and I made cookies this morning. They were up early."

"Thank you and please tell them thank you from me." He gives me a hug. "I promise I'll share…some." He smirks.

"I also wanted to ask you if you have anything new?"

He shakes his head, frowning. "I promise you'll be the first to know when I do."

I look at Griffin standing next to Matt and looking down at me. "What are you doing here?"

He gestures outside. "How about we grab some lunch and I'll tell you."

"I have to head home. Ashton is there putting in security cameras." I narrow my eyes at Griffin.

"Ah, yeah, Matt agrees with me…"

"Don't drag me into this."

"Sorry."

"I'll see you two later." He waves and retreats towards the back.

"I just want you and the kids safe, Mallory."

"Yeah, but…"

"Can we just go somewhere and talk?"

"Okay." I wave to Linda as Griffin holds the door open for me and step past him.

"Did you walk?"

"Yeah, it's not far and I needed the fresh air."

"Can we take my truck back to your place then?"

Instead of answering, I walk to his truck and climb in. We ride in silence to my house, my stomach turning, knowing something is coming I'm not prepared for. Griffin parks along the curb and we find Ashton still working. We make lunch side by side, but the tension between us starts to feel like a wall and I'm waiting for it to come crashing down on my head.

When Ashton's done, he shows us both how to work the system before he leaves. The moment the door closes behind him, I look at Griffin and ask, "I need you to respect my decisions. I told you I didn't want a security system."

"But I need to know you're safe, which is why I paid for it."

I huff a humorless laugh. "But I was fine before you, and you're here every night anyway."

"But I won't always be."

"What?" My heart drops into my stomach like lead.

He closes the distance between us and looks me in the eyes as he repeats, "I'd like to be here every night, but the fact is I won't be."

"And why is that Griffin?"

"Because I'll be working some nights."

My eyebrows draw down in confusion. "At your parents' farm?" I gasp as a sudden realization hits me. "Is your dad okay?"

He nods vehemently. "Yeah, yeah, my dad is okay. He really is doing much better. I'm sorry. I didn't mean to scare you like that."

"Okay, then I don't understand."

"I'm not going to be working at my parents' farm, Mal. I'll still help when I can, but staying there, working there full-time was never part of my plan. I work there to help my family, not to make a living."

"Okay," I mumble, drawing out the word.

"And not only is Wyatt back, but my dad is doing well."

"What aren't you telling me, Griffin? What will you be doing?"

"I told you I got a job so I can stay in Piper Falls, stay here with you."

"Well, that's not exactly what you said, but okay."

He takes a deep breath and exhales slowly, looking into my eyes, and watching me closely. "My transfer came through."

"Your transfer?"

"I got my transfer from Waco. Bill Camden is retiring and I'm taking over as the Lieutenant for the night patrol shifts at Station 28."

My breathing picks up its pace and my heart pounds so hard, the blood flowing through my ears is suddenly deafening. I shake my head to clear the noise, but it doesn't do much. "You're going back to being a cop?"

"I never wanted to stop. I love my job, Mal and I think I'll love it even more being here in Piper Falls."

"After everything? You're going to be a cop again?"

"I'll be doing more paperwork than anything. Being a lieutenant is not the same as being out on patrol every day."

"But you will be out on patrol sometimes." He shrugs, knowing it's true, whether he's covering a shift, or for training or a multitude of other reasons. Then I could lose him just the same. I can't do that.

"Mallory, it's going to be okay," he attempts to reassure me, his hand falling to my shoulder.

"You can't promise me that!" I shriek, yanking my arm away from him.

He flinches. "Mal," he murmurs, his eyes pleading.

I clench my fists at my sides and shake my head in denial. "How could you do this to me, Griffin? After I let you in my life, in my kids' lives and you just go back to work without thinking of us?"

"You and your kids are the first thing I think of with every decision I make, including this one."

Huffing a humorless laugh, I shake my head. "Bullshit!" She narrows her eyes at me. "I trusted you!"

"Me going back to work shouldn't change that."

I shake my head in disbelief, panic setting in making my chest tight. "I can't do this again. I can't ever feel the way I did when Matt and Reid told me my husband was gone. Griffin, you know that!" I glare at him, not able to see through my own pain as my tears start to fall, imagining the worst-case scenario.

"That's not gonna' happen."

Gasping, I struggle for breath. "I wouldn't be able to gather the strength to tell my kids again. They don't deserve to ever have to go through that pain, that nightmare."

"You're right, they definitely don't deserve that and I would do everything in my power to make sure they never had to endure anything like that ever again."

"You think Noah didn't try to do the same? What makes you any different?" I challenge, gasping for each breath.

Griffin's arms come around me, holding me, attempting to soothe me. All I want to do is collapse and let him support me, but I squirm, hitting him in the chest. "I hate you Griffin! I hate you for letting me fall in love with you. I hate you for letting my kids fall in love with you. How could you do this to me?" I whimper, giving into his embrace for just a moment, feeling his silent tears mix with mine.

"I'm sorry baby. I love you."

Taking a deep breath, I plant my hands on his chest and shove him away. "Fuck you Griffin Erickson! You don't give a shit about any of us!"

"Mal…"

"Get out!"

"But Mal…"

"I said get out!" I scream, punctuating each word.

Sighing heavily, he trudges towards the door, just before he closes it behind himself, he rasps, "You don't have to believe me, but I love all of you."

The door clicks shut and I collapse against the wall, my sobbing no longer controllable, my breaths coming out in short gasps.

What do I do?

Chapter Thirty Eight

♡ Mallory ♡

"Kids, go get your things and clean up the playroom for Aunt Carla." I watch my three kids retreat down the hall and look at Carla, my eyes tired, my head and heart heavy. "Thanks for having the kids last night, Carla."

"You're welcome, but are you sure you don't want me to keep them for another night? You don't look so good."

Grimacing, I mumble, "Thanks. I had a rough night."

"From the looks of it, it doesn't look like the good kind of rough night. Isn't Griff still good in bed?" She wiggles her eyebrows and I glare at her, not in the mood to think about sex with Griffin, especially when it involves the two of them. Her grin falls and she rolls her eyes. "I'm kidding. I was trying to lighten the mood."

The thought of them together runs over me like a freight train. "Are you kidding me right now? You thought that would lighten my mood?" I ask, my tears once again flowing down my cheeks and my fists clenched at my sides.

She shakes her head. "I'm sorry, I'm trying to get over the weirdness of this and I'm only making it worse."

"Ya' think?"

"Oh, Mallory, I said I'm sorry. It was a stupid question but green is not your color."

"I'm not jealous."

"Great. What happened?"

I shake my head, my chest squeezing and tears welling in my eyes once again. "Nothing happened."

Stepping towards me, she tentatively puts her arm around me. "Listen, I know I'm likely the last person you want to talk to about Griffin, because I'm going to assume this is about him, but it's been like thirteen years. That's all ancient history. Sort of. Besides, you are my family," she emphasizes. "Talk to me."

"It's not that I don't want to talk because it's you, Carla. We're okay or we will be." She flinches, but I ignore it. "It's because I don't think I can talk about it at all."

"Did he do something to you? If he did, I'll kill him."

"No." I gulp, blurting out the words. "He's going back to work."

"Okay…" she mumbles, dragging out the word.

"At the Piper Falls police station."

"Oh." She frowns and nods in understanding. Heaving a sigh, she asks, "Do you love him, Mal?"

"Does it matter?"

"Yeah, it does. Do you love him?"

I gulp down the lump in my throat. "Yeah, I do."

She winces, quickly hiding it. "Then, it's worth the risk. He's a good man and believe me, I know what it's like to lose a man you love because you're scared."

My stomach twists, wondering if she's talking about Noah or Griffin or someone else entirely as she brushes a tear away. But I can't think about that right now.

"What's the alternative, Mal? You live without him? You give up all the good things that go along with loving someone and having them love you because yeah, I still know Griffin and he loves you and all three of those incredible kids."

My eyes widen and my stomach flips hearing her say he loves me, but I ignore it, just like I ignored him sleeping in his truck last night in my driveway. "I can't go through losing someone like that again."

"What happened to Noah wasn't normal."

My hand falls to my chest, barely breathing. "I can't."

"Would you give up everything you and Noah had together so you wouldn't have to go through losing him?"

I scoff. "No, but that's different."

"Is it? Yeah, there's the kids, but besides that." She arches her eyebrows in challenge, but I don't respond. "If you decide to date anyone Mallory, you could lose them. Life is not a guarantee, but the moments you create with the people you love are not something anyone can ever take away from you."

"But they still get taken away."

She shakes her head. "You know better than that. Every moment, every memory of Noah is still alive and I wouldn't trade a single one of them for anything."

"You're right. Neither would I."

"Don't throw away moments to live and love with the man you really want to have those new memories with. I have a lot of regrets in my life, but I promise you, throwing that away would be your biggest."

Her words squeeze my heart, but the only thing that comes out of my mouth is, "I'll think about it."

"We're ready, Mom."

Swiftly, I wipe my tears away and turn towards my kids with a smile. The three of them chatter about their time with their Aunt Carla as we head home, but my mind remains foggy, not able to process much of what they're saying and I don't like it. It's important to me that my kids always know how special they are and listening to them is the first way to do it. "I'm sorry guys. I'm tired today."

"That's okay, Mom. I can't wait to show Griffin," Tiegan announces, grinning as she jumps out of the car and runs to the door.

My heart sinks knowing I have to break my kids' hearts, but better now than later. Right?

As we walk into the house, Tiegan asks, "Will Griffin be here for dinner?"

A heavy sigh escapes through my lips. "I'm sorry sweetheart, but no. He's not going to be here tonight." Even as I utter the words, I wonder if they're true or if he'll be sleeping in his truck just outside like he did last night. He can't keep doing that.

"Why not?" she asks, her brother and sister fidgeting as they stand nearby listening to our conversation.

"He's just busy."

"Well, can I call him? I know if I called him and invited him over for dinner, he would at least come for dessert."

I shake my head, feeling lost, having no idea how to navigate this. "I don't think that's a good idea, Tiegan."

"Why not, Mom? Griffin loves us."

Her words hit me like a punch to the chest. I nod. "Yeah, he does, but…"

"Then, why not? I want to see Griffin." She crosses her arms over her chest, narrowing her eyes at me.

"Me too," Ollie murmurs.

"Me three," Mia adds.

"He's starting work at the station and y'all go back to school soon."

"At the station? Mom, is he okay?" Tiegan asks, her voice shaking.

"Is he with Daddy?" Ollie asks, tears in his eyes.

I rush over to her and put my arm around my kids in comfort. This is the exact reason I can't do this again. "He's all right. I promise, he's okay. He just can't come over right now. Okay?"

Tiegan shakes her head. "No, it's not okay. I don't understand. If he's fine, why can't he come over at all? He said he loved us."

"He does. I asked him not to come over."

Gasping, Tiegan pushes out of my arms, staring at me with wide eyes. "Why would you do that? Why would you take him away from us?"

"I'm not. It's just the right thing to do for us."

Tiegan's voice becomes louder as she talks. "No, it's not. He understands me, Mom. I want him to be here with us. You're taking him away. We already lost dad, why are you making him leave too?"

"No…" I shake my head, tears spilling over without my consent.

"I hate you, Mom. I'll never forgive you for this. I love Griffin. He should be here. First dad, now Griffin. You ruin everything!" She screams and spins on her heel, running to her room and slamming the door, making me jump.

Ollie follows without a word, his shoulders slumped, while Mia climbs into my lap, popping her thumb into her mouth for comfort for the first time in a year.

I hold my sweet little girl, crying silent tears and feeling completely helpless. My heart aches, but it will hurt less to let him go now, right? Will I be able to let him go when all I want to do is run back into his arms? I'm already starting to doubt my own logic. Maybe Carla is right, even though some of her reasoning was a little fucked up.

A knock on the door interrupts my thoughts and I stand, carrying Mia to answer it. I glance out the window finding Tanner standing with one hand in his pocket and the other holding a large bag of takeout. Opening the door, I paste on a smile, but it's no use. "Tanner, I told you I was okay. You didn't have to bring dinner."

"I know what you told me, Mal, but I also know you and it looks like you're not the only one that could use a sweet treat for a pick-me-up."

My tears spill over and Tanner sets the bag down, pulling both Mia and me into his arms. "Thank you."

Chapter Thirty Nine

♡ Griffin ♡

My hand runs over my face, trying to wake up, my entire body completely exhausted. It's not like I don't expect it but that doesn't make it easy. Sleeping in my truck is not exactly comfortable, but what else am I supposed to do? I couldn't bear if anything happened to any of them and with everything that's happened, I feel like with me gone it would be an opportunity for whoever to push in.

My phone beeps with a text and I glance at the screen, hoping it's her. I heave a sigh, disappointment slamming into me.

Bitch: Are you ok?

Me: What do you want Carla?

Bitch: Just checking on you. Mallory told me she broke up with you and I was worried.

Me: I'm fine. She okay? The kids?

Bitch: They're okay. Congratulations on the job. I'm glad you'll finally be at Station 28. That's where you always wanted to be. I'm happy for you.

Me: Thanks. I think I'm gonna' go say hi to your brother.

Bitch: Blow him a kiss for me.

Bitch: And Griff, you will be okay no matter what. You will get the family you always wanted one day.

I don't bother responding, but I do change Carla's name from Bitch to Carla again. I've let it go; it's time.

After avoiding Memorial Gardens cemetery for so long, I'm a little surprised to find myself here for the second time in only a few days, but I don't know where else to go. My family has other shit to deal with, I still haven't smoothed things over with Reid and Matt has a lot going on, including trying to find out who's been messing with Mallory.

I glance at Noah's headstone and shake my head. "I don't know what the fuck to do man. She won't answer my calls or texts. I know it's only been a few days, but it's killing me. Do I give up everything to be a part of their lives? Is that what I do?" Heaving a sigh, I drop my head in my hands, feeling completely defeated. Sitting up, I rub my head over the constant ache in my chest since she kicked me out. "Is it fucked up I'm coming to you for advice? But you know her better than anyone, right?"

"Maybe a little bit," Matt answers from behind me. I spin around to find him smirking at me, his eyebrows raised in question.

"Thanks for the warning."

He laughs. "You're usually more aware."

I grimace. "Yeah, I haven't been sleeping. How'd you know I was here?"

He nods, glancing at Noah's headstone as he sits down next to me. "I didn't. But I heard what happened with Mal. After I talked to her, I checked your parents. This was my second guess. She didn't like the idea of you going back to work, huh?"

I huff a humorless laugh. "That's an understatement, but can you really blame her?"

He shrugs, "No. I understand where she's coming from, but I also know that what you two have together is worth fighting for every fucking moment. Nothing is guaranteed."

"Funny. I said almost the same thing. Didn't seem to matter."

"Don't be so sure about that. If she's anything like me she'll get out of her head sooner or later."

"She's nothing like you, man." I smirk.

"Asshole," he mumbles, laughing. "Just don't give up. I think you two are good together and I can't imagine myself saying that about anyone else when it comes to Mal. She's worth it. Just prove that you're worth it too."

"I couldn't give up on her if my life depended on it. She's it for me. Now I need her to fucking believe it."

He nods, glancing at his phone, his face going pale. "We gotta' go."

"What's wrong?

"There's a report for a missing child."

I jump up as we jog towards our cars. "For who?" I ask my heart stopped, waiting for a name I almost know is coming.

"Tiegan."

"Tiegan?" I echo, surprised. I almost expected to hear him say Mia with how she tends to run off, but Tiegan? Mallory must be sick. My chest tightens and my stomach sinks, twisting with worry.

"Ride with me."

I do as he says, jumping in the passenger seat of his dark gray Dodge Charger. "Do they know anything?"

He holds up a finger, reading through his phone. "Looks like the security cameras caught her leaving the house around eleven last night."

"She was out all night? By herself? What the fuck was she leaving for?" My heart begins to race, praying she's going to be okay. If your daughter ever needed you Noah, right now is the time. Please let her be okay.

"Sounds like she got into a fight with Mallory. A couple others are canvassing the neighborhood and talking to her friends. Where do you think she would go?"

I pick up my phone and press Mallory's number, mumbling under my breath, "Pick up the phone, Mal. Please, pick up the fucking phone."

"Griffin," she cries into the phone, "Tiegan…"

"I know. What did you fight about?"

"What?"

"What did you fight about just before she ran away?"

"You," she whimpers.

My heart clenches and I struggle to breathe. Squeezing down the lump in my throat, I attempt to comfort her. "We're going to find her, Mal. I promise we will fucking find her and she will be okay."

"Please," is all she says before she disconnects the call as she starts to cry harder.

"Fuck."

"Anything?" Matt prompts, shaking me out of my momentary panic.

"They fought about me."

"Do you think she was coming to look for you?"

"Maybe, but she would've seen me if she went out the front. Hell, I would've seen her, so she definitely continued out the back after going out the back door."

"If she was going to the farm from there, she might've gone through the woods." I nod in agreement. "I'll notify the station and let's start looking from your farm. The team will fan out starting in town."

"I'll text my family to help."

Tuning Matt out, I tap out a text to my family.

Me: Tiegan ran away last night. There's a good chance she's in the woods between town and the farm. Need all hands-on deck. Be home soon.

I don't bother reading their responses. What's the point?

It feels like forever before Matt's pulling into the long drive at the farm, driving straight past the main house and moving towards the woods before parking. We jump out of his car and he informs me, "Luke is on his way."

I nod. "Great." Catching sight of Colton, Wyatt, Beau, Harper and my dad out of the corner of my eye, my chest tightens further, the reality of the situation hitting me hard and I quickly fight back my emotions and focus on what we need to do. I didn't even realize Beau and Harper were home.

"Mom is at the house to help with communication or if anyone comes back," Colton informs us without preamble and holds out a bag, "and we have radios just in case. Service can suck out here."

My dad announces, "I'll stay here to direct anyone else that comes to help, that way, all of you can search."

"Luke is on his way," Matt states.

Colton takes over, breaking up the area and directing where each of us should go, knowing the property and at the same time, knowing my head is spinning and I can't focus on anything except finding her. As I begin trudging through the brush at the edge of the woods, I call out for my girl, "Tiegan!" Calling again and again every few steps.

Hours of bleak updates push at my armor but I refuse to let any of it get to me. I'm not stopping until I bring her home to Mallory where she belongs. "Tiegan!"

Soft whimpering causes me to halt my footsteps. Holding my breath, I listen carefully, not wanting to take a chance of missing a thing. I hear it again, my heart skipping a beat as I move towards the sound, calling again.

"Tiegan!" Moving swiftly, I close in on the whimpering. "Tiegan, sweetheart, is that you?"

A glimpse of blue catches my eye between the trees at the edge of a steep incline. "Tiegan," I breathe, my heart pounding even harder the moment I set eyes on my girl sitting on the ground, dirty with swollen eyes and tear-stained cheeks.

"Griff," she rasps, barely able to speak as her tears flow freely.

I rush to her, shuffling sideways down the incline and kneel down beside her, carefully taking her in my arms. "You're okay," I whisper, overcome with love and relief.

"You're here," she cries. "I called for you all night."

My heart squeezes, irrational guilt overwhelming me for not being here. "I'm so sorry, Tiegan. I'm sorry I couldn't find you sooner. Are you hurt?"

She nods, pointing to her foot. "My flashlight died. I couldn't see and I fell."

"Okay, I'm going to have you call your mom from my phone, but just tell her you're okay. I need you to talk as little as possible. Sounds like you hurt your throat too. We can talk about it later. Okay?"

She nods in understanding. I hand her my phone with Mallory's number pulled up and radio as she presses call. "G to all units. The package is safe, but in need of medical and returning with me to base."

After the first, "Copy," I turn the radio down, focusing on Tiegan.

"Mom, I'm okay."

Mallory's cry echoes through the line and I take the phone from Tiegan. "Mallory, it's okay, darlin'. She's going to be just fine. She strained her voice and it looks like she sprained her ankle. I'm going to carry her back to the farm if someone can drive you there. My mom can direct you where to go."

I disconnect and slip my phone in my pocket, checking her ankle again, to make sure it's okay hanging loose. "I'm going to pick you up, okay, sweetheart?"

She nods, her lower lip trembling, twisting my insides. "Okay."

Getting my hands underneath her, I carefully pick her up and cradle her to my chest. "Put your arms around my neck."

She rests her head over my pounding heart. "I just wanted you to come home," she whispers, obliterating what's left of my heart.

I want that too. I'm going to do everything in my power to make that happen. "I'm always here for you, Tiegan. Always."

"I love you, Griff."

"I love you too, sweetheart."

She settles into my chest and quickly falls asleep. Soon, we're stepping into the clearing at the edge of Erickson's Family Farm. The paramedics are already standing by and I stride towards them, Tiegan clinging to me as they check her over, refusing to let go.

A car I don't recognize pulls up and Mallory jumps out of the passenger seat, running towards me, Tanner stepping out of the driver seat and following behind, his eyes narrowed on me.

I really don't like that asshole.

＃ Chapter Forty

♡ Mallory ♡

I've never been so scared and so mad at myself for how I handled everything with the kids in my life. Because of me, my daughter ran away and ended up hurt, scared, and alone in the woods. Thank God Griffin found her when he did.

When we finally got her home, I had to promise her Griffin wouldn't leave so she would let go of him to take a bath. My chest tightens, guilt consuming me. I don't know what the right thing is anymore, but I know I feel like the worst mom in the world because of the decisions I did make.

Feeling restless as the sun begins to peek over the horizon, I tiptoe to Mia and Ollie's rooms finding them both still asleep. I'm not surprised knowing yesterday was a long day and night for all of us. I walk back into my bedroom and lean against the bedpost, staring at Tiegan curled up against Griffin's side with his arm protectively wrapped around her and his other bent above his head, as they sleep peacefully, squeezing my heart.

I don't know how to do this.

Griffin's eyes flutter open, his gaze meeting mine. "I can feel your eyes on me. Come lay with us."

"I don't know if that's a good idea."

"It's a great idea, Mal," he purrs, his voice a low grumble making me wet. Not a good time for that, Mal with your daughter in the room.

"I'm glad she's such a deep sleeper." I curl up on the other side of Tiegan, pressing a kiss to the top of her head, another tear slipping out of the corner of my eye. "I keep imagining her scared and alone in the woods."

"She's okay. She's safe and she's home. Her foot will heal and the memories will get better too."

"Thanks to you."

"We were all lookin'."

"Yeah, but you knew where to find her."

He shakes his head. "All that matters is she's right here and she's safe. Stop beating yourself up."

"But I can't help it. I really messed up, Griffin."

He reaches over with his free hand, wiping my tear away. "You're doin' just fine darlin'. Being a single mom of three kids after losing a great man the way you did, you're not only doing so much better than most could ever do, but you're killing it. Don't you dare doubt yourself for even a second. I've never met someone more incredible in every way."

"Thank you."

The corners of his lips twitch up as he adds. "Well, maybe you can doubt yourself a little for breaking up with your sexy boyfriend."

I giggle, not able to stop myself. "I'm sorry, Griffin. I just don't know what else to do. You can't promise me you would come home to us every night."

"You're right. I can't."

"But that's what I need this time."

He reaches over, brushing a loose lock of hair out of my eyes and holding my gaze. "Doesn't matter who I am or what I do Mal, no one can make that guarantee. I can promise you I will always do everything in my power to come home to you."

"But…"

He puts his finger over my lips. "No buts this time, just listen." My heart squeezes as I nod in agreement. "I promise I will love you with every single breath I take for the rest of my life and yours. And Mal, I promise you that you and I together will be more than worth it if you just give us a chance."

"Griffin…" My voice cracks as tears once again flood my eyes and he gently wipes them away.

"Because I do love you, darlin'. I love you so damn much and I don't want to lose you or the kids."

"I love you too Griffin."

"Then everything else is just background noise. So, why aren't we together?"

Instead of answering, I ask, "When do you go back to work?"

He frowns, pausing before answering. "Next week. I'm going to train here, get to know the station, the team, their routines." He shrugs. "Then when Bill retires in the middle of August, it's an easy transition for everyone.

My heart clenches terrified I'll lose him before we've even begun and I have no idea if I should take that chance.

My phone pings with a text, and I pull away, rolling over, and glancing at the screen, suddenly in need of a distraction.

Tanner: I just wanted to check in on you and Tiegan. How is she feeling?

Me: She's doing okay. She's still sleeping.

Tanner: Good. I'm sure she'll start feeling better in a few days.

Me: I hope so.

"Is everything okay? Who are you texting?"

"It's just Tanner."

"Just Tanner?" he questions, arching his eyebrows in challenge. "Do you have to talk to him right now? It's early."

"No, but I'm going to text him back anyway. He was worried."

He huffs a humorless laugh, mumbling under his breath, "Yeah, but not for the reasons you're thinking."

"Can we please not do this today, Griffin? I'm not in the mood to argue with you."

"I'm never in the mood to argue with you, unless there's the possibility of having some fun making up." He smirks.

My phone pings again and I force my focus away from the man lying in my bed.

Tanner: What about you? How are you doing? Yesterday was a rough day.

Me: Yeah it was. I'm still processing everything.

Tanner: Do you need me to come over?

Me: No. We're okay. Griffin is still here.

Tanner: He is? I thought you two broke up?

Me: We did. Tiegan wouldn't let him go. I feel like I really messed up.

Tanner: It's going to be okay.

Tanner: My parents are visiting next weekend. Do you have time to see them? They miss you.

Me: Sure, we can do that. We'll talk later.

Tanner: Sounds good.

"Everything good with Tanner?" he asks, his sarcasm thick on his tongue just as my sweet girl starts to stir.

We both focus on her as her eyes blink open. She looks up at Griffin and smiles bright, her eyes shining with happiness. "You're still here," she rasps, hugging him tight and squeezing my heart as he kisses the top of her head.

"You needed me, darlin'. I'm still here."

I bite my lower lip and hold my breath to keep from making a sound as my chest tightens. This man is everything, and every minute I spend with him, I fall more in love with him.

What am I going to do? I need some space for my head to figure out what I need. My heart is screaming like a banshee. We all know what it wants, but I'm not sure if it's what we need; what I need. My decision could impact everything like a tsunami or let it fall into place.

My hesitation has me questioning if we are two puzzle pieces that fit perfectly together or the perfect storm?

Chapter Forty One

♡ Mallory ♡

A week later Griffin is still sleeping out front in his truck when he's not working, but now my kids know he's there. Luckily, it only took a few days for Tiegan to get back on her feet since she just twisted her ankle.

After lunch, I drop my kids at Carla's, hoping to get started on preparing my classroom for the next school year. My three kids run towards the swing set in her backyard, as I stand on the back porch with her, watching. "Thank you for watching them."

"You know I love those kids like they're my own." She gets a faraway look in her eyes, pressing her lips tightly together as she stares at the kids laughing.

"You okay, Carla?"

"Yeah. Sometimes I just wonder. My baby would've been a few years older than Tiegan. I guess seeing Griffin again has brought back a lot of memories for me."

Involuntarily, I wince, the thought squeezing my heart for more than one reason. "I can't imagine how hard that was on you, and everyone else."

"You know, we might not have known, but I believed my baby was Griffin's. I was heartbroken when he told me he was leaving, so I did something stupid to get back at him. I hated myself for it for a long time. Noah is the one who brought me back to myself. Sometimes I wonder how he did that and at the same time met the love of his life when I had lost mine."

My heart drops into the pit of my stomach. "I'm sorry, Carla, I know we normally talk about everything, but I'm not comfortable talking about this."

She shakes her head and waves away my concern. "Mal, I'm not talking about Griffin. Yeah, I loved him, but I'm talking about our baby."

I open my mouth to argue, but snap it shut the moment I see the tears in her eyes. "I know I messed up when it came to him, but he always wanted a big family. When I found out I was pregnant, I thought for just a moment that maybe I could have it all."

She pulls out her necklace tucked into her shirt and grasps it tight. "My baby would almost be twelve. Noah got me this when I was really struggling, reminding me that our baby would never be forgotten and to always keep an open mind and an open heart."

My heart skips a beat, remembering the rose quartz. "What is it?" I ask, my voice shaking.

She looks at me, forcing a smile as she opens her fist, a small pink rose quartz on a rose gold chain resting in the palm of her hand. "It's a rose quartz crystal in memory of my baby."

"Um…" My heart stops and I feel the blood draining from my face. Was the crystal from her? She told me she didn't give it to me. Was she lying?

Her eyebrows draw down in concern. "Mal, are you okay? You look a little pale."

As she moves towards me, I step back, stumbling over the chair behind me. "I'm, ah, I'm okay," I stammer, righting myself.

"You don't look okay. Maybe you should sit down."

"No. I'm okay. You have so much on your mind though, maybe I should just take the kids and go. We can do this another time."

"Why not today? I love spending time with my nieces and nephew. These are my favorite days. Besides, I have nothing going on today."

I'm overreacting. This is Noah's sister. I need to take a breath and calm down. "I think it's just my time of the month."

She laughs, shaking her head. "Well, I relate to that. I'm sorry for dumping everything on you. Noah would always check on me this time of year and now no one does. It's been thirteen years since I lost the baby."

"I'm sorry," I reiterate. It has to just be a coincidence.

She tucks the necklace back in her shirt. "I promise I'm okay to watch the kids. I just needed someone to talk to and taking care of them is exactly what I need. Please?"

"Yeah, okay."

"Besides, don't you have all that stuff to do at school?"

"I do. My classroom is a mess. Tanner said he would meet me there and help me out."

She grins. "That man is so good to you."

"He's a good friend."

She smirks but doesn't comment. "The kids will be fine. I promise I'm okay and the color is starting to return to your cheeks."

"Yeah, I should probably go. Thanks for watching them, Carla."

"You're welcome."

"Bye guys. I love you!"

Without looking in my direction, my kids respond with a chorus of, "Love you, Mom!"

I wave and walk back to my car, sliding in behind the wheel, my thoughts all over the place as I make the short drive to school. As I pull into the parking lot, I spot Tanner's lone car and park next to him right in front of the main entrance. Pulling out my phone, I send him a quick text.

Me: I'm here.

Moments, later, Tanner strides out of school and waves as he walks up to my car, opening my door for me. "Are you getting out or did you just come to say hi."

Shaking my head, I huff a laugh. "No, I'm coming."

I climb out of the car, Tanner's eyebrows instantly drawing down in concern. "Everything okay? Kids good?"

"Yeah, I'm sorry, Tanner. I'm okay."

He step up to me and reaches for me, wrapping me in his arms. I settle into his embrace, squeezing him back. "You sure about that?"

"You really do know me."

"Yeah, I do. So, what's going on?"

He kisses the top of my head. "It's fine. I'm just in my head. I dropped the kids off at Carla's."

"Okay…" he prompts, dragging out the word.

"It's just we were talking and she started talking about something she's never really talked to me about before."

"Why is that so bad?"

"It's not, but she completely threw me off. I'm not sure what to think."

"Why don't you run it by me? Maybe I can give you some good advice."

"Sure." I'm not about to tell him everything. A lot of it isn't my story to tell, but I need to talk to someone about this and there's no way Matt would remain neutral with who it involves. I push back and his arms loosen, his hands giving me a gentle squeeze in support before he completely lets me go. "How about we grab a couple boxes and go inside and talk?"

"Tell me what you want me to carry."

"Thanks." I point out a couple boxes to Tanner, and pick up one myself, following him inside. I'm grateful Tanner has keys to get me into the building so I can work when I need to instead of on the principal's schedule.

"Let's set these down and then we can talk in the main office and raid the fridge in the teacher's lounge."

I laugh. "Too bad there won't be anything in there."

"Don't be too sure about that, Mal. I may have filled it up knowing you would be setting up your classroom."

We set the boxes down in my room and I look at him and smile. "Thank you, Tanner. That's so sweet of you."

"It's no problem."

He follows me out of my room, his arm going around me. "So, tell me what happened with Carla that has you off your rocker."

I shove at him playfully, making him laugh. "I'm not off my rocker, just a little unsettled, I guess."

"Why?"

Heaving a sigh, I shrug my shoulders, piecing together what I want to reveal.

"Here." He hands me an iced tea, taking one for himself as we sit down next to each other, spinning our chairs to face each other.

"Thanks." I take a drink and set it down on the table. Glancing at him, I ask, "Do you remember when I asked you about the rose quartz?"

"Rose quartz?" he echoes, quirking a brow.

"Yes, the crystal thing someone left on my doorstep?"

"Oh, yeah. What about it?"

"She had a necklace with a much smaller version, reminding her of someone she lost a long time ago and Noah was the one who gave it to her."

His eyes widen in surprise. "Huh. Do you think she was the one that gave it to you?"

"Maybe, but she denied it."

"And because of it, you're questioning if she did any of the other things like your tires, or the letters." He nods in understanding.

"I guess, but it seems stupid hearing it out loud." I frown.

His hand runs over his jaw in thought before he leans towards me, resting his elbows on his knees. "Why would you even think she could do the other things to you? She's your sister-in-law and I don't see you having those thoughts blindly."

My gaze drops and I spin in my seat. "I'm not."

"Mal, it feels like I'm pulling teeth here. Talk to me." Reaching out he squeezes my knee in encouragement.

I peek at him from underneath my long eyelashes, watching his reaction. "I'm not sure she's really over him."

"Him, who? Griffin?"

Sitting back, I roll my eyes. "Yes, Griffin."

"Did you ask her?"

I flinch. "No, it got weird, so I convinced myself I'm blowing this up, but honestly I'm not so sure. They had a really tough breakup, and this is the first time they really saw each other or talked in like thirteen years."

His eyes widen. "That's a long time."

"Yeah, it is."

"Well, honestly, I'd feel better knowing it was her that did those things to you, instead of some asshole."

Pushing his hand away, my eyes narrow and I cross my arms over my chest, challenging his insinuation.

"What? Guys can be assholes." His gaze shifts dramatically to my cleavage and slowly drags back up my body. Meeting my eyes, he gives me a salacious smile.

I smack him in the arm. "Okay, you made your point."

"Look, I just don't know if she would really hurt you. Even though he's gone, you were married to her brother and she loves your kids." He smirks, adding, "Besides, the guy couldn't be that great."

I bite my lower lip, refusing to respond. "You're right, but the idea that she would do this to me still hurts, Tanner."

He sighs, giving me a look, I can't quite decipher as he reaches for my hands, giving them a squeeze. "I know, Mal, but sometimes people do stupid things when they're in love with someone."

"You think she's in love with him?"

He shrugs. "If I know you, you'll talk to her and figure it out. You two will be okay, even if it was her."

"Maybe you're right."

"But," he mumbles, dragging out the word, "I heard they were a pretty hot item when they were together, I wouldn't be surprised if she did still have feelings."

I narrow my eyes at him. "That doesn't help Tanner."

He grips my hands tighter, holding my gaze. "I'm just saying, if she does have feelings for him, maybe she'll back off you since you two are no longer together. I'd be okay with that as long as you're safe."

My chest tightens. "Yeah, maybe." I heave a sigh and push up from my chair, feeling even more off-kilter than I did before I talked to him.

Chapter Forty Two

♡ *Mallory* ♡

Tanner walks into my classroom carrying two more boxes. "Where do you want me to put these?"

I point to the wall by the door. "Anywhere along that wall is fine. Thank you. You didn't have to unload my car for me. I would've gotten more stuff after I finished with all of these boxes.

"It's no big deal. I needed more of a workout this morning." I chuckle, shaking my head knowing he's just saying that so I don't feel so bad. "Do you ever wonder why you have to move out every year when we know you're coming back to the same place?"

I laugh. "Yeah, I know, but it never gets this clean for the rest of the year no matter how hard we all try."

"Very true."

"At least I'm in the same classroom, so I know where I want everything to go and I know it will all fit." I grin, shrugging.

He smiles. "Well, I always thought this room had the best view."

My gaze veers towards the windows, glancing out at the grassy fields next to the school. "Hm, I never thought about that."

Tanner steps up behind me, his hot breath on my neck gives me goosebumps as he whispers, "I do every single day."

I flush, reaching for my desk calendar to keep myself busy. Clearing my throat, I try changing the subject. "I'm really looking forward to seeing your parents this weekend. It's been a while."

Placing my calendar in the middle of my desk, I take my time straightening it before spinning around to grab my box of pens. I yelp in surprise finding Tanner stepping into my space.

"I'm sorry, Mallory, I didn't mean to scare you," he states, but he doesn't take a step back. Reaching up, he tucks a loose lock of my hair that had fallen from my ponytail behind my ear, making me blush and leaving me on edge. He doesn't do things like that, so why is he now? "How are you doing?"

My breathing picks up and I put my hand up, moving backwards, and bump into my desk. Tanner remains a half step back, allowing me to breathe and relax. "I'm doing okay."

"You seem to be doing better."

Nodding, I give him a comforting smile. "I am. There's been so much on my mind with what happened with Tiegan and now Carla. Plus, school starting again soon for all of us." I purposely leave off the one man consuming my thoughts, hoping he won't want to talk about it; about him anymore.

"Tiegan appears like she's rebounded well. She's a warrior with everything she's been through. I'm proud of her."

A smile tugs at my lips. "I love that description of her."

"It's true, Mal. She's just like her mom."

My cheeks heat. "Thanks Tanner." He nods and everything he's done for me over the years suddenly rushes through my mind. Reaching for his hand I give it a squeeze and hold his gaze, needing him to know how grateful I am for what he's done for me. "No, I mean thank you for everything. Not just the sweet things you say about my kids, or me, but you've always been there for me, Tanner. You protected me from the bullies at school when we were kids, you defended my honor when I dated an asshole in high school and you supported me when I met Noah and was pregnant with Tiegan."

He chuckles, shrugging like it's no big deal. "You know I would do anything for you, Mallory."

My chest tightens, but not the way it does when Griffin would say things like that. I know I can't compare anyone to him, but I don't believe that means I have to spend the rest of my life alone. Maybe Tanner really does love me and the kids. I guess it's true that the look in his eyes lately hints at wanting more than friendship. Would it be so bad to date someone safe? Someone who's always been a good friend? Someone that couldn't shatter my heart? Someone who doesn't put their life at risk every day just by doing their job? Someone like Tanner? Maybe my heart would eventually feel different if we took that step.

"You didn't run away when I was at my absolute worst two years ago. I don't think I would've gotten through all of that without you."

"I believe you would've made it through to the other side. You're the strongest woman I know."

"Thanks, for saying that but I'm telling you this because I need you to know that I'm always here for you too, Tanner."

Sighing heavily, he shakes his head and closes the distance between us, a small smile curving his lips. My breathing picks up and I tilt my head back to look up at him, my eyebrows drawn down in confusion. "No, Mallory, you don't get what I'm saying to you. Yes, I'm always here for you and that will never change, but I would do anything for you and your kids. Don't you understand that by now?"

"Of course, I do."

"Then give this a chance," he pleads, framing my face with his hands. I gasp, just before his lips brush mine. He kisses me and for a moment, I kiss him back, shocked, confused, and feeling nothing but hate for myself.

What am I doing?

His phone rings, and I pull back, slightly stunned. He straightens, looking down at me as he reaches for his phone, glancing at the screen. "It's just my mom. I can call her later." He moves to set his phone down.

Reaching up, I grab his arm to stop him, needing a moment to pull myself together. "Tanner, no, it's okay. Answer the call. What if they need something before they come tomorrow?"

He sighs, and steps back, putting his phone to his ear. "Hi, Mom."

Standing frozen, I listen to his side of the conversation, my thoughts racing. He grins wide, glancing in my direction. "I'm actually helping Mal set up her classroom right now, Mom, so I can't really talk." He pauses nodding. "Yeah, she's excited to see you too." I watch as he pauses again, his eyes remaining on me. "I'll give her a hug for you and we'll see you tomorrow." He disconnects and sets his phone down on top of one of the boxes.

"What did your mom want?" I ask, suddenly feeling like this reunion is much more than just seeing people I used to know.

He grins wide. "She asked if they were still going to be able to see you. She got you something and wants to bring it with her."

My eyes widen in surprise. "Really?"

"Apparently." He shrugs like it's no big deal. "They've always loved you, Mal and I guess with what happened with your parents in college, they're like me and feel protective of you."

"Wow. That's so sweet. They've always been so good to me, but..."

"It's hard not to love you, Mal."

"Tanner...I...um..." I stammer, not sure what to say, my body slowly heating from head to toe.

"You're cute when you blush."

"I don't think this is a good idea."

"Why not? I think we are a great idea. Don't you think it's about time I stepped all the way up. I've been fighting for you since we were kids, Mal. I've always jumped whenever you or the kids have needed me, only asking how high because you mean the world to me. Give me a chance to be there for all the rest. Please?"

My eyes widen, my palms sweat and my heart begins to race. "What? Tanner, we've been friends for so long."

"Yeah, we have. I'm the one who's been your friend since we were kids. I've stuck by you through everything. All the highs and lows, I've been the one who has been there for you because I love you, Mal."

I shake my head, my chest tightening, overwhelmed. This is not happening. It's not supposed to be this way.

Grabbing my face in his hands, he looks into my eyes, his own frantic, pleading. "I love you so much it hurts. Please, Mallory, give me a chance. Give us a chance. Noah is gone. You dated Griffin and he couldn't be the man you needed, but I can be that for you. It's my turn. I'm the one who won't leave you."

Without giving me a chance to respond, he presses his lips to mine, his tongue diving in as I gasp. His hard length presses into me, prompting a wave of guilt to wash over me. I try pulling my head back but he holds my head in place, kissing me hard. Demanding. Begging with his lips.

What the hell?

Planting my hands on his chest, I shove him hard and he stumbles back, finally breaking the kiss. With tears in my eyes, I gasp for breath. "Tanner, I'm sorry, but I can't do this."

"You can't do this," he repeats, his eyes narrowing as he lets go of my face and grabs my hands. "Why not? Are you going back to *him*?"

"What? I don't know, but I can't do this."

"You don't know," he mutters, scoffing. "He's a cop, Mal! Do you really want to do that again? I remember what it was like for you."

"You think I don't remember? I *lived* that nightmare and I still do every single day," I emphasize, punctuating each word.

"Then let me help you through this. Don't go back to the guy who would rather do a job than be with you and the kids."

"That's not fair. I would never ask him to do that."

"He shouldn't matter. I'm right here and I love you. What the hell do I have to do to get you to notice me?"

"I do notice you, Tanner. You're one of my best friends, but you don't choose who you fall in love with."

His mouth drops open and he gasps, rearing back as if I punched him. "What did you just say?"

Chapter Forty Three

♡ Griffin ♡

If I have to watch that asshole show up to her house one more fucking time, I just might lose my shit. I'm not sleeping now, what happens when I start working nights? In a matter of days, I'll be on nights just to get to know the guys better and their regular routines better. Then what?

Does he really have to hug her every time he sees her? Now they're at school together alone?

Forget it, I've already lost it. I'm running it through my head like they're fucking in the principal's office. I need to think and stop acting like a jealous asshole.

"Everything okay, Lieutenant?"

"What?" I glance over to the driver's seat, Officer Brian Channing glancing in my direction before focusing back on the road.

"I just said that the staff will be here more often again. The principal let us know they started setting up the school for fall. Then I asked if everything was okay."

"Yeah, sorry."

"Isn't that Mallory's car?"

I quirk my brow and nod my head. "Yeah."

"Well, I just heard you two were dating. She deserves the best."

"Damn right she does."

He nods and we continue circling town, writing a few tickets for traffic violations, but the day relatively uneventful. That's the way it should be after so much chaos, especially in this damn heat. I asked questions about different people in town and new business that have popped up since I lived here. Honestly, I never really paid much attention while I was in and out of town visiting. We stopped in to visit a few businesses and the day really gave me a good overview. I still have some people I want to talk to, but the day was mostly a success. Progress with Mallory is the one thing that could make it better. "Thanks for letting me ride along today."

My phone vibrates in my pocket and I pull it out, glancing at the screen, Matt's name lighting it up. I lift my phone to my ear. "Detective, please tell me you have something."

"Detective? Forget it, I don't have time for that bullshit. I'm on my way to talk to Tanner Pratt and I thought you would want to know."

"What did you find?"

"Let's just say you were right about him."

"Matt," I prod, desperate for details.

"Did you know he went to the same college as Mallory and followed her here? It looks like he threatened the superintendent at the time to get the job. He's remained under the radar until now, but he's always been around. Noah was never a fan of him either, but he never could pinpoint why."

"My heart pounds in my chest. Did you find anything with his writing? Compare the letters."

"The last one was legit, but I believe the other two were from him. I had an analyst look them over."

"They're at the school," I interrupt. "Mallory is with him at school."

The static on the radio just before I hear dispatch leaves a sour taste in my stomach as if I'm anticipating the worst, and then it happens.

♡ Mallory ♡

My own words ring in my head. You don't choose who you fall in love with. Am I really in love with Griffin? I know I already love him, but am I in love with him? How will I ever move on if that's the case?

"Are you kidding me?" Tanner presses my hands to the desk behind me, his jaw clenching. "You're in love with him? What about me?"

His question hits its mark and I try to remind myself Tanner is hurting and it's my fault. "I'm sorry Tanner. I love you, but not like that."

"You're sorry?" He growls, fuming. "Why did you have to kiss me if you didn't fucking mean it, Mal? You're doing the same thing you did back in high school."

"What are you talking about?"

Shaking his head, he looks at me with pure disbelief, He presses my hands further into the desk causing me to arch my back to alleviate some of the pain and focus on him. "Do you like fucking with me?"

"Of course not! I don't know what you're talking about," I insist, taking a deep breath. "Tanner, you're hurting me."

He huffs a humorless laugh. "You don't think this hurts me?"

"No, my hands, you're hurting my hands."

Flinching, he mutters an apology, "Sorry." Releasing me, he continues, "So let me see if I have this right," he begins, barely backing away. "You find out he's been lying to you this whole time, first about Noah, then about Carla and then about going back to being a cop."

Shaking my head, I insist, "He told me about Noah and Carla, just not right away, but I understand why."

He gives me a pointed look. "Not until he had no choice but to tell you. And you break up with him because he lied again. Yet, you still want to go back to that prick?"

"It's not like that. He didn't lie. I knew he was a cop."

"Why are you defending him? You didn't know he applied to transfer to the Piper Falls police station. Isn't that the same as lying? Do you want what happened with Noah to happen to you again? You want to put your kids through that torture?"

"No!" I wince, shaking my head. "You know it's not like that," I cry, my eyes welling with tears once again.

Silently, he stands staring at me, a range of emotions passing over his features. His body sags as he sighs in defeat, stepping closer. "I hate seeing you in so much pain. I'm just trying to help, Mal and you're fighting me every step of the way." Heaving a sigh, he holds out his arms, waving me towards him. "Come here."

Wiping my tears away, I step into his familiar embrace, guilt overwhelming me. "I wish things could be different. Things would be so much easier if they were."

"That's all I want is to make things easier; make things better." He squeezes me tighter, inhaling deeply.

"I'm sorry, Tanner."

"Me too, Mal. Me too."

I feel him playing with my hair when suddenly I'm yanked back by my ponytail, making me gasp, my head slamming into my desk before my world goes black.

Chapter Forty Four

♡ Mallory ♡

Squinting, I attempt to open my eyes, but the bright light keeps them sealed shut. My head is pounding and my stomach churns. I move to lift my head, finding my cheek wet and sticky. Was I drooling? I try lifting my hand towards my face, but I can't move, triggering the memory of Tanner's face and his look of anger and betrayal just before I passed out.

Gasping, my eyes fly open as reality quickly sets in, Tanner squeezing my heart in the palm of his hand with the devastation of his betrayal. My head rests on my desk, my hands and feet tied to my chair.

Tanner paces back and forth, running his hand through his hair and muttering under his breath. "What am I gonna do? This wasn't supposed to happen."

Slightly stunned, I attempt to clear my thoughts and think about everything Noah taught me about protecting myself. Quietly, I try to assess my situation without bringing Tanner's attention to me. Carefully, I wiggle my hands and feet, testing how much room I have to get out of this mess. It's not much, but if I keep working, I can do this.

Tiegan, Ollie and Mia flash in my mind, eliciting a whimper from my lips. Tanner instantly halts and crouches down in front of me, tenderly pushing my hair back. "You're awake. How are you feeling?"

My eyes narrow. "Do you really care? You did this to me."

"Of course, I care, Mal. I love you." I snort, the movement making me flinch in agony. "Be careful. I don't want you to hurt yourself any worse."

"Why did you hurt me at all?"

"I didn't mean to. I swear, I didn't. Sometimes my temper gets the best of me. I'm usually good at controlling it, but…" He scrunches up his face in displeasure. "I'm just glad you're okay."

"But I'm not okay, Tanner. I'm hurt and I can't move."

His eyebrows draw down in concern. "I cleaned up your cut. I'm sorry about that, it was an accident. But you will be okay."

"Why am I tied up?"

"I was afraid you would run when you woke up, but they're not too tight, so it shouldn't hurt. I didn't know what else to do."

"Get me some help."

He shakes his head. "You don't need it. I'm here."

"Why are you doing this?"

Ignoring my question, he readjusts my restraints, moving them from the desk to the chair so I'm able to sit back. "There, that should feel more comfortable."

"I need to get up."

He frowns. "I'm sorry, but I can't do that, not until we talk."

My eyes widen in surprise. "You just want to talk?"

His hands go to my knees, his eyes pleading. "This wasn't supposed to happen, Mal. I've been patient. I waited for you for so damn long. This was supposed to be our chance." His hands slide up my thighs.

I shake my head. "No, Tanner."

He flinches. "No? Don't you think I've been tested enough, watching you strut around town with your rebound fuck? Living in sin with him? I can't believe you want to go back to that asshole. Why in the hell would you date another cop?"

"Tanner, please."

"Please, what? You want something else from me, Mal? You always take, take, take from me and you never give me anything in return. Don't you think it's time you give me something?"

I open my mouth to respond but my heart sinks, realizing there's no point. The dark look in his eyes turns my stomach. I shouldn't have let him kiss me or kissed him back. It's my fault he's feeling like this, now I have to figure out how to get out of it. "I'm sorry, Tanner."

"You're sorry? There's no reason to be sorry if you open your damn eyes. I'm the one who's been there all along."

"I wish it were that easy."

Standing over me, he places his one hand on each side of me. Narrowing his eyes, he punctuates each word as he speaks. "It. Fucking. Is!"

"Please, just let me go. We can figure this out."

He huffs a laugh. "You want to figure this out? Do you know that I waited for you? I bided my time, watching on the sidelines while other men asked you out, and practically threw themselves at you. I'm the one who's always here, protecting you, loving you and it's still not enough for you. I'm never enough for you."

"That's not true." I shake my head, continuing to wiggle my hands, scraping them on the zip tie as I try to get them free.

He quirks a brow, leaning closer. "Isn't it? I'm the one who's there, I leave you a gift to open your heart to me and instead you open your legs to that man whore."

I gasp, his admission slamming into me. "You left the rose quartz?"

"Of course, I did. I'm always thinking of you, Mal. I bought you the roses for the same reason. You deserve nice things and I want to be the one to give them to you. And of course, roses represent love." He shrugs, looking almost shy.

"Why didn't you sign a card? Or tell me when you knew I was scared, with no clue where any of it came from. In fact, you lied to me about the crystal."

"I didn't want to, but I had no choice because you were still with him. You weren't ready to be with me yet."

"And you think I will be now? After this?"

He grimaces and looks away, his eyes watery. I shift my feet while his eyes are averted, freezing anytime his gaze returns to me. "You can forgive me. I haven't done anything wrong, not really. It was an accident. And besides, you have a good heart. You know I only want what's best for you."

"If that's true, then let me go and I'll forgive you."

Turning back to me, he demands, "Show me you'll fight for us and I'll let you go."

Grabbing my ponytail, he wraps it around his hand and holds me in place, pressing his face into my neck and inhaling deeply. His free hand trails up my side, cupping my breast.

"Tanner, please."

"That's right but say my name with more confidence."

I press my lips together, refusing, tears forming in my eyes. I'm confused how we got here and terrified I'm gonna' lose this fight. I can't let that happen.

He yanks my ponytail back a little further and licks my neck. "Damn you taste good. Just let me in and we'll be just fine. I know you want me darlin'."

A choked sob leaves my lips. "It doesn't work that way, Tanner."

"This was our chance, Mallory! All you had to do is take it! Groaning in frustration, he releases me and pushes away, muttering, "Doesn't really matter, I'm fucked now, aren't I?"

I shake my head. "No."

"You're either with me or you're not, and it doesn't seem like you are, Mal. After all this time I dedicated to you. Why couldn't you just give me a taste to make it all worth it?"

"Tanner, just let me go."

Ignoring me, he continues, "Do you remember the first time you kissed me, Mal? It was a couple weeks after that asshole broke your heart. We were at a party and I brought you home. You made out with me for hours." He grins, licking his lips. "But as soon as you had me reeled in, you told me it was too soon for a relationship. Then you go and meet Noah." His eyes flash and his dark laugh erupts. "I think I've been patient enough. I can't go through that again. No more waiting. I deserve to have you. Don't you think?"

"Tanner, my kids need me. Please."

"Darlin', don't worry. I would never hurt you."

"You're hurting me now."

He shakes his head, my accusation wounding him. "I am sorry about your tires, though. My temper got the best of me."

My eyes widen. "You slashed my tires?"

He winces, a haze passing through his eyes. "I was pissed. You betrayed me. I give you a gift, and you repay me by fucking another man. You were supposed to date a couple of the other men who were asking you out and realize what you had with me was priceless. Instead, you push them away and date that asshole and practically maul him on your front porch with your kids just inside. A hell of a role model, don't you think?" He curls his lips in disgust.

"And that makes it okay to slash my tires? Were you trying to scare me? What about the letters? Did you write those, too? The ones you pushed me to give to the police?"

His lips twitch. "Nah, I wouldn't do that to you. Didn't the guy sign them?"

"Just the last one, you know that." I don't know if I believe him, but why would he do that to me? And why is he doing this? "We've been friends our entire life." How did I not see this coming?

He throws his hands up in the air, emphasizing his point. "Exactly! I'm always the friend, but I'm the one you depend on. It's like being your husband without any fucking benefits and I can't take it anymore. I want you Mal."

Finally, I maneuver my hands free, wiggling them to get the circulation going. "You have to let me go, Tanner."

"I can't. I've waited too long. You're supposed to be mine. I thought I lost you for a while, but when Noah died, that was our second chance. I just have to figure out what to do." He returns to pacing, giving me enough time to finally get my feet free.

My eyes skim over my desk, spotting my scissors just before he steps closer to me.

"I'm sorry." The moment he has his back turned, use all my strength to push up. As he turns towards me, using my back leg for leverage, I lift my front leg as hard and fast as I can between his legs.

"Fuck!" He grunts in pain, his hands reflexively going to his balls as he falls to the floor, instantly pale.

I swipe my phone, keys and scissors off my desk, stumbling for the exit. Tanner sweeps my feet just before I reach the door and I go flying, hitting my chin and my hands, my teeth coming down hard on my lower lip, my phone and scissors slipping out of my right hand. The coppery taste of blood hits my tongue as I use my free leg to try to kick at him, hitting him in the face twice before he pins both legs down with his body and slithers up, my hands continuing to swing, not giving up. I'll never give up.

"Why are you doing this, Mal? Don't fight me. Fucking stop! I don't want to hurt you."

"Just let me go!"

"No, I'm never letting you go. I'm done waiting, Mal. I'm fucking done. I've waited long enough. I can't do this without you anymore. You're mine. You were always meant to be mine."

"But this isn't the way to do it with me." I flip my key open, still clenched in my left hand and swing it towards him, plunging it into his side and twisting.

"Ah!" he screams, loosening his grip enough that I'm able to scramble up a few inches to grab my phone, quickly tapping 9-1-1 and praying the service is good enough for the call to go through, but call failed quickly flashes on the screen. I retry just as he yanks me back towards him.

"Tanner, let me go!" I scream again at the top of my lungs, the decibel momentarily stunning him, his eyes going wide.

"Shit, what did I do? Mal I'm so sorry. I'm so fucking sorry. I didn't mean to hurt you." He scrambles up my body, pinning me and checking my face. "I'll take good care of you, darlin'. It's okay."

Silent tears stream down my face. "It's not okay, Tanner. My kids."

Ignoring me, he stands, holding me tight as I squirm, but he keeps taking my hits, stumbling into his office and locking the door behind him before letting me go. Shaking my head, I scramble, getting my feet underneath me and stumble away from him to the corner of the room. He stares at me with a soft look of concern, a look I'm more familiar with tinged with fear.

"I'm so sorry, Mallory. I love you. I love you so damn much baby. Please forgive me. I didn't mean to hurt you."

"You can't force me to love you!"

"I didn't! You told me you loved me."

"Not like that, Tanner. I'm sorry, but not like that."

Sirens sound in the distance, but I hold back my sigh of relief knowing this isn't over. "Fuck!" he screams sweeping everything off his desk in one swift motion, his computer slamming against the opposite wall making me flinch.

"How did I fuck this up so bad? I went from having you in my arms to this? It wasn't supposed to be like this. We aren't supposed to be like this" He unlocks his desk drawer and pulls out a small black handgun eliciting a gasp from my lips. He looks at me, meeting my gaze. "I'm not going to let anyone hurt you, even me."

He lifts the gun to his head and I jump up, screaming, "No!"

His eyebrows draw down in confusion. "Why the fuck not? My life is over. It's nothing without you."

"That's not true. You're really good at your job."

Shaking his head, he huffs a humorless laugh. "You know I'll never be able to work here again, or with kids at all; not after this."

"What about your parents? They're going to be here tomorrow. They love you."

"But you don't."

"Not the way you want me to, but I do."

"No, you don't. You'll never be able to forgive me."

"You know me better than that. You just need help, Tanner. I want to get you some help."

A tear leaks out of the corner of his eye. "It wasn't supposed to be this way. I really do love you, Mal." Closing his eyes, he sighs, handing me his keys. "Get the fuck out before I do something I regret."

I hesitate for just a moment before slipping out and running towards the front doors.

The sound of a gunshot rings in my ears startling me as I fall through the door and hit the ground sobbing as a police car and Matt's Charger screech to a halt at the end of the walkway. Welcome footsteps pound on the pavement coming towards me as I close my eyes wondering how everything went so wrong.

"Mal! Fuck, please be okay."

"Griff," I whimper as he pulls me into his arms, checking me over. "I'm okay, but Tanner," I cry, pointing towards the school.

"Let's go," Matt urges.

Chapter Forty Five

♡ *Griffin* ♡

The memory of seeing Mallory just outside the Piper Falls Elementary School doors dropped to the ground in tears plays like a reel of my nightmare in my head, haunting me. My heart stopped the moment I saw her. I didn't think I could get to her fast enough, terrified something had happened to her. The sight of blood on her face, her mouth, her hands and who knows where else, not able to focus, sent me off the rails. Frantic, I checked her over, making sure she was okay. She's banged up in more ways than one, but she'll be fine.

Forcing myself to walk away from her to make sure she was out of danger, was one of the hardest things I've ever had to do, but her safety always comes first. We walked in, calling out, guns drawn, but the asshole was passed out on his office floor after shooting himself in the foot, apparently an accident as he moved to put the gun away. I've never wanted to kill anyone more than I did him, but getting back to Mallory was the most important thing. Matt arrested him, the physical and emotional mess of his betrayal left behind.

Insisting she was okay, Mallory put off the paramedics taking her in until she gave us a report, wanting to get it over with. I don't blame her, but to hear what she went through feels like a stab to my fucking heart. I'm so proud of my girl; Noah taught her well.

Since we left school grounds, I haven't let go of Mallory unless I had to, but I'd give anything to help pull her out of this state of shock.

Luckily Matt explained the situation so I'm not putting my new job in jeopardy, but I would've stayed with her no matter the result. She's what's important. I remained by her side at the hospital while they stitched up her chin, everything else just cuts and bruises, although I'm sure they hurt like hell.

I take her home, thankful her kids are staying with Carla. My lips brush across the top of her head, inhaling her sweet scent as I lay her down on her bed. She clings to me as I move to stand. "I'm right here, Mal. It's going to be okay. I'm just going to help you get more comfortable."

"Thank you," she whimpers.

Looking through her dresser, I pull out a black graphic t-shirt and a pair of her white cotton shorts she likes to wear around the house. As I tug off her shoes and drop them to the floor, I rub my thumbs along the bottom, hoping to alleviate some of the ache. "Here." I hand her the clothes and press my lips to her forehead, turning to walk out of the room.

"Don't go."

I nod, keeping my back to her while she changes.

"Okay, I'm dressed."

She scoots back and pats the mattress next to her. Without question, I kick off my shoes and climb onto her bed, pulling her into my arms.

Finally, she's starting to calm. Her breathing has slowed, her heartbeat returning to a normal pace as she curls into my chest. My hand runs up and down her back, attempting to soothe us both, while my other arm holds on tight. "I'm here as long as you want me to be, Mal."

"You promise, he's really okay?"

I flinch, hating that she's so concerned about him. "Yeah, he will be, but he's not getting away with what he did to you."

"He needs help."

"He'll get it."

"I guess you were right about him."

"I've never wanted to be more wrong. I'm sorry you lost your friend."

She frowns, a tear escaping out of the corner of her eye. "Thanks. Apparently I lost him a long time ago. I just never realized. What am I going to tell the kids?"

"Mal," I sigh, feeling her pain.

She waves her hand, attempting to brush it off. "At least we know the truth about everything and now we're all safe. Well, as safe as we can be anyway."

"What can I do to help ease your worry?"

She shakes her head. "Nothing. You've done everything you can, Griffin; even things I didn't want you to do."

"You mean the cameras? The security system?"

"Yeah, but I'm glad you did it."

I nod, my chest tight remembering the hours when Tiegan was missing. "Yeah, me too."

"How do you ever know, Griff? I've known Tanner most of my life, so how do I know if my instincts are good or complete shit?"

My heart clenches, feeling her pain. "Sometimes you don't. But with Tanner, you stood up to him when it mattered most. You pushed back when you needed to. I'm so damn proud of you, Mal. I'm sorry you had to go through it and fight him, but you're a damn warrior."

She gives me a sad smile. "Thanks. There was no way I was letting him win, not with my kids." She chokes up, gulping down the lump in her throat. "I'm just happy I'm okay."

"What I'm feeling right now…happy is an understatement darlin'."

She presses her lips to my chest, my heart skipping a beat. "I keep thinking that if something like that can happen with someone I've known my whole life, in my classroom at the elementary school in this small town—it truly can happen anywhere."

My eyes close, desperate to protect her and the kids, but I've seen my share of tragedy. "Unfortunately, that's true, but we can sure as hell do our best to prevent the worst from happening and that's exactly what you did. You're safe. Your kids are safe. Your daughter might say you're a knight in shining armor." A small smile lights up her face making it easier to breathe again. "So much cooler than a prince."

She huffs a laugh. "I always liked prince charming."

The corners of my lips curve up in a smile as I press a kiss to the top of her head. "That works in my favor."

She settles, curling back into me and resting her head on my chest. A soft sigh escapes just before she whispers, "I'm thankful you're safe too."

Taking a deep breath, I inhale her sweet scent and squeeze, holding her tight while she lets me and hoping it never has to end. "I'm safe too, Mal."

"Griff?"

"Yeah, darlin'?"

"I have something to tell you."

My heart stops, worry seeping into my pores. "Yeah?"

"Today, it was my fault."

My eyes widen and I turn her to face me, holding her gaze. "No, darlin', it wasn't your fault."

She shakes her head, refusing to believe me. "It was. I did something that started it all. Something I regret."

My breath catches in my throat. "There's nothing you could've done that would've made any of that your fault."

"I kissed him."

My body stiffens and I struggle to breathe.

"I knew it was a mistake right away, but it was too late. I triggered his confession and our fight. If–"

"It still would've happened sooner or later. I think the letters prove that don't you?"

"The letters?"

"He wrote the letters?"

"The unsigned ones," I confirm with a nod.

More tears slip out of the corner of her eyes. "I'm sorry, Griffin."

"I may hate it, but you didn't do anything wrong."

"Do you think that maybe we should try again?"

My heart skips a beat, filling with hope. "You already know my answer to that question. What are you really trying to ask me?"

"I'm scared, Griffin. I'm terrified of losing you or even the kids." She bites her lower lip and lets it slide through her teeth, driving me crazy.

"Mallory, being scared can be healthy, as long as you don't let it control you or your life. Use it to your advantage, like you did today."

"But I fought him without even thinking."

"Exactly. You are incredibly smart, strong, and determined. Your courage and tenacity helps you do things others can't. You're independent and confident without even thinking. Those are only a few of the reasons I've fallen in love with you."

"I love you too, and I don't want you to stop doing what you love to be with me because to me that feels like I'm disrespecting you, but I don't know how to be part of Station 28 again, let alone being with a cop again."

"I know you'd never ask."

"No, I wouldn't let you." She frowns, her eyebrows drawn down in thought. "Then again, I know that the station and everyone there never stopped being a part of me or my family. Going there the other day almost felt like coming home at first. But mostly, I don't want to do this without you."

"Are you sure about that?"

"You are one thing I am sure about and after today, I know I don't want to throw that away for something that might happen."

My heart squeezes and I clench my jaw, trying to get my emotions under control. "So, you know what I want, but in case you forgot, I want you, Mallory. And I want Tiegan, and Ollie and Mia. I want the highs and the lows. I want the happiness and the tears. I want it all, but I only want it with you."

A tear runs down her cheek. "I want everything with you, too. But I'm not exactly ready to jump in the deep end."

"So, you're saying I have to move out?" I tease, my lips quirking up as I closely watch her reaction.

Ignoring me, she questions, "Griffin, what do we do?"

Tipping my head towards her, I brush my lips across her forehead and tilt her head up to look into her eyes. "We take it slow while we work through what happened today and I start back to work. Plus, school starts soon." My heart stutters at the thought of her back at the same school, in the same classroom Tanner attacked her and she defeated him.

"Griffin?" she asks, lifting her head to get my attention.

"Just thinking about school."

She frowns. "Oh, yeah, school."

"You want to go back?"

She nods, giving me a sign of her familiar confidence. "Of course, I do."

My lips twitch at the power she put behind her response. It's obvious she loves teaching. "So, you'll teach."

"Do you think they'll let me switch rooms? That's one thing I don't know if I can do; go back into that room."

Her statement slams into me once again, imagining what she went through. Swiftly, I shake it off and clear my throat. "I'm sure of it." She smiles and I feel her body relaxing once again. "Whatever we do, Mal, we will find a new normal that works for us."

She nods. "I like that."

I run my hand over her hair, needing the connection. "I'll follow your lead when it comes to you and me, but I'm not going to let you push me away and I won't be shy about nudging you if I think you're ready."

A small smile tugs at her lips. "Good."

My lips twitch, savoring her positivity. "Just keep being honest and never stop telling me what you want or what you need."

"I promise."

Smirking, I tease, "So does that mean I have to move out tomorrow?"

She giggles. "You moved in?"

"Technically, no."

"I'm not sure what I need, but I'll tell you as I figure it out. I do know that tonight I need you to hold me if you're willing."

I grin, pulling her closer. "Always my pleasure."

"We'll worry about the rest tomorrow. Goodnight, Griffin."

"Goodnight, my darlin'." My lips brush across her mouth making them tingle. "I love you."

<h1 style="text-align:center">Chapter Forty Six</h1>

♡ Mallory ♡

I'm sick to my stomach. I'm so nervous, but I don't understand why. Bill Camden is the one retiring, and my boyfriend is the one taking his place, yet I feel like I'm walking into an event where I'll be the center of attention. I've known most of the men and women that work at the police department since before Noah and I moved here. Without my family around, we came back to Piper Falls to celebrate with his family for holidays and special occasions and he knew he wanted to work there, immediately intertwining our lives together. But I guess being at a Station 28 event for the first time with Griffin instead of Noah leaves me slightly on edge.

Griffin's hand runs up and down my back, before settling on my waist and giving it a squeeze. "Relax, Mal. Everyone here loves you."

"I know. I'm not sure why I'm so nervous."

"There she is," Matt states from behind us, making me laugh at the parallel to my thoughts.

We turn towards Matt, dressed in dark jeans and a white button down with his arm draped around Amber and her arm around his waist, both of them smiling brightly. "Hi, Matt," I murmur as he gives me a one-armed hug and kisses my forehead without letting go of Amber.

"It's good to see you two together." He smirks at Griffin. "A little strange, but damn good."

"Look who's talking," Griffin replies.

"Amber, you look gorgeous," I proclaim, glancing at her simple black tank dress that fits her curves beautifully with her long blonde hair falling loose over her shoulders.

"Thank you, so do you, Mallory. I love your dress."

My hands smooth over the light blue dress, flaring at my waist, my stomach flipping once again at my nerves. "Thank you."

"Good to see you Amber," Griffin states, mirroring Matt's greeting.

"You, too. I can't believe you guys are finally going to be working together."

"It's about time he wised up and came home." Matt grins.

"Yeah, yeah. I'm going to go say congratulations to Bill. You comin' with me?" Griffin asks, looking down at me.

I nod. "Of course. We'll see y'all later."

We wave and weave our way through the room, stopping to say hi to several people on the way, Reid, giving me a hug and whispering in my ear, "You two are good together," easing my nerves once again. Griffin had told me the same after they worked things out with Matt's help but hearing it directly from him makes me feel better.

My stomach twists with every step through the sea of familiar faces as I force myself to paste a smile on my face. The wide eyes, the double takes and the gaping mouths become too much to take. I jerk on Griffin's hand, urging him to look at me. He turns, closing the distance between us, his eyebrows drawn down in concern. "What is it? Are you okay, Mal? You look a little pale."

"I'm sorry, but I don't feel so well." Spinning on my heel, I rush towards the women's bathroom, barely making it to the tiny stall before I throw up in the toilet. Wiping my brow, I lean back against the cool tile wall.

A knock sounds at the bathroom door. "Mallory? Are you all right?"

With a heavy sigh, I pull the door open and come face to face with Amber. "Yeah, I'm okay. Thanks for checking on me."

"Of course. Can I get you anything? Maybe a ginger ale?"

"No thanks. My nerves are just going haywire being here with Griffin and seeing everyone floods my memories."

"I get that, but is that normal for you? To get sick from your nerves?"

My eyebrows draw down in confusion, when suddenly I gasp in realization. "You think I could be pregnant?"

"It's not impossible. Am I right?"

Taking a deep breath, I grab the wall for support and shake my head. "Oh my. I um, I have to go."

"Let me know if you need anything."

"Thanks." I smile, reaching out and squeezing her hand.

I rush out of the bathroom, Griffin pushing off the wall across from me, taking me by surprise. "I thought you were going to talk to Bill."

"I already did. Are you okay?"

"Yeah, but is it okay if I go?"

"Sure, but I'm going with you."

"You don't have to do that. The entire department is here. You should be here."

"Don't argue with me. I want to be there for you. I've seen everyone I need to, so there's no reason to feel bad."

Forcing a smile, I nod and we walk out, making our way towards his truck. "Is it okay if we stop at the pharmacy on the way?"

"No problem. I can run in for you." We climb in the truck and he turns it over and backs out, pulling out on the road.

"What do you need?" I bite my lower lip, running it through my teeth. "Mal?" he prods, glancing at me out of the corner of his eye. He reaches for my hand and squeezes it. "Mal? Darlin'?"

"Hm?"

"What do you need?"

"A pregnancy test," I blurt out on an exhale.

He slams on the brakes as he pulls into the parking lot, staring at me wide-eyed. "Did you just say a pregnancy test?"

I suck my lower lip into my mouth again and nod my head. Without another word, Griffin leans over, covers my mouth with his and sucks my lip into his mouth before releasing it and kissing me soft and slow eliciting a whimper from me.

"Whatever the test says, I'm right here with you Mallory. And let me say, that would make me a damn happy man."

"Griffin." My heart squeezes, wondering how I got so lucky to not only fall in love twice in my lifetime, but have both men love me back with incomparable ferocity. "No matter what happens, I need you to know I love you."

"Well, that's good because I love you, too." He kisses me again and leans back. "Should we go do this together?"

I nod and we both move quickly, suddenly desperate to know. It feels like only a matter of minutes when I find myself waiting at home for one line or two with Griffin holding me tight. A smile tugs at my lips as I inhale his sweet musky scent.

"It's time. Do you want me to look, or do you want the honor?" Griffin asks, kissing the top of my head.

Instead of answering, I reach for it and hold my breath. "Ready?"

"When you are."

I flip it over and hold it up, seeing one bright line. My heart sinks. "It's negative," I mumble, pressing my face into Griffin's chest as tears start to fall.

His hand rubs up and down my back, soothing me. "Hey darlin', it's okay." His fingers slide along my jaw, tilting my head up until I look into his eyes. "Mal, do you want another baby?"

Surprising myself, I don't even have to think about it. "Yeah, I do. I want to have a baby with you, Griffin."

A slow grin lights up his face making my heartbeat pick up its pace. "I want that too and I'm sure we can have a hell of a lot of fun trying. We've never gone without a condom."

Heat pools in my core, making me wet at the thought of feeling him inside me with no barrier between us. "Mm, no we haven't but that's about to change. I'm done going slow, Griffin. Are you ready for me?"

"I've been ready for you since the day you hit me with your car."

I huff a laugh as I reach down, grabbing the bottom of my dress and pulling it up, slowly tugging it over my head and tossing it to the floor. "Are you ever going to let me live that down?"

He licks his lips as his eyes roam hungrily over me standing in pale blue bikini underwear and a matching strapless bra to fit perfectly under my dress. "Right now, I'll do about anything you want."

"Then, it's time for you to get naked, Mr. Erickson."

"Fuck, Mal."

"That's right, you are listening."

His head falls back as he laughs, the movement sexy as hell, the sound making my nipples perk up and pay attention. As I step towards him, I cup his hard length. "Fuck."

He flicks his jeans open and tugs the zipper down before he goes to work, unbuttoning his shirt. As I watch him, my hand slips past his waistband and I wrap my hand around him, squeezing towards the tip, precum dripping out the end. His shirt drops to the floor, and his arms slip around my back, removing my bra with a flick of his fingers. My eyes widen, my breathing picking up as I take in his beautifully sculpted chest. "I think I forgot just how sexy you are, Mr. Erickson." I press my lips to his chest, kissing and licking as my hands roam.

The moment his jeans and boxer briefs hit the ground, his thick cock springing free, he cradles my face in his hands and tilts it up as his lips come crashing down on mine. His tongue sweeps inside my mouth and finds its mate. Our tongues move together, pushing back and forth, finding their own beat and dancing to their own song.

My pussy clenches, vibrating with need. Desperate to get closer, I grab his shoulders and jump up, wrapping my legs around his waist, putting my wet heat right over him, finding him thick and hard. His fingers slip into the sides of my panties and he yanks, making me gasp as he tears them the rest of the way, tossing them and leaving me bare, right above where I want to be. "Griffin, please."

Swiftly spinning me around he presses me to the door, holding me just above his shaft. "Are you sure, Mal? Because there's no going back."

"We wouldn't be here if I had any doubts. Fuck me, Mr. Erickson."

His muscles go taut as he thrusts up as he pulls me down, impaling me. "Ah," we both grunt, pausing to relish the feeling and take a deep breath.

He begins to move, slow, quickly picking up the pace. "It's been so long and you feel so damn good like this, Mal."

My juices flow as he plunges into me again and again. My legs squeeze him as I feel my walls do the same, swelling, tightening, burning. "I'm gonna' come, Griff."

The feel of his skin on mine, ignites my whole body, making me tingle, feeling alive. His hips move faster, our skin slapping and breathing rapid as he pushes inside me. My walls clench around him, his cock slick with my juices swells as he moves in and out. He grunts as my body tenses, releasing and I start to come down from my high.

His lips find mine and he kisses me hard. "Ready for round two?" he asks, never pulling out.

My eyes widen, but I nod, smiling as he pushes off the door and carries us over to the bed, laying me down without ever removing his cock. He begins moving again, slower as he presses his lips to my lips, my neck, my chest. "I'm not gonna' last, but you will come again. Got me?"

"Yes, Mr. Erickson."

His eyes flare at my response, further igniting me. He thrusts, our bodies finding a perfect rhythm as we move together. "Fuck, Mal," he grunts, his hips speeding up. "It's been too long since I've been inside you and having you this way feels so damn right I can't hold on much longer. Please come for me, darlin'."

I arch my back and my hips, meeting him with every thrust, his cock going deeper. "I need more."

He reaches down, pinching my clit and rubbing his thumb over it in circles. "Yes, Griffin, do that again." He does as I ask, making me scream his name. "Griffin!"

My body convulses around him as his body spasms, giving into his orgasm just as mine consumes me, the world going black around me. He pushes into me one more time before he collapses against me, still inside me as we gasp for breath.

After a moment, my eyes flutter open, meeting Griffin's blue eyes. A lazy smile tugs at my lips. "Wow, that was, wow."

He chuckles. "I second that. I'm at a loss of words, but damn, I can't wait to do that again."

I giggle, pressing my lips to his. "Me too, Griffin. Me too."

He presses his lips to mine and grabs a wipe, cleaning up his legs and mine, avoiding any cleanup between my legs. "When will the kids be home?"

"Not until tomorrow."

"Hope you're feeling better darlin' because we're going to have some more fun."

"Sounds perfect."

Epilogue

♡ Griffin ♡

(Five Years Later)

After I got off shift this morning, I stopped at the farm to cut some flowers for my girls before making my way home. I walk into our five-bedroom farmhouse up the road from my parents, smiling. Tiegan jumps up from the U-shaped couch in the open living room, the stone fireplace the only separation to the kitchen. "Griff!" She grins, setting her book down.

"Howdy, sweetheart." Wrapping my arms around her, she gives me a hug as I press a kiss to the top of her head. "These are for you."

I hold out a small bouquet of flowers and watch as she smiles, inhaling the scent.

"Are you ready for school?"

She nods. "Yeah, I got up early to read."

"Must be a good book."

"It is." She sets the flowers down on the coffee table, returning to her spot on the couch as Mia walks out wearing brown leggings, a pink dress and tan cowboy boots matching Mallory's old ones.

"Good morning, darlin'."

"Good morning, Dad." She walks over, wrapping her arms around my waist, squeezing tight as if she's squeezing my heart in the palm of her hand. She knows how to get to me.

She doesn't always call me that, but when she does it hits me every time. They all started calling me dad, sometimes. At first it made me feel like an imposter, but it's truly the biggest honor I could imagine. We never stop telling stories about their real dad. My gaze travels to the pictures on the mantel, the first one with Noah and the kids in front of a lake on their last family vacation. The one on the opposite side is a photo of Noah, me, Matt and Reid with our arms around each other right after we graduated from the police academy. Hung in the center, is an image with me, Mal and the kids, right after we bought the house. Noah will never be forgotten and he will always be loved.

"Are those for me?" Mia asks, drawing my attention as she points to the flowers in my hand.

"This bouquet is," I reply, handing her the smaller bouquet.

"Thank you." She hugs me again before releasing me.

"You're welcome."

"Can you bring me to dance after school today?" she asks, looking up at me with her sweet smile.

"Yes, but then Ollie and I have to head to his soccer game."

"What am I doing?" Ollie asks as he trudges down the hall, rubbing his eyes, still dressed in his pajamas.

"Getting ready for school," I answer, smirking. "Did you sleep okay?"

Shaking his head, he groans, "No."

"Your brother keep you up?"

He yawns, nodding his head. "Yeah."

"I'll go check on your mom."

My hand falls to Ollie's head as I walk by him, messing up his hair just like his dad and I used to do to each other. "Hey," he grumbles, laughing.

"Don't forget we have a game tonight."

His eyes brighten at the reminder and he rushes back to his room making me laugh. Colton and I started coaching his soccer team, Asher and Mason on the same one. It's helped all of us grow closer together and I wouldn't trade it for anything.

Quietly, I make my way down the hallway, reaching the door at the end. Not wanting to wake Mal if she's sleeping, I open the door slow, closing it behind me. A grin tugs at my lips, as I stare at my wife. Mallory lays curled up on her side with her hair spread out on her pillow and her eyes closed. I set her flowers down on our dresser, tiptoeing over to the bed. Not able to help myself, I lean down, brushing my lips across her forehead.

"You missed," she mumbles, her caramel eyes fluttering open, landing on me, giving me a tired smile.

Chuckling, I press my lips to hers. "Good morning, Mrs. Erickson."

"Good morning, Officer Erickson. Have I ever told you how sexy you look in your uniform?"

"Maybe, but I like hearing it every time it's coming from your mouth." I kiss her again, and she reaches up, tangling her fingers into my hair, tugging me closer. "I love coming home to you in my bed every morning," I mumble over her lips, making her giggle.

"You say that like I broke in. Maybe you need to cuff me."

"Oh, be careful what you ask for darlin' because now I know exactly what I'm going to do to you while the kids sleep at the farm this weekend."

"You do?" Her eyes flare as she shifts, laying on her back.

I nod, pushing the blankets down, staring at her in her short white cotton shorts and pale green tank top, my dick instantly springing to attention. Reaching down, I start at her toes, softly dragging my fingers up her leg, sliding inwards at her thigh, clenching my jaw as she whimpers the moment I come close to her heated core. "First, as you suggested, I'm going to cuff you to the headboard with your hands above your head and worship every inch of your body."

"Griff."

My hand slips underneath her tank, running over the small swell of her stomach, five months pregnant with our baby. My hand trails up, cupping her breast, my finger grazing her nipple. "I'm going to make you come with my hand, and my tongue before I fuck you so hard and deep you'll feel me for a week."

"Please."

Cries echo through the baby monitor, interrupting us, making her groan in frustration. "How can he be awake right now? His two-year molars kept us up half the night."

Chuckling, I kiss her again. "One more day Mal, and I have you all to myself for the entire weekend."

"I don't know if I can wait that long."

"I've got Noah. I'll bring him with me to take the kids to school. You relax and get some sleep. I'll be back to pick you up for your doctor's appointment."

"Okay," she easily agrees. "I love you, Griffin."

"I love you, darlin'," I whisper, giving her one more chaste kiss before readjusting myself and pulling the door open.

Crossing the hall, I step into my son's room. The moment he sees me, he stops crying, holding up his arms. "Daddy!"

"Good morning, Noah." I grin, sweeping him up into my arms. He looks just like his mom with her brown hair and caramel eyes, but he's got the Erickson smile. I'm pretty sure he'll be a handful growing up, just like me and Noah used to be. "How's my boy this morning?" I ask as I change him. "Did you keep Mommy awake?"

He looks at me wide-eyed, shaking his head. "Mommy seep?"

I chuckle. "Yes, she's sleeping."

We wanted our son to have a piece of Noah, like his siblings, giving him his namesake. It was our way to honor him as we started our family.

"Let's go take your brother and sisters to school."

I don't know if I ever really got a sign that Noah approves, but I feel like he's watching down on us, grateful to see all of us whole once again.

The End

Other Books by Nikki A. Lamers

<u>The Unforgettable Series</u>
Unforgettable Summer
Unforgettable Nights
Unforgettable Dreams
Unforgettable Memories
Unforgettable One
Unforgettable Mistakes
An Unforgettable December (Coming October 2024)

<u>Mending Shattered Hearts Series</u>
Breaking Cycles
Breaking Barriers (Coming Soon)

<u>The Home Series</u>
Dreams Lost and Found
Finding Home

Piper Falls: Station 28 Series

Available Now

Embracing My Duty by Melony Ann
Torn By My Duty by Kayla Baker
Against My Duty by Anneke Boshoff
Defying My Duty by D.L. Howe
Leave Of My Duty by Nikki A. Lamers
Fulfilling My Duty by Havana Wilder
Following My Duty by Louise Murchie
Replete In My Duty by Stacy Kristen
Accepting My Duty by Darley Collins

Connect with the Author

Official Author Website
www.nikkialamersauthor.com

Linktree for All Author Links
https://linktr.ee/NikkiALamersauthor

Acknowledgements

As always, thank you to the most important people in my world, my family, Michael, Tyler, Allison, and our dogs, and my mom, my dad in heaven and my sister, as well as my extended family. I appreciate your constant love and support more than anything! I wouldn't be able to do what I love without you.

Melony Ann, thank you for asking me to be a part of this unique collaboration with this incredible group of authors! I'm truly grateful for the opportunity. Your idea has become a springboard for a small town filled with characters with so many different voices, a project like I've never seen and I'm truly thrilled to be a part of it. I've had so much fun working with (in book order, although all standalone novels) you, Kayla Baker, Anneke Boshoff, D.L. Howe, me, Havana Wilder, Louise Murchie, Stacy Kristen and Darley Collins.

The number of editors needed for a project like this was immense, making sure to get each character, scene and location just right. Thank you to Melony Ann for answering all my questions. Thanks to Melony Ann, Louise, Darley, Stacy Kayla, D.L. Howe, Anneke, and Havana for answering questions, helping with clarification and reading to make sure I got it right. Thank you Dina for your hard work and dedication in helping me get the story the way it needed to be. Thank you Jill and Annie and my other Beta readers, as well as all my ARC readers and fans. I appreciate every single one of you and I truly hope you enjoy this story!

Vinny, I'm thrilled I got to work with you again. You again are the perfect cover model for Griffin. Thank you! You really helped me out at the last minute and I appreciate you more than I can even explain. Hopefully you love the cover as much as I do. I can't wait for the day I actually get to meet you in person. Thank you to Creative Instincts for the beautiful images and Carter Cover Designs for putting it all together for the beautiful cover design.

Thank you Nick and everyone at Carxander Publishing for your help, patience, and support, not only on this project, but for all you do to help with getting my books out there!

To all my fellow author friends, I'm incredibly grateful for every one of you. You are all fantastic writers, supporters, and friends! I'm thankful for all of you keeping me sane, providing help and encouragement and cheering louder than I thought possible! I love writing and being able to share it with all of you!

I hope you continue to read, share, and enjoy! Thank you!

About the Author

Award Winning Author, Nikki A Lamers grew up in Wisconsin and lived in Florida for a few years before ending up on Long Island in New York where she now lives with her husband and their two children. She writes mostly spicy contemporary and new adult romance, many times incorporating tough health, wellness, and life issues. With her public health background, she loves diving deep into her characters and seeing how some of the tough issues can impact an individual and their relationships. Recently she has expanded her romance writing with romantic suspense, romantasy and paranormal romance, while maintaining her roots. Writing, reading, coffee, chocolate, and at times a good drink are all she wants alongside her friends and family. Since meeting her husband, they enjoy spending time in Maine and exploring different places, meeting new people, and always crafting her next story. For her other job she freelances as a script writer, advisor, and supervisor on and off set, hoping to one day see one of her own stories on screen.

Her recent release, *Breaking Cycles* is the first stand-alone novel in the Mending Shattered Hearts series and won a Literary Titan Gold book award upon release in October 2023. It is also being released on audio by Neo Publishing with Grant voiced by the talented Chance J Terry. Listen to the first chapter now on Neo Publishing's TikTok page.

The Unforgettable Series has won several awards including Firebird Book Awards for *The Unforgettable Summer* (New Adult Fiction, Series, Summer/Beach Read and Contemporary Novel), *Unforgettable Nights* (New Adult Fiction, Series, Contemporary Novel) *Unforgettable Dreams* (Contemporary Novel, Series), and *Unforgettable Memories* (Romance and New Adult Fiction). *The Unforgettable Summer* also won an Imaginarium Imadjinn Award for Best Romance. Now with six books in The

Unforgettable Series, you have the chance to fall in love with the characters just like her!

Leave of My Duty, is part of The Piper Falls Station 28 Series. Each book in the series is a standalone novel with different MCs, each one written by a different author. All the books take place in the same small town with one MC having a connection to the local police department. She loved the challenge and collaboration of this project.

Dreams Lost and Found and *Finding Home* are part of The Home series and the only two by the author that need to be read in order. This duet hits close to home for the author. The main character Samantha was adopted as an infant, just like Nikki. Although Samantha's story is not her own, she enjoyed writing every word and using her personal experiences to portray the emotions of the character and the circumstances. Nikki would love to travel more, meeting new people and exploring new places, finding new inspirations for her stories. While at home she's having fun working on her next books.